D1040648

TAKEN BY THE HOUSE

Casey Faraday took a glass of white wine across to the window that looked out over the flagstoned patio. She took one sip of the Pinot Grigiot, then dropped the glass to the floor and screamed. By the time the others reached her Casey was crying hysterically, pointing out through the window.

Sheila grabbed her by the shoulders. 'Casey, calm down. What's wrong?'

Andrew Johnson followed the line of Casey's pointing finger.

Eddie Farrant joined him, mouth open in astonishment, face draining rapidly of color. 'Oh my God!'

They stared through the window at the patio. Tables and chairs had been overturned and umbrellas lay on their side, rocking gently back and forth in the afternoon breeze. In the center of the patio was Guy Lomax, but only his head, shoulders and right arm were visible; it was as if the rest of him had been swallowed by the patio, as if he had sunk into the flagstones....

Other *Leisure* books by L. H. Maynard and M. P. N. Sims:

DEMON EYES
SHELTER

BLACK CATHEDRAL

L. H. MAYNARD
& M. P. N. SIMS

LEISURE BOOKS   NEW YORK CITY

Black Cathedral *is dedicated to all lovers of*
supernatural stories, real and imagined,
the stories not the lovers...

A LEISURE BOOK®

January 2009

Published by

Dorchester Publishing Co., Inc.
200 Madison Avenue
New York, NY 10016

ISBN 10: 0-8439-6199-6
ISBN 13: 978-0-8439-6199-7

The name "Leisure Books" and the stylized "L" with design are
trademarks of Dorchester Publishing Co., Inc.

Printed in the United States of America.

10 9 8 7 6 5 4 3 2 1

Visit us on the web at www.dorchesterpub.com.

ACKNOWLEDGMENTS

We would like to thank Don and the fantastic team at Leisure for another stunningly produced novel. The cover artwork is great and the process of delivery of manuscript to finished book is a real pleasure.

Many thanks to Mario Guslandi for his prepublication reading and review.

Grateful thanks to Clare Sims and Emily Sims who helped and inspired Mick with his part of the writing, revisions, editing, proofing, promotion—well, all of what he did really.

Len did all his hard work all on his own.

Huge thanks to Iain Maynard for the marvelous new website and the appearance of what seems a worrying new website with links to it.

Finally thank you to everyone who took the time to review, blog or just tell us what they thought of *Shelter* and *Demon Eyes*. All feedback is like oxygen.

BLACK
CATHEDRAL

CHAPTER ONE

It was what had happened here, and what was about to happen again, that made it obvious this was the start of it all.

There was nothing very special about the house—a medium-sized English suburban semidetached, built some time in the 1930s, complete with bay windows and a stained glass panel depicting sunrays, set in the solid green-painted front door, so that it looked like sunlight captured on grass; nothing much to set it apart from its neighbors. Except for what had happened there.

The tree-lined avenue was the picture of normality; cars parked either side against the neat verges, hedges precisely clipped, a child's bicycle on a front drive, the sound of an electric mower buzzing like a sun-lazed bee. The house they were visiting looked welcoming, and would have been a pleasant place to spend the afternoon. Except for what was going to happen again.

Robert Carter hesitated, pushed open the front door and, after taking a deep inward breath, stepped into the house. Sian Davies, his assistant, followed close behind, her pad in hand, pen poised to take down notes and to keep an accurate record of events as they unfolded. Both of them were certain events *would* unfold.

Carter carried a small device, holding it out in front of

him, sweeping the air in broad strokes, like a warrior brandishing his sword. The device looked very much like a photographer's light meter. It was no more than three inches square and an inch deep. On one end was a small white dome, on the front a dial with calibrations from one to one thousand. But while a photographer's meter measured light, Carter's machine could detect the slightest changes, the tiniest fluctuations, in magnetic fields. Perfect for suspected hauntings.

Carter was thirty-five, tall and slim with an athletic physique he owed to the four hours a week he spent at the gym, combined with regular games of squash and racquets. The exercise was complemented by a healthy diet, apart from far too many cigarettes, a light intake of alcohol, and occasional sex with willing partners.

Sian Davies had none of these attributes, and none of the virtues of a healthy lifestyle. She was short, dumpy, with spiky black hair and a small tattoo of a rose on her shoulder. And she had a crush on Robert Carter the size of a small country. Yet despite their close working relationship, Carter was a total mystery to her. There were rumors of a great love affair—some forbidden passion that had ended and left Carter a scarred, emotional wreck. Some of the rumors had even linked him with Jane Talbot, Department 18's brightest star, but Sian was not sure she set much store by them. She liked and respected Jane Talbot—aspiring in her own small way to be like her—and she knew Jane was happily married.

Sian was worldly enough to know that men like Robert Carter were always the targets for the mythmakers and rumormongers. The scurrilous stories told around the Department's water coolers were fed and nurtured by jealousy and envy. Sian preferred her own fantasies. They sustained her during long, lonely nights and gave her a reason to get up every morning. Often they weren't the type of fantasy to share around the coffee machine at work.

'Ambient temperature in the house low and dropping rapidly.' Carter was speaking into a small microphone attached to the collar of his shirt and wired to a digital recorder he carried in his jacket pocket. As if to prove his point his breath was starting to mist in front of his face. There was also an oppressive atmosphere in the house. An atmosphere that couldn't be measured with meters but one that was almost palpable.

He trusted the readings on the various instruments he carried, and when they read that there were disturbances in the electromagnetic fields and unusual fluctuations in temperature he knew he had something definite to deal with. The instruments had their uses, but more often than not he preferred to rely on his own feelings; the vibes—primitive instincts inherited from mankind's prehistoric ancestors, so dulled in the majority of people to be absolutely worthless. In him they were honed to razor sharpness. So much so that he rarely began an investigation like this without scrupulous preparation, building his mental defenses as carefully as a bricklayer builds a wall. Sometimes he worried he had built the wall so high, so strong, that nothing could penetrate it, not even if he wanted it to.

The house had been decorated some time in the 1970s, but the browns, yellows and pinks had faded with age and looked more muted now than when they were first applied. The Flemings, the owners of the house, were a couple in their seventies, both retired. It was Mrs. Fleming who had taken the steps to bring in the Department. Her younger brother was high up in the Whitehall pecking order, and a frantic phone call to him had set the wheels in motion. Another phone call was made to Department 18's head, Simon Crozier, with the request that the Department

investigate the house. In deference to the request, Carter—
the Department's top field man—had been sent, even if
Crozier did hate his guts.

Carter reviewed the file in his mind. Six months ago
the couple started hearing things that disturbed their
prosaic little life. At first it was nothing more than a few
scratches on the ceiling, the odd footfall on the bedroom
floor when they were both downstairs, but nothing that
couldn't be explained away rationally; a loose board settling into place, birds or mice setting up home in the eaves
of the house, nothing to be alarmed about. They were
both getting old and the mind could play tricks.

The smells were more alarming. According to the
Flemings, the kitchen was often filled with the reek of
ozone that smelled something like an electrical short circuit. In the lounge it was the odor of sour cream, and in
the bedrooms the musty mud and straw smell of an animal
pen. But it was the entrance hall that had the most distinc-
tive and most repellent aroma. Mrs. Fleming described it
as 'the smell of something washed up on a beach; dead
and rotten' and, standing there in the hall, Carter had to
agree. 'God, it stinks in here,' he said. Sian made a note in
her pad.

The needle on the meter twitched significantly, leaping
a quarter of the way around the dial. He frowned. 'There's
a huge amount of electromagnetic energy coming from
the kitchen. Let's go take a look.'

Sian felt the hairs on the back of her neck start to prickle.
No matter how many of these investigations she attended,
she never got over that first thrill of fear and dread. Experience had shown her that there was never anything much to
fear—in fact she had only ever witnessed one manifestation,
and that was of someone's dead pet Labrador. Not a very
frightening image at all. But a feeling buried deep within
her, and one she could not rationalize, told her that this

house was very different from anything she had experienced before.

She knew from her reading of the file on the house that there had been a number of physical manifestations, and an alarming amount of damage to both the property and the residents, culminating with old Mr. Fleming being pushed down the stairs. The fall had broken his hip, and a prolonged stay in hospital had precipitated their moving out. He flatly refused to set foot in the house again until it was '*sorted out!*'

Carter reached the doorway and glanced round. Sian was shifting from foot to foot, pretending to read from her notebook. 'Coming?' he said. He knew she was frightened, and probably with good reason. This house *was* different, he was sure of that.

The tone of his voice jerked her out of her inertia, and she followed him reluctantly. By the time she entered the kitchen Carter was standing in the center of the split and cracked vinyl floor, turning slowly in a circle, the meter extended at arm's length.

'There,' he said as the needle on the dial twitched again.

He was pointing at a door. Sian stared at it. It was probably nothing more than a broom cupboard and she knew Carter was expecting her to open it, but she really didn't want to. Crazy and macabre images were flashing through her mind; all sorts of gruesome tableaux were waiting for her behind that rather bland, cream-colored door. She started to back away.

Sensing her fear Carter laid the meter down on the kitchen table and stepped forward, grabbing the handle of the door and twisting it sharply. He yanked the door open and a nightmare of teeth, claws and fur flew out at him. He yelled a warning to Sian, turned, and tripped on a torn piece of vinyl, tumbling to the floor, landing sharply on his knee. He hissed with pain and shock, glancing round as the cat skidded across the kitchen floor to the back door. Without even checking its stride, it shot out through the cat flap. Sian ran to the door but only just managed to catch a fleeting glimpse of tortoise shell fur as the animal dived into the overgrown shrubbery at the end of the garden.

She looked back at Carter, who was struggling to get to his feet. Pain had etched lines across his face and colored it an ashen gray. She ran across to help him. Pulling a chair away from the table, she helped him into it.

'Shit!' he said, rubbing his knee, a rueful smile hovering on his lips. 'And I've got a league match tonight.'

She smiled sympathetically, and absently stroked his hair. 'How long do you think the cat was in there?' she said, approaching the broom cupboard cautiously. 'The house has been empty for weeks, but there's no sign that it's been shut in there for any more than a few hours. No mess, and it certainly couldn't have survived that long without food and water.'

'It wasn't real,' Carter said. 'It didn't actually exist. Check your file again. The Flemings had a cat matching the description of that one, but they found it with its throat cut six months ago. Besides,' he added as almost an afterthought, 'it passed straight though me, and the cat flap didn't open as it went through.' Gingerly he got to his feet. 'Come on,' he said. 'Let's have a look upstairs.' Sian wasn't surprised at his casual acceptance of the supernatural. She didn't understand it, or share it, but she found it reassuring. It made her feel safe, well, safer.

The master bedroom was dead, cold and empty, and caused not so much as a flutter on Carter's meter. 'There's nothing here,' he said, and closed the door, shutting in the memories and the dust.

It was the same story in the other bedrooms and the bathroom. Even the smells that the Flemings had described so eloquently in their report were subdued. There was a faint trace of an odor in some of the rooms, but nothing as strong as they had described.

'What do you think?' Sian said when they had checked all the rooms.

Carter leaned against the banister, looking down the stairwell. There was *something* here. He could feel it. The incident with the cat proved it. But what? 'I'm not sure,' he said. 'Let's check downstairs again.'

He was halfway down the stairs when he heard china smashing. Gritting his teeth against the pain in his knee, he ran down the last few steps, pausing only to point his meter at the kitchen door again. The needle was swinging wildly, arcing backwards and forwards across the dial. He shivered and took a breath. Whatever was in there was giving off a huge electromagnetic charge, more powerful than anything he had encountered before.

They entered the kitchen together this time. The source of the noise was obvious straightaway. Plates were lifting from the dresser as if grasped by invisible hands. One after another the plates were being destroyed, smashing down on the floor with such force that pieces of china were embedding themselves in the vinyl.

Whatever was causing the damage was instantly aware of them as soon as they entered the room. There was a momentary pause, and one of the willow pattern plates floated from the dresser, hung in the air for a second, and then, with frightening force, flew across the room towards them. Carter ducked and pushed Sian out of the way. The plate sailed through the gap between them and smashed on the wall behind, showering them with sharp shards of broken china. Sian cried out as a large fragment of crockery sliced through the sleeve of her shirt, then gasped with relief as she realized it had missed her flesh by millimeters.

Starting as a low rumble, a sound started to fill the

room. It developed quickly into a chorus of whoops and
squeals, underpinned by a deep guttural growling. As another plate was lifted from the dresser Carter grabbed Sian
by the arm and propelled her out of the kitchen, yanking
the door closed behind him. He heard the crash and felt
the wood shudder as the plate smashed into it.

They were in the dining room. He turned to speak to
Sian, but her attention was focused on the wall ahead. He
followed her gaze.

There was a bulge underneath the wallpaper, about the
size of a large walnut, and it was moving slowly across the
wall at eye level. As it moved it formed a hump in the paper,
but behind it the wallpaper was smooth, flattened down as if
the hump had never been there.

Whatever was beneath the wallpaper was picking up
speed. The paper made a soft hissing sound as it lifted away
from the wall. Carter jerked his head round as he heard the
same sound coming from behind him. There were three
humps, moving parallel to each other diagonally across
the wall, and more of the things were creeping up from the
skirting board.

'We'd better get out of here,' he said, but Sian wasn't
listening. She'd moved across the room and was staring at
the first hump as it zigzagged back and forth, her face
inches away from it.

Carter felt a spear of apprehension skewer him. 'Sian,
get back!' he shouted, but as the words left his lips the wallpaper split and a large beetle emerged, black and glistening,
with a hard iridescent carapace. The creature scuttled across
the wall, and then the carapace opened and it took flight,
launching itself at Sian and attaching itself to the soft skin
of her neck. She turned to Carter, too shocked to cry out,
a look of absolute terror on her face, her fingers fluttering
at her throat, anxious to pull the thing off but far too terrified to actually touch it.

Underneath the wallpaper the rest of the creatures were moving in frenzy, sensing the attack. As the paper lifted and fell in their path it whispered and hissed, filling the room with a soft susurration. Carter was across the room in two strides. 'Keep still,' he said as he grabbed the hard shell and squeezed, but the beetle's head was burrowing into her flesh, its legs forming sharp hooks, anchoring it to her skin. Sian was silent, but huge tears were forming in her beseeching eyes and rolling down her cheeks.

The grip of the creature was fierce and the effort of making it loosen its hold made the sweat bead on Carter's brow; then suddenly, with a sound like a sigh of resignation the creature released its hold on Sian's flesh. It writhed in Carter's grip, the scurrying movement of tiny legs making him shudder. The thing was squirming in his grasp and twisting its head in an effort to bite him.

As if acting on a signal from the first creature, the other bulges in the wall burst open, like paper eggs hatching, and the air was filled with the sound of twenty or more of the beetles testing their wings.

Carter threw the beetle to the floor, stomped on it, and grabbed Sian's arm again and hauled her towards the French doors, batting the things away as they flew at them. He grasped the door handle but another beetle landed on his hand, clicking mandibles biting down hard, puncturing skin. He swore loudly and brushed it off before its head could start burrowing. The door swung open but, as he forced Sian out into the garden, a dozen or more of the beetles landed on his back. He could feel the legs scrabbling up his jacket as they tried to reach his throat and he threw himself backwards against the wall, grunting with satisfaction as he heard the carapaces crack on impact. As the creatures dropped to the floor he threw himself through the open door, slamming it shut behind him, listening to the glass rattle as the beetles launched themselves at it in pursuit.

He stood on the patio, panting, trying to get his breath back. Sian was watching him with tear-smudged eyes. 'What were those things?' she said. 'I've never seen beetles like them before.'

'Well, I don't think you'll find them in any reference works on coleopterans,' Carter said, drawing the warm afternoon air into his lungs. 'At a guess I would say they were elementals, some kind of physical embodiment of the power, or powers, in that house. How's your neck?'

Her fingers went to the soft skin at the side of her throat and came away bloody. Carter pulled a clean handkerchief from his pocket, folded it into a pad and handed it to her. 'We'd better get you to the hospital. You're going to need a tetanus shot for that.'

Sian was shaking. 'But they were real,' she said, shock reducing her voice to no more than a whisper. 'At first I didn't think they had any substance . . . like the cat . . . but it hurt. Christ, it hurt!' She held the pad to the wound as tears welled in her eyes again. Carter wrapped an arm around her shoulders and led her back to their car parked in a bay at the back of the house. He opened the passenger door and ushered her inside. 'Wait here,' he said.

She grabbed the sleeve of his jacket. 'Where are you going?' she said, close to panic. She didn't want to be left alone. She was badly frightened and the fear was making her feel nauseous. She didn't want Robert to take the risk of going back to the house.

'Back in there,' he said, and saw the panic flare in her eyes. 'Don't worry. I'll be fine now I know what I'm up against.'

Sian chewed her lip, unconvinced. She was trying to conquer her fear, furious with herself for appearing so weak, so bloody girly! He'd never take her out on an assignment again. She'd screwed up and was anxious to make amends. 'I'll come with you.'

'No, you won't. You've had enough for one day. This won't take long, then I'll take you to A and E, to get that wound looked at.' He slammed the door and started to walk back to the house. Halfway there he pulled out his cell phone and punched in a number.

CHAPTER TWO

The call was answered instantly. 'Crozier.'

'It's Carter. This is worse than we thought. It's degenerated very quickly, too quickly. There are some nasty physical manifestations.' He described the events briefly.

There was a pause at the other end of the line and Carter could almost hear the other man thinking as Crozier's sharp and well-ordered mind weighed the ramifications of what he'd been told and considered his options. 'Is the girl badly injured?' It was typical of Crozier not to use a person's name if he could show some superiority over them.

'Nothing major.' He was damned if he was going to give Crozier the full details.

'Careless, Robert.' The evident pleasure at a possible Carter mistake was like the purr of a satisfied cat.

'I know. I wasn't expecting anything quite this violent.' He had, though. As soon as he entered the house he knew there were powerful forces there. He needed to check a couple of things inside the house; then he would know which direction to take his investigation.

'Hmm. Do you need a cleanup team or do you think you can deal with it yourself?' Crozier said. He made the possible need for help seem like a definite sign of weakness.

Carter had reached the French doors. He shaded his eyes with his hand and peered in. There were no signs of anything unusual; nothing flying about the room, the wallpaper smooth and undamaged. 'I think I can handle it,' he said. He wouldn't be reckless enough to deny help just because it was Crozier's suggestion; he was far too professional for that. But there were suspicions he had that had to be confirmed before he could let others into the house.

'Okay. Let me know how it pans out,' Crozier said and rang off. Letting him make the decision about when help was given was as near to a show of courtesy as Crozier would afford Carter.

Carter slipped the phone into the pocket of his jacket and let himself back into the house. He stood in the center of the dining room breathing deeply, eyes tightly closed. It was time to open up, to let down his guard, to try to discover the secrets of the house. Four investigations in as many months, each one progressively worse than the last. Something was happening. Something out of the ordinary, and he felt it was down to him to discover exactly what was going on. This was no poltergeist upset at not reaching closure before death. This was no ghost whose violent death couldn't be forgiven. What was attacking this house, using it, was far more dangerous.

The process of opening his mind was easy, rather like taking off a pair of sunglasses and letting his eyes see the brightness, but it had to be done carefully. If he exposed himself fully he would be vulnerable to attack. If he didn't open himself enough he would learn nothing. He'd been preparing for this moment for days; increasing his work rate at the gym, pushing his body, getting it as fit and as strong as possible to be able to withstand the sheer physical toll that his mind would demand.

He spread his arms wide and opened his eyes.

Nothing.

He frowned, puzzled. The electromagnetic disturbance and the manifestations he'd witnessed in the house told him that there were very strong influences here. So why was he not picking up anything?

He tried again, concentrating more deeply, lowering his defenses still further.

Nothing.

It was as if the house was depleted, a flat battery, devoid of energy.

It made no sense. He took another deep breath, stretching his arms wider. 'Come on,' he muttered under his breath. 'Show me.'

A second later the forces in the house rushed at him like an express train and he cried out as he was lifted off his feet and hurled against the wall. He hung there for a second before sliding to the floor, his breath knocked out of him. 'Shit!' he said and struggled to stand.

It hit him again, this time with a more mental attack. His mind was filled with spiraling images. The beetles were back in the room, hundreds of them, flying at his face, nipping and biting his hands as he raised them to protect himself. In the next second they were gone and the image of a desolate landscape rushed into his mind. He felt himself transported, picked up and dragged through the air.

He was pulled upwards, through the ceiling of the dining room and the roof of the house, until he was hundreds of feet in the air. Unseen forces were holding him there, suspended over the house. He looked down and could see the streets of the town, the shops, the houses, the cars, and the people going about their daily lives. The church, easily identified from its steeple, was crumbling, brick by brick, as if it was dissolving into the ground. He blinked, once, twice and the scene changed.

He was staring down at the sea, choppy gray waves capped with white, rolling in on a clean sandy beach and crashing over rocks that guarded the coastline of a bleak, inhospitable island.

And then he was falling down to the ground beneath. He landed without impact, his body cushioned by pads of soft heather and bracken. Above him a pale sun glared down at him, its white light hurting his eyes. He squeezed them shut and when he opened them again he was staring up at a circular dish filled with electric lights.

He was lying on an operating table, a sharp antiseptic smell filling his nostrils. And he was seven years old again, at his most vulnerable, in hospital for a tonsillectomy, while about him white-clad figures stood watching him, their faces obscured by white masks, but their eyes earnest and threatening. A scalpel hovered in front of his own eyes, then with a swift downwards slash cut a line in his flesh from sternum to pelvis. Hands reached inside him, searching out vital organs. He could feel soft fingers caressing his liver, his spleen, his lungs, his heart.

He could hear a voice, whispering, the sound too muted to be clear, and then many voices, the sounds merging into one long sonorous drone. Finally silence.

Then 'Take him back.' Sharp, clipped. An order.

'Will he return?' A softer voice, almost female, but not quite.

'He has no choice. Take the girl.'

And the light was switched off.

In the car Sian relaxed in the seat and leaned back on the headrest, closing her eyes. This was the worst ever. She couldn't remember ever being this frightened. Whatever the creatures were, elementals as Carter had said, or something else entirely, they had awoken in her a deep-seated, almost primeval fear. Somewhere, lodged in her trace memory, was the image of them, dark and scuttling, hiding in shadows, crawling into the light. They were at once foreign yet familiar.

She froze as she heard a soft whispering, like tissue paper tearing. She looked down at her chest. Something was moving underneath her clothes. With trembling fingers she undid the buttons and opened her shirt.

In the expanse of flesh between her bra and the waistband of her skirt, five lumps, no bigger than quails' eggs, were moving under her skin. And, as she watched, the skin itself was turning gray, translucent, as the lumps moved actively beneath it. Panic surged through her and she prodded one with her finger. At her touch the skin split and a black antennal head forced its way through the bloody hole.

She screamed, but the sound was blocked by a horde of scrabbling creatures chasing the daylight glimpsed through her open mouth. They crawled up her throat, over her tongue, scrambling over her teeth and hanging from her lower lip before dropping to her chest. Within seconds the car was filled with the things as they exploded from every orifice—from her mouth, her ears, forcing their way down her nostrils, crawling out from her anus and, in a cruel mockery of childbirth, pouring from her vagina, ripping through the sheer material of her panties.

She struggled and in her panic the small gold cross and chain she wore was torn from her neck.

She reached for the door handle, but as her fingers connected with it the central locking mechanism activated and sealed her into the car. She looked round frantically, hoping to catch a glimpse of Carter through the bushes surrounding the car. 'Come back!' her mind screamed. 'For pity's sake, Robert, please come back.' And then she slumped back into the seat as, inch by inch, the beetles devoured her.

He opened his eyes and he was back in the dining room. His body was soaked in sweat, his hair plastered to his scalp. He shook his head, trying to shake away the cobwebs that were draped over his thoughts. Gradually the cobwebs thinned and dispersed as rational thought reestablished itself.

Take the girl. The voice echoed in his thoughts, distant and inhuman. He pushed himself to his feet and raced from the house.

The car was where he had left it. He ran across to it and yanked the door handle.

Locked.

Locked and empty.

Of Sian Davies there was no trace at all.

'Oh Christ!' he said, and leaned against the car, his legs weak and trembling. He let his body slide down the metallic paintwork until he was crouching, almost slouching, on the ground. He was going to vomit; he could feel the bile rising in his throat. He retched, and his cell phone began to ring.

He fumbled for the talk button. 'Yes?' he choked back whatever was lodged in his throat.

'It's Crozier. I told you to report back.' The impatience, the reprimand, was deliberate.

'We only spoke a moment ago,' Carter said, trying to gather his thoughts, wondering how he was going to explain what had happened to Sian.

'It's been over four hours, Carter. What the hell's going on there?'

Carter took the phone away from his ear and stared at it as if it were some strange, alien artifact. *Four hours!* 'I've changed my mind,' he said shakily. 'I need help.'

'Details?' Crozier's clipped tones were legendary in the Department. He never used politeness when efficiency could do the job in half the time.

Carter was still trying to come to terms with the lost memory of the past four hours but a verbal battle with Crozier was always guaranteed to sharpen his brain. 'Debrief me later. Just get a team out here as soon as you can.'

There was a slight pause on the other end of the line, and Carter knew he was weighing taking decisive action with a familiar rebuke that would be something like 'I give the orders around here.'

Carter had to admire Crozier when he said, 'Very well. Will you be around to brief them?' Performing his job was more important than point scoring; at least he could give the man grudging respect for that.

'Yes,' Robert Carter said wearily. He suddenly felt exhausted, more tired than he had ever felt in his life. 'I'll be here.' He switched off the phone and hugged his knees, lowered his head and closed his eyes.

He was in the same position when the cleanup team arrived an hour later.

CHAPTER THREE

If there was a bleaker, more godforsaken part of the world than Kulsay Island, John Harrison had yet to visit it. Lying three miles off the east coast of Scotland and subject to a ferocious battering by the North Sea, the island was a hard, desolate place, hunched and compact and resolutely self-contained.

As he flew the helicopter in from the mainland he could see the band of empty crofters' cottages on the

south of the island, decaying and rotten, their gray slate
roofs gaping with holes, the stone walls, moss covered and
crumbling, a testament to the harsh, ripping winds that
blew in from the sea, and to the years of neglect. They
were falling apart, tumbling down, as if the wretched landscape of the island was reclaiming them as its own. In a
field to the right of the cottages were handfuls of scraggy
sheep. They looked thin and unkempt, their fleeces matted
and tangled, caked with mud. They had defied the odds
(and the gods) to survive at all, but Harrison imagined that
it was a cruel, grinding existence, trying to find ready grazing in such harsh and unforgiving circumstances.

He was heading to the north end of the island. A group
of people had been stranded here as some sort of initia-
tive course. No one had heard anything from the island in
two days and the company the group worked for, Waincraft Software, was in a state of panic. The owners of the
island had been contacted and Harrison had been dis-
patched by them to investigate, and if necessary, airlift the
group off.

As he left the crofters' cottages behind he stared down
at the gradually changing landscape. The further north he
flew the harder and more extreme the conditions. There
was a wooded area at the heart of the island, mostly larch
and spruce, but the trees seemed stunted and tortured,
their crowns sorry affairs, sparse and spare, home to the
ragbag nests of huge black crows who took flight in a ca-
cophony of flapping wings and throaty cries as he passed
overhead.

Harrison had been flying charters for the best part of
ten years since his demob from the U.S. Air Force. Flying
gun ships during the Gulf War had prepared him for any
hazards he might encounter. But as he stared down at the
gnarled and twisted trees he couldn't suppress a shudder.

There was something decidedly unpleasant about Kulsay: the hostile landscape certainly, but it was more than that. Experience had taught him that you get a feel for places, something deep-seated, instinctive. And Kulsay Island was working on him at this deepest level, making him feel uneasy and anxious to complete his mission and get the hell out of there again as soon as possible.

Beyond the trees the land was more uneven, with rocky crags and verdant peat bogs jostling for space within the island's confines. There were the ruins of a small church, evidence that the community of Kulsay had once spread across the entire island, and half a mile away stood the old Manse, a great gray edifice of Aberdeen granite, imposing and austere. It was here the group was meant to be based, but as he flew over the building there was precious little evidence of habitation.

He decided to circle the island one more time before setting down. He increased throttle and the Bell AP139 bucked in the air before climbing higher into the dull, overcast sky.

Harrison had been told he could set down in the Manse's sprawling garden, but he was concerned there were no signs of life below. If, as he had been told, the group had run into difficulties, then the sound of the helicopter should have provoked at least one of them to come out into the open. Unless something was stopping them.

As he came in for the landing his eyes searched the stand of trees surrounding the grounds, looking for any sign of life. Below him the scrubby grass of the lawn was flattened by the downdraft from the blades as he took the machine in. As the wheels settled on the grass he switched off the engines, unstrapped himself from his seat and climbed out of the aircraft, instinctively ducking his head as the blades slowed above him.

Several feet beneath the grass something stirred;

something ancient and malign that sensed a new presence on the island.

In the cellar of the Manse, Eddie Farrant listened to the chopping sound as the helicopter flew over the building. His eyes widened in terror and he buried himself still further under the mildewed sacks that had been his refuge for the past twelve hours. They stank now, and were wet with urine, but this was his sanctuary and Farrant wasn't moving, despite the hunger pangs gnawing at his stomach. He'd eaten a Mars bar shortly after secreting himself down here, but nothing since.

If he truly believed it was a real helicopter, coming to rescue him, he might have come out of hiding. He might have run all the way up to the roof and stood there waving his arms to attract attention, screaming for help. But he didn't believe it was real. It was just another trick, another illusion, and he wasn't going to reveal his hiding place that easily. So he wormed down deeper into the pile of sacks until they covered his head, with just enough of a gap for him to breathe in the rancid air of the cellar.

Before the helicopter there had been nothing to listen to but the screams of the others coming from the rooms above as one by one they were taken. Sounds so wretched and desperate they forced him to clap his hands over his ears to block them out.

Now, as he lay there in his own filth and squalor, his mind drifted back over the past few days, remembering the people with whom he had come to the island—their faces, their idiosyncrasies, snatches of conversation, things they had done to irritate him. They were people he had worked with every day. Some he got on with, some he didn't, but he had been surprised how different they had all been out of the work environment.

Michael Bennett, Andrew Johnson, Casey Faraday,

Sheila Thomas and Jo Madley. He repeated the names over and over in his head like a mantra, hoping the repetition would block out some of the images of horror that were crowding into his mind.

He let his thoughts drift back in time to the day of their arrival when the launch brought them across from the mainland. He'd looked around the small boat at the excited and apprehensive faces of his work colleagues and wondered how he was going to cope living with them all for an extended period of time. Nine to five was one thing, but this was something entirely different.

The launch was piloted by a hulking brute of a man called Scart; ex-SAS, or so he said. He'd introduced himself gruffly and told them he was taking them across because he was being paid for the job and not because he wanted to make friends with them.

'Right,' he said, handing out seasickness pills with a barely concealed smile. 'The crossing's going to be choppy. Who's the senior member of staff here?'

Michael Bennett raised his hand.

'Okay. You're Group Leader. It's your responsibility to look after the others.' He turned to the rest of the group. 'You all clear about that? Any problems, don't come whining to me. Tell . . .' He glanced back at Bennett. 'What's your name?'

'Bennett. Michael Bennett.'

'Right. You tell Bennett here first. He'll then have to decide whether to bring your problems to me.'

'I really must obje . . .' Bennett began, but Scart silenced him with a scowl.

'As I said, the crossing's going to be choppy. Some of you will throw up. Inevitable. Just make sure the wind's behind you, otherwise you'll get a face full of vomit.'

Casey Faraday's face turned a pale shade of green in anticipation.

Casey worked with Sheila in Farrant's department, pushing paper for the most part; a small step above the secretaries who occupied the floor below. Andrew Johnson worked alongside them, but spent most of his time trying to cement his reputation as the office Romeo, spilling lurid tales of bedroom conquests and easy lays. Michael Bennett was Farrant's supervisor and had his own office at the end of the corridor. Eddie Farrant hated him with a passion, resenting his senior position, knowing he could do Bennett's job without breaking a sweat, but knowing also that the directors had no intention of letting him try. At least not while Michael Bennett remained with the company. Michael Bennett looked around the small boat at the excited faces of his colleagues and wondered how he was going to cope with leading them over the week. They were such a diverse group, united only by their employment at Waincraft. Why they had all volunteered for the grueling management Outward Bound course he had no idea. He could guess a few reasons.

Johnson would be hoping he could improve his rather sad reputation as the company ladies' man, and probably had a few moves planned on the three women members of the group. Two of them were married, not that Andrew would find that a barrier, but Bennett thought he knew Casey Faraday and Sheila Thomas well enough to know they wouldn't fall for Johnson's oily charm. The new girl, Jo Madley, was different; something about her defiant profile and firm manner told Bennett that maybe Johnson would have met his match if he tried it on her.

It was Jo Madley with whom Johnson was least familiar. She was about his age, blonde and lithe and he fancied her quite badly, but there was something about her self-confident style and brusque manner that told him she was out of his class, but he hadn't quite ruled himself out of the running. Andrew Johnson, however, was crass enough to make a pass at her on the launch and lived to regret it. Her rebuff was short and acidic and he'd withered in front of their eyes.

Jo Madley had been the first of the group to disappear.

CHAPTER FOUR

The boat couldn't get as close to shore as Scart intended; the forlorn wooden jetty had crumbled further into the gray sea since his previous visit and he couldn't maneuver near enough for his passengers to get onto it. They would have to get their feet wet if they intended to get onto Kulsay. Though why anyone would want to stay a single night on the damned island was beyond him. There were enough stories, enough missing people and animals, to ward off all but the most foolhardy. As a mainlander he had had no patience with the crofters at the other end of the island and their ancient beliefs. Not that he hadn't been as worried as the next man when they all disappeared.

Let them all be blown off into the ocean during the next storm, let the island and its traditions rot and sink into the cold dark water. Now that they were all gone, he regretted thinking ill of his fellow men and women, but he hadn't changed his mind about the island. He cursed the day he had ever set eyes upon it.

Michael Bennett realized almost straightaway that things wouldn't go smoothly. Jo and Sheila screamed as the boat bucked on a large swell. It was at that point that Scart told them they would have to jump for it. What that meant in practical terms was leaping about three feet from the boat onto a few clearly rotting planks of wood that were already roughly a foot underwater.

To Bennett's surprise Eddie wasted no time in jumping from the boat. With equally surprising agility he moved from there onto the jetty itself.

'Come on, Andrew,' Eddie shouted. 'Get your fit young ass up here and help me with the others.'

Andrew, cocky as ever, looked at him with almost oriental scrutiny and then wordlessly leaped onto the submerged planks. He seemed to know straightaway what Eddie intended; a two-man line from the boat to the relative safety of the jetty.

Bennett began to shepherd the others from the boat. The women were light enough to jump cleanly and for Eddie to catch them and maneuver them up to Andrew safely. Whether they would have been so willing if it was Andrew doing the initial grabbing from the boat Bennett doubted.

When they were all on the jetty with their bags, Bennett turned to thank the skipper. He had already turned the boat and was heading back to the mainland without a backwards glance.

At that moment it began to rain, and Bennett's misgivings began again in earnest.

Kulsay Island in the eighteenth century wasn't a great deal different from the one visited so disastrously in the twenty-first. There were more trees, and the only buildings a roughly hewn church and the original Manse. Both were inextricably linked.

The obscure group who built and populated the Manse led a sheltered if not entirely blameless life of devotion and prayer. That their prayers were not offered to any conventional God was a secret they managed to protect until word of their practices spread across the inlet of the inhospitable sea to the mainland. The consequences of that discovery reverberated through the centuries, the sacred lines carrying surging power, swirling like veins beneath the earth's skin, creating a beating rhythm of pulsing strength, feeding and breathing with a mystery as ancient as the curse that enveloped them.

Bound by the blood promise that wrapped itself around them, they slowly emitted hollow echoes that traveled ceaselessly—waiting, patiently waiting for the century that would provide sufficient sustenance for release.

With feet already wet from the landing, and with the persistent rain obscuring the gray light that clung to the last few minutes of the day, the six company employees trudged away from the water's edge and up towards the Manse.

Casey Faraday was still holding onto Andrew's arm and Bennett hoped he hadn't been wrong about her. Andrew had offered to help Sheila with her bag but she politely declined while Jo Madley gave no indication she needed or would welcome any offer of assistance. As they neared the large, indistinct shape of the house, the watery light seeping from the grimy windows didn't exactly cheer them.

'Looks welcoming,' Andrew said in his ironic way.

Casey gripped his arm tighter, and his mind began to run ahead of itself while his arm pressed against her breast and relished the soft warmth it found there. 'Anywhere out of this rain is home at the moment.'

'If the phone is connected you can ring home, Casey,' Sheila said sweetly. 'Let your husband know you're missing him.'

Before Casey could reply, Bennett said, 'There is no phone. That's part of the deal. It's a survival week. Live rough and develop as a team.'

'In that case some of us have become good team players already,' Sheila said.

Any response was postponed by a sudden shout of thunder and the slight rain altered direction and intensity; screaming at them in jets of pure fury. They ran for the house, luggage slowing them.

Behind them none of them noticed the ground undulate, rippling as if forces beneath it were struggling to get free.

Andrew Johnson was first through the door. He threw down his holdall and searched with one hand for the light switch. As the others bustled inside the lights flickered and illuminated in pale shadowed fringes a hallway that would once have been considered grand. Worn black and white tiles shuffled off into corners where dust piled in inelegant mounds. Once-ornate covings were coated with accumulated grime that lent them the appearance of mould, and judging from the underlying smell of the house mould was prevalent throughout.

'Home sweet home,' Jo Madley murmured, voicing the thoughts of them all.

'It's a survival course,' Bennett said. 'And the house seems to be part of the survival.'

'Stayed in worse on the road,' Eddie said cheerfully. 'We just need to get warmed up.'

Their footsteps echoed on the marble tiles as they began to open doors and check inside. None of the rooms were inviting; most of the furniture was covered in yellowed dust-sheets, the windows covered on the outside by wooden shutters and on the inside by thick velvet curtains, drawn tightly shut. At least the electricity seemed to be connected and the lights in all the rooms working.

They weren't conscious of moving through the rooms as a group, but that's what they did. It was as if none of them wanted to be alone, even though they would have argued they were merely team building if one of them had mentioned it.

Because they kept together, none of them noticed the curtains rippling as though breathing, and the fresh finger marks on the old dustsheets.

They decided to share rooms. Once Eddie's coarse jokes were all used up the three women took one large bedroom to the front of the house; there was a huge four-poster bed there and a smaller divan type; and the men selected a room at the back with four single beds in it.

'No good if we strike lucky,' Andrew complained and while Eddie ignored the comment, Bennett knew it was made only half in jest.

Unpacking didn't take long as they had been instructed to travel light and wear warm, practical clothing. Jo went through to the en suite bathroom and as soon as the other two women heard the sound of running water they jumped on the bed and began talking.

'What the hell were you doing hanging onto Eager Andy like that?' Sheila wanted to know.

'And what were you doing making snide remarks about it?'

'You know what he's like. You can't fancy him surely?'

Casey looked at her friend as if she needed to explain the reality of things very slowly. 'We're here for what? Seven days? And six nights! Eddie is cute but uptight and bound to take all of this ultraseriously, Bennett is so full of his team leader role he can't see past his own nose, so that leaves Andy as the only one to have a laugh with. Besides, he's so keen to preserve his womanizer image he'll do anything in return for a harmless flirt. I'm about as good on a survival course as I would be running the marathon, so I—we—might just need a friend to get us out of the more strenuous ordeals they have planned. Andy will cover for us.'

Casey spread herself on the slightly damp quilt. Sheila absorbed what she had said and laid beside her. 'How does that husband of yours ever stand a chance married to a schemer like you?'

'He doesn't, but I don't take advantage . . . too often.'

Eddie was unpacked and had his things stowed away in two drawers of an ancient wardrobe before Andrew had even opened his case.

'What's on the agenda, Mike?' he asked Bennett.

Bennett hated being called anything other than Michael, which is why so many of his colleagues used the diminutive as often as they could.

Eddie knew that more than anyone. 'Yeah, *Mike*, what have you got planned for us?'

Bennett carefully folded his clothes and wash things into a voluminous drawer in the chest next to his bed before he turned to them. 'Look, guys, I'm just one of you. Okay? They made me team leader but you know and I know that means shit. We're stuck with each other for the next seven days. I have no idea what happens tomorrow— I'm supposed to get instructions somehow. "You'll be contacted" is all they told me. For tonight lay off me and let's just relax. Okay?'

Andrew held up his hands in a gesture of appeasement. '*Okay*,' Eddie said.

Downstairs they were surprised to find about nine people assembled and waiting for them. A gray-haired man with a close-cropped beard stepped forward and introduced himself. 'I'm Lomax, the head of the household for the week, and this is Mary our housekeeper, and the rest of the staff, including the kitchen staff and cook.' He smiled but it was a dour smile that reminded Bennett of the deep waters of a loch he had once seen near Oban. 'I dare say you could all do with some food after your pleasant crossing.'

'I could do with a drink,' Eddie said and most of the others laughed. Team building included finding weak jokes funny.

Mary ushered the majority of the staff away, to the kitchens, Casey imagined, while one of the younger men walked in a different direction.

'Young Ben will serve you at the bar. You'll find the whisky excellent of course, but the bar is stocked with all manner of fancy drinks that you might be more used to than I am.' Lomax gestured that they should all follow Ben.

Bennett hovered behind as the others all walked through.

'Is there anything I can help you with, sir?' Lomax asked, his accent soft and deep.

Bennett swept his hand in the air to indicate the house. 'The house is large, and obviously has been wonderful in the past.'

'Your point, sir?'

'Judging by the dust and the neglect I doubt the Manse houses nearly ten staff on a permanent basis.'

Lomax inclined his head. 'Waincraft employed us for the week. We have a small launch moored along the jetty.' Bennett noticed there was no 'sir' this time. 'I understand they want a team bonding week but seven days is a long time without some home comforts.'

They wouldn't have their allotted seven days. The walls of the Manse began to move during the night; the ground around the perimeter rising and falling as if it was a duvet being shaken into place.

CHAPTER FIVE

It was like waiting outside the headmaster's study at school.

Robert Carter had mixed memories of school. He had enjoyed the social side of it, though he had kept in touch with none of the other boys. He had quite liked the education, finding learning, in most subjects, satisfying and stimulating. The discipline was a different matter. He had hated being told what to do, and as a result he quickly collected a reputation for challenging teachers, for disrupting classes with his questions. The corridor outside the headmaster's room was soon familiar to him, and six of the best from the bamboo cane became a regular punishment.

Now, sitting on a chrome and leather chair that was excruciatingly uncomfortable despite looking chic and modern, waiting for Crozier to usher him in, the memories flooded back. The door opened and Crozier popped his head out for a moment, beckoning Carter in. A sudden flashback of being fifteen and walking nervously into the headmaster's study washed over him and he was unsettled as Crozier closed the door behind him.

'Robert,' Crozier said with apparent warmth. 'And how are you?'

For a Georgian building in the center of London's Whitehall area the office was loudly modern. There was the ambience of a newly opened and longing to be fashionable restaurant about it. Though discreetly set on the desk were all the apparatus of a high-powered executive. Which in many ways was exactly what Crozier was.

Carter was aware that his superior was looking at him and realized he was waiting for a reply. 'Any news on Sian?'

Crozier glanced out of the window for the barest of moments and Carter knew what the answer would be. 'Have you seen the report from the cleanup team?'

Carter shook his head. If Sian hadn't been found that probably meant she was still alive. The chances were her body would have shown up on the various scans of the area the Department would have organized as standard procedure if she had been killed and dumped.

There was disapproval on Crozier's face that the report hadn't been read and inwardly digested but Carter knew that was unreasonable given he had slept for sixteen hours once he got home. 'Your car was thoroughly investigated, of course.' Crozier looked up like a cat might glance at a mouse. 'It was clean. No blood traces, no traces of . . . what were they you mentioned, beetles? The house was taken apart inch by inch, you know the drill.'

Carter knew from the deliberate hesitation that the news would not be good for him. Crozier was enjoying this. He was toying with Carter as a prelude to something worse to come. Not that it concerned him. His only worry at that moment was Sian.

A brief flicker of annoyance that his prey had not yet bitten rippled across Crozier's lips but it soon passed as he slipped back the professional mask. 'Apparently the house was untouched.'

He had no alternative but to react to that. 'What about the wallpaper? The kitchen?' The beetles in the dining room were still vivid in his mind. The crockery smashed in the kitchen, the smells and the noise when he went back into the house after making sure Sian . . . after thinking he had made sure she was safe.

Crozier flicked a nonexistent piece of dust from his

desktop. 'Sorry, Robert, can't help you there. The house was as clean as the day the Flemings moved out. Cleaner in fact, as the team found no psychic traces of any kind.' This was said with a note of disbelief as if he wanted to believe Carter's version of events but just couldn't.

Except Carter knew his wasn't a *version* but reality.

There had been powerful forces in that house and if they were gone a day later then they must have been there for a reason. As Sian had disappeared at the same time, then either she or Carter must have been the reason.

There was a knock at the door and Trudy, Crozier's secretary, walked in with a tray of cups, saucers and a teapot. The reputation of the English government flourishing on a diet of afternoon tea and digestive biscuits was kept alive in this part of the establishment.

Carter needed to get away and think. For months now incidents had been building that could only partially be explained. They had culminated in the episode at the house but other events had occurred on a regular enough basis to alert someone with Carter's abilities. He needed to go home and run through the notes he had been making.

The tea had been poured, the milk and sugar added and Crozier was nibbling on a digestive. 'You see the position I find myself in, Robert?'

'What position is that?'

'Do I have to spell it out?' The cat was preparing to pounce.

Carter finished his cup of tea, placed the cup delicately onto the saucer and smiled at Crozier. 'I rather think you do, yes.'

Crozier stood and walked to the windows. Looking out he could see the traffic starting to build up. The roof of Buckingham Palace was visible a short distance away. The flag was flying, indicating the Queen was in residence.

Strangely, since the Helen Mirren film had been so successful the popularity of Hĕr Majesty, already generally
high, had soared.

'Very well.' Crozier turned to Carter. 'You fouled up,
Robert. Made a complete balls-up of what should have
been a simple poltergeist investigation. Christ, it was only
a favor for a colleague because the house belonged to a
member of their family. How could it go wrong?'

Carter stood, and although he hadn't intended it to, the
chair toppled over backwards. Crozier took a step back as
though he had been threatened. 'That was no simple
haunting . . .'

'So you say . . .'

'I'm the expert, remember? It's what I do. There were
forces, very strong . . . that's why Sian . . .'

'Which brings us to the most serious aspect of the
matter.'

If he hadn't realized it before, he was under no illusions
now. This was a disciplinary meeting. How Crozier must
have enjoyed setting the agenda for this.

When Carter didn't reply Crozier continued. 'You lost an
employee on a case. Not just lost but "mislaid." Your verbal
report cannot be substantiated, and the cleanup team has
found not a single trace of evidence to support your apparent sightings. You lost it, Robert. Your nerve, your powers,
whatever way you want to dress it up. You cost Sian Davies
her life.'

Carter walked across to Crozier, nodded once, then hit
him hard on the jaw.

Chapter Six

The last few hundred yards were agony. They were breasting a hill and could see the Manse in the distance, but for Michael Bennett and Eddie Farrant it looked to be miles away. The other runners had left them behind halfway round the cross-country course, and the two men were tired, thirsty and thoroughly humiliated. Farrant glanced round at Bennett, who was trying and succeeding to match him pace for pace. He swore under his breath. Bennett was ten years older and twenty pounds heavier than him. The sweat was flowing freely down the older man's face and his mouth sagged open, wheezing in breath after breath, trying to force air down into his lungs. His eyes were bleary and unfocused and his skin was bright pink, like a lobster just out of the pot.

In the distance Farrant could see the others reach the Manse and stop and collapse to the ground in exhaustion, but could also hear the whoops of triumph. They'd made it; they'd completed the course and were celebrating. He still had two hundred yards to run, on legs that felt like jelly, with his rival both here and at work, dogging his heels. With a sob of desperation, he tried to summon one last burst of energy. He couldn't be beaten by Bennett. Not by him; anybody but him.

'What kept you?' Andrew Johnson said, as Eddie Farrant finally reached the Manse and collapsed on the ground beside him.

'Twisted my ankle early on,' Farrant lied, watching with satisfaction as Bennett took his last few steps, the agony plain to see on his face.

'What's up with him? Looks like he's about to have a coronary.'

'Yeah,' Farrant said. 'I nursed him home. Didn't want to leave him behind in case something happened to him.' He put a mask of concern over his features.

'Regular Good Samaritan, aren't you, Eddie?' Jo Madley said, rubbing the sweat from her face with a towel. She turned to Casey Faraday and winked.

Casey smiled and pushed herself up. 'I'm going for a shower,' she said. 'I stink like a pig.'

'We all do,' Sheila Thomas said. 'I just hope there's enough hot water for us all.' Last night she was last in the bathroom and the water had been running cold.

'I could murder a pint,' Andrew Johnson said.

'Your round,' Farrant said.

'Care to join us for cocktails, girls?' Johnson said.

Jo Madley ignored him. 'Where's Lomax? I thought he'd be here to meet us with his stopwatch.'

'Don't question it, Jo,' Sheila said. 'The bastard's probably inside somewhere pulling the wings off flies.'

'Or drowning kittens,' Casey said.

Lomax, it turned out, was the keeper of the instructions from Waincraft. Part of his role was to set the group tasks for the day and measure the results. Today it had been a cross-country run. They were certain there were even more sadistic trials planned for later.

'The point is, he's not here, so let's take advantage,' Sheila said. 'Race you to the bar.'

'Yeah, right,' Jo said, lethargically forcing herself to stand. She turned to Michael Bennett. 'You okay, Mike?'

Bennett was still panting, trying to get his breath back. He nodded his head, unable to speak.

'I'll walk with you,' she said, and took his arm.

'You don't have to,' Bennett said, finally able to speak, and fell into step beside her, walking slowly.

'I know,' she said.

The others had almost reached the front door. Johnson looked back at them, a smirk on his face.

'Cretin,' Jo muttered under her breath. 'Who does he think he is?'

'God's gift to the female species,' Bennett said. He felt dreadful and was very conscious he didn't cut a particularly heroic figure right now.

'Then Heaven help us all,' Jo said. 'If you don't mind me asking, why are you putting yourself through this?'

'Vanity and pride, with a very large chunk of masochism thrown in,' Bennett said. 'Can you imagine the ribbing I would have endured at work if I'd chickened out? Those idiots would have made my life hell.'

'Sod 'em,' Jo said. 'You mustn't let them get to you, Mike. It's all wind and piss with them. What they lack in intellect they make up for in macho posturing. There were dozens like that at the last place I worked. I got fed up with them in the end; that's why I left and joined Waincraft.'

'And you find Waincraft better?' It was the first time Jo had opened up about anything personal, even work related, although he knew her employment history from the staff files.

'Marginally.' That was the truth. One office was very much like another in her experience.

They reached the door and went inside. And immediately realized something was wrong.

'What's going on?' Jo said.

Sheila and Casey were standing in the hallway, anxious looks on their faces. Of the other two men there was no sign.

'There's no one here,' Sheila said.

'What do you mean?'

'Just that. Everybody's gone. Lomax, the housekeeper, the kitchen staff, everybody.'

'They're probably somewhere else in the house. They can't just have gone,' Michael Bennett said.

'Andrew and Eddie are checking now, but when we got here the place was as silent as the grave. And then there was this.' Sheila walked across to the entrance to the dining room and pointed at the floor. There was a dark, wet smear across the parquet. Michael Bennett crouched down and poked the smear with his finger. When he took his hand away his fingertip was stained red. 'It's blood,' he said, staring at his finger with disgust.

'Yes,' Casey said. 'But whose?'

'And how did it get there?' Sheila said. She shivered.

Johnson and Farrant appeared at the top of the stairs. 'There's no one up here,' Johnson said. 'The place is deserted.' They came down and joined the others at the foot of the stairs.

'And the phones are out,' Farrant added.

'Okay,' Bennett said. 'Let's not panic. There's probably a logical explanation.'

'Who's panicking?' Johnson said. 'I'm going to get a drink. Anyone care to join me?' He walked through to the small bar area to the left of the dining room. There were a few easy chairs, a couple of coffee tables and the bar itself, well stocked with spirits and bottled beer. He helped himself to a triple vodka, grabbed a bottle of tonic water from the shelf behind the bar and went to sit down in one of the easy chairs. Pulling a pack of cigarettes from the pocket of his sweatpants he lit one and sat back to enjoy the nicotine rush.

'What about your cell?' Bennett said to Farrant as the younger man pushed past him on his way to the bar.

'No signal. Haven't had one since we arrived. Hardly surprising really. This *is* the back of beyond, after all.'

One by one the others helped themselves to drinks, except Bennett who never touched alcohol these days, not since he'd ended his love affair with the bottle four years previously.

Casey Faraday took a glass of white wine across to the window that looked out over the flagstoned patio. She took one sip of the pinot grigio, then dropped the glass to the floor and screamed. By the time the others reached her Casey was crying hysterically, pointing out through the window.

Sheila grabbed her by the shoulders. 'Casey, calm down. What's wrong?'

Andrew Johnson followed the line of Casey's pointing finger. 'Holy shit!' he said.

Eddie Farrant joined him, mouth open in astonishment, face rapidly draining of color. 'Oh my God!'

They stared through the window at the patio. Tables and chairs had been overturned and umbrellas lay on their side, rocking gently back and forth in the afternoon breeze. In the center of the patio was Guy Lomax, but only his head, shoulders and right arm was visible; it was as if the rest of him had been swallowed by the patio, as if he had sunk into the flagstones.

'I'm sorry,' Michael Bennett said, 'but that's impossible. I'm going to take a closer look.'

'Don't go out there!' Casey grabbed his arm.

Bennett yanked it away. 'Don't be stupid. We can't just leave him there. Anyone else coming?'

'You're on your own, mate,' Johnson said. He'd resumed his seat, but he no longer looked so self-assured. He would never admit it, not even to himself, but he was scared.

'Eddie?' Bennett turned to Farrant, hoping he wouldn't have to go outside on his own.

'No way.' Farrant swallowed his drink and moved to the bar for another.

'I'll come with you,' Jo said.

Bennett stared at her. 'Are you sure?'

'Let's just do it.' She walked to the door. Bennett stared at the other two men with barely concealed contempt, then spun round and followed Jo out of the bar.

'Wanker!' Andrew Johnson said as Bennett disappeared from view.

'Just shut up, Andrew,' Sheila said. 'At least he's got the guts to actually do something.'

Johnson looked at Eddie Farrant and raised his eyebrows. Farrant looked away.

'It's impossible,' Bennett said again.

'So you said. But obviously it's not.' Jo Madley was crouching down, staring at Lomax.

'Is he dead?' Bennett was worried about getting too close.

'Yes, I think so.' Jo studied Lomax's face. The skin was white and pasty, eyes closed, lips clamped together in a thin line. His head was slumped forward, almost touching the flagstones. Tentatively she reached out and touched the stone. 'It's solid,' she said. She inched her fingers forward until they reached the point where flesh and stone merged. There was no gap, not even a millimeter. The join was seamless. 'This is too weird,' she said, and then threw herself backwards as Lomax opened his eyes. 'Jesus Christ!'

The thin line of his mouth split and opened wide. The scream that emerged was deafening and harrowing. And as the scream ended Lomax sunk another six inches into the ground so that only the top half of his head and one hand was visible. Seconds later he disappeared altogether, the flagstones rippling slightly before becoming solid once more.

Jo looked up at Bennett. 'Mike, this isn't right. We've got to get out of here,' she said, and tears started to trickle down her cheeks.

Michael Bennett's face was a pale, frightened mask. He nodded his head in a jerky, marionette-like movement, and helped Jo to her feet.

'Okay,' Andrew Johnson said. 'We need a plan.'

They had gathered together in the bar once more. Both he and Eddie were nursing large vodkas. Jo was sitting in the corner, hands clasped around a brandy snifter containing a large measure of the spirit. She halfheartedly put the glass to her lips but the sickly smell of the brandy made her gag and she lowered it and stood up quickly. 'I think I'm going to be sick,' she said and ran from the room.

'I've checked all the phones in the place,' Johnson said, ignoring the interruption. 'None of them work. The same goes for my cell. As Eddie said, no network.'

'So we've got no way of contacting the mainland?' Sheila asked.

'Not unless you've got a radio transmitter stashed in your hand luggage. No, we're stuffed. So, any ideas?' He looked from face to face. They all stared back blankly at him. 'Great,' he said. 'Just great!'

Jo Madley wiped her mouth on a paper towel, cupped her hand under the faucet, filled her palm with cold water and splashed it over her face. It helped, a little. She felt hollow inside, as if her guts had been reamed out. She couldn't rid herself of the image of Lomax, screaming as he sank beneath the patio. She knew the sound of that scream would come to her in the nights ahead, invading her dreams, waking her; and in her dreams she would again see Lomax's face, contorted in unimaginable agony, his hand flopping uselessly from side to side until it too was swallowed by the ground.

There was a knock at the door. 'Are you okay, Jo?'

Sheila's voice jerked her back to reality. 'Yeah, fine. Just puked, that's all.'

'If you need anything . . .'

'I'll call you if I do.'

Actually, being alone in the bathroom was something of a relief. She was wondering now why she'd volunteered for this course. Being holed up on a remote island with a bunch of people she didn't really care for was not her idea of Heaven. Bennett was all right in a wimpy kind of way, pleasant but harmless. But Andrew Johnson was an asshole, and Eddie Farrant wasn't much better, content to hang on to Johnson's coattails and bask in his reflected glory. Of the other two women she preferred Sheila. There was a kind of no-nonsense aura around her that commanded respect. Casey, on the other hand, was a fairly weak character with no hard, firm opinions of her own, and the possessor of a tabloid mentality who got her kicks from reading about the bedroom exploits of the rich and slightly famous. Jo had nothing in common with her, which made conversation all but impossible.

And then there was her, Jo Madley. Twenty-six, single, fairly pretty, if she looked at herself objectively, but unable to sustain relationships with the opposite sex for little more than a few days. Her problem was that she really didn't like people very much, and trusted them even less. And that applied especially to men. She knew the fault was with her, and blamed her father who had run off with his secretary when she was just eight years old, leaving her mother to bring up Jo and her two brothers alone. To her credit her mother did a fine job. David, her eldest brother, was now a solicitor, whilst Ian, who was two years younger than her, was a professional pianist, earning his living providing mood music for the diners aboard various luxury ocean liners. If anything it was she who was the underachiever, flitting from one job to another, unable to settle into anything that could vaguely be called a career.

She poured water into her hands again and ran them

through her hair, slicking it back from her face. She couldn't languish in here forever, no matter how tempting it might seem. But she really didn't want to go back and sit with the others. What she had witnessed on the patio had left her badly frightened. She just wanted to go home.

As she stared at herself in the mirror a movement behind her diverted her attention. The wall was moving, rippling slightly, white tiles starting to buckle and lift. As she watched, one came loose and fell, but instead of crashing to the floor it seemed to float down like tissue paper in an almost endless descent. It finally reached the stone floor and then exploded into a thousand jagged white pieces. But the explosion was silent, gentle.

One by one the tiles dropped from the wall, each taking a balletic eternity to land and smash. In falling they exposed a rough brick wall, russet red and dusty. She turned away from the mirror and went to investigate, her feet crunching over broken tiles. She traced the line of mortar between the bricks with her fingertip. It was powdery, insubstantial, crumbling away under her touch. As she prodded one of the bricks it wobbled slightly. *The place is falling apart*, she thought.

As if to echo her thoughts, the brick she was prodding slid backwards and fell into the cavity behind the wall. Again, like the tiles, the sound of the brick falling was muffled, as if it had dropped onto a cushion of foam rubber. She peered through the gap left by the brick but could see only blackness. She pressed against the surrounding brickwork and felt it give under the pressure. As more bricks started to tumble, a white hand thrust out through the gap and grabbed her around the throat.

CHAPTER SEVEN

'She's been in there for ages,' Sheila said. 'I'm going to see if she's all right.'

'You only checked ten minutes ago,' Johnson said, lighting another cigarette and blowing smoke in her direction.

'Yes, and now I'm going to check again. Or do you have a problem with that?'

Johnson shrugged. 'Suit yourself.'

Sheila glared at him. 'Don't worry, I will.'

Asshole! She thought as she walked along the dimly lit corridor to the bathroom. Andrew Johnson was starting to get on her nerves and she wondered now how she had once found him attractive. Thoughts of last year's Christmas party insinuated their way into her mind and she shuddered at the memories of hurried sex behind the photocopier in the machine room; his hands inside her blouse and down her panties; fumbling fingers trying and failing to bring her to orgasm. Her lips wrapped around his . . . *Stop it! Stop thinking about it*. She'd been drunk; one too many Tia Marias, and the hangover of a blazing row with her husband, making her act out of character. Andrew Johnson was a chancer, an opportunist whose sexual radar had locked in on her vulnerability. Andrew Johnson was a slug and she forced herself to push him from her mind.

'Jo? You've been ages. Are you sure you're all right?' She tapped on the bathroom door again, pressing her ear to the wood, listening for the reply and getting only silence. 'Jo?' She curled her fingers around the door handle, ready to turn it. Still nothing. Perhaps she'd passed out. She turned the handle and pushed the door open.

The bathroom was empty. Sheila frowned. Maybe she'd gone back to the bedroom, but it didn't seem likely given what had happened. This was not the time to be anywhere in this house on your own. She could still hear conversation buzzing in the bar, drawing her back. She closed the bathroom door and hurried back along the corridor.

'She's not there,' she said as she entered the bar.

'Where is she then?' Eddie Farrant said. The attention he was giving to his drink showed how deep his concern went.

'How the hell should I know?' Sheila snapped. She was beginning to feel real impatience with Andy and Eddie, not to mention the bloody island.

'Tetchy,' Johnson said, a slight sneer on his lips.

'Piss off!'

'All right, settle down,' Michael Bennett said. 'Getting edgy with each other won't solve anything. We'd better search the house for her.'

'That's a bit extreme, isn't it, Mike?' Johnson said. 'She's probably gone up to her room.'

'Then we'll go and check.' When he needed to be, Bennett could adopt the leader role, he just didn't choose to do it enough of the time.

'You can go. I've just made myself comfortable. Free booze. What could be better?' Johnson was being deliberately provocative, fueled by the alcohol.

'Free booze and no guts,' Sheila said, glaring across at Johnson.

He raised his glass to her and smiled. 'Need any photocopying done, Sheil?'

'Prick!' Sheila said with anger.

'Sheila!' Bennett said.

'Well he is,' Sheila said with passion, but hoped no one realized what Johnson's remark meant.

'Agreed, but standing here sniping with each other

won't help find Jo. Come with me. We'll check out her room.'

'Shouldn't we all go?' Casey Faraday looked pale and frightened. She chewed her bottom lip and tears were welling in her eyes.

'Good idea,' Bennett said. 'Best that we all stick together. Eddie, Andrew, come on.'

With a theatrical sigh Andrew Johnson put his glass down on the table and shuffled himself to his feet. 'Bloody waste of time,' he said.

Bennett walked over to him and spoke softly so the others couldn't hear. 'If you want a job when you get back from here, stop acting like a moron. You may think you're Jack the lad, but just remember, when we get back to Waincraft, I'm still your superior, and I can make life bloody difficult for you.'

Anger flared in Andrew Johnson's eyes. His mouth opened, but he bit back the words and forced a smile. 'No problem, Mike,' he said.

'Good,' Bennett said. 'Now, come on.' And to his surprise the whole team moved as one.

Jo Madley's bedroom, the room all the girls were sharing, was empty. Her bed was neatly made and a few pieces of clothing hung from hangers hooked over the handles of the wardrobe door. On the dressing table was a cluster of her cosmetics; on the bedside table a paperback book, open, face-down, spine straining.

Johnson glanced down at the title of the book and smirked. *Change Your Life in Five Days.* We'll she'd certainly done that.

'We'll try the other rooms, then move on up to the staff quarters,' Michael Bennett said. 'She's got to be here somewhere.'

'Has she?' Sheila said quietly. 'After what we witnessed

on the patio, I would have thought that all bets were off.'

Bennett looked at her tight-lipped and walked from the room.

The rest of the Manse was empty.

'This is pointless,' Johnson said. 'She's not here. Let's go back to the bar.'

'To do what?' Bennett said. 'Sit there and get pissed?'

'That's better than roaming about the house aimlessly,' Eddie Farrant said. 'We're not going to find her.'

'What makes you so bloody sure, Eddie?' Casey Faraday said. Her voice had a hysterical edge. Bennett looked at her sharply. She was on the edge and the slightest thing might push her over.

'I would have thought that was obvious,' Farrant said. 'This is the second time we've searched this place. The staff has gone, Jo's gone. We'll be next. One by bloody one.' He said it calmly but the fear was evident.

'That's enough, Farrant,' Bennett said. 'We don't want to hear your opinions.' He went across to Casey and wrapped an arm protectively around her shoulders. 'Take no notice of him, Casey. He's just sounding off. All wind and piss,' he added, remembering Jo Madley's graphic description earlier.

Eddie Farrant glared at him. 'I resent that,' he said, his temper flaring. 'I'm entitled to express my opinions.'

'Not when it's upsetting others.' Bennett stood upright and his posture dared Farrant to take it further.

'I need a drink,' Farrant said.

'So you're just going to sit in the bar and lose yourself in a bottle. Is that the plan, Eddie?' Sheila said.

'Yes,' Farrant said. 'That's the plan.' He shoved past her and made his way down the stairs.

Andrew Johnson looked at the others, then shrugged

and followed Farrant. Michael Bennett stood at the top of the stairs with the two women. 'Did either of you see a radio transmitter in any of the rooms? They must have had a contingency in case the phones went down.'

Casey and Sheila exchanged looks, and then both shook their heads. 'There could be one on the boat Lomax has down at the jetty,' Sheila said after a moment.

'You're probably right,' Bennett said. 'Let's go down and tell the others. One of them might know how to use it.'

'Don't you?' Sheila said.

Bennett's cheeks flushed. 'No. I don't. Outside my sphere of experience.'

'My dad had a CB radio,' Casey said. 'Years ago when it was all the rage. Breaker one nine . . . all that nonsense.'

'Did he let you use it?' Sheila said. She'd seen the films and found them boring, preferring her dad's old tapes of Tony Hancock and *The Radio Ham*.

Casey shook her head. 'But I used to watch him. I'm sure I could pick it up if I had a bit of practice.'

'Then what I suggest is that we all get in one of the Land Rovers and drive down to the jetty,' Bennett said.

'Andrew and Eddie won't want to leave the comfort of the bar,' Sheila said.

'That's up to them. We can still go,' Casey said.

'I'd prefer it if we all stayed together,' Bennett said. But he didn't relish another run-in with the two men, especially as they'd have drunk quite a bit by now.

'But you can't force them to go to the boat,' Casey said. 'And if we try to argue with them we'll just be wasting time. I don't know about you two, but I want to get off this bloody island as soon as possible.'

'Amen to that,' Sheila said.

'Well, let's go and see what they say,' Bennett said,

although he had no intention of trying very hard to persuade them.

Eddie Farrant reached the bottom of the stairs. He'd had enough of Michael Bennett. It was bad enough having to suffer his pettiness and rank-pulling at work without having to endure it here.

'Eddie.'

He glanced round, peering along the corridor, which led to the kitchen. Jo Madley was standing there, her back to the wall. As their eyes met she beckoned him with a quick motion of her hand, then peeled away and disappeared into one of the rooms. Johnson was already in the bar and he could hear the others as they made their way down the stairs. He wasn't going to wait for them, and Bennett's inevitable order couched as a suggestion that they all go after Jo together. There had been something in her eyes; something that his mother would have called a *come hither* look. He'd lusted after Jo ever since she started at Waincraft, though not as obviously as Andrew, and he felt an unmistakable stirring between his legs. That look!

He took off down the corridor, walking quickly, found the room she had entered and slipped inside.

It was dark. The drapes were pulled. His hand reached for the light switch.

'Leave it!'

He let his hand drop. 'Where are you? I can't see.'

And then he felt her body press against him. 'Here,' she said, her mouth closing over his.

His hands slid over her back, pulling her closer, whilst his tongue tasted the sweetness of her mouth. Her hands were in his hair, fingers entwining themselves, gripping tightly, almost painfully, her lips bruising his. Finally he broke away. 'Where have you been? We've been looking everywhere.'

'That doesn't matter now,' she said breathlessly. 'Eddie, I don't want to die.'

'Die? What are you talking about?'

'I want to show you something,' she said, and grabbed his hand, tugging him across the room.

'What?' he said, wanting her back in his arms, wanting to feel her soft breasts pressing against his chest.

She didn't let go of his hand; instead her fingers closed more tightly around his, making him wince. They reached the window. He could hear her breathing heavily, but still could not make out her features in the gloom. He sensed rather than saw her hand reach out and pull open the drapes. Twilight nudged its way into the room. He peered out through the window at the Manse's sprawling grounds.

'I can't see anything.' It was too dark outside to see anything clearly.

'Not out there. Here!' Her voice was insistent, almost impatient.

He turned to her and saw her face for the first time.

The scream bubbled in his throat but refused to leave his lips.

Maggots. Hundreds, thousands of them, covering Jo Madley's face. The nose had gone, eaten away. Fat white bodies dropped from lips that bare seconds ago had been pressed against his. They writhed over and under her skin making it ripple and pulse. They moved under her eyelids, dropping from her eyes like white tears.

'Pretty, eh?' The words sounded thick, and they triggered the scream.

The scream brought the others running.

Farrant spun round as the door was flung open and Bennett, Sheila and Casey ran into the room.

'Eddie, what's wrong?' Bennett shouted.

'That!' Farrant shouted back and turned back to face Jo Madley, but she'd gone.

'What?' Sheila said.

'She was there . . . right there,' Eddie Farrant said. 'Horrible. Maggots.'

Bennett turned to the women. 'Have you any idea what he's talking about?'

Sheila shrugged, went across to Farrant and put an arm around his shoulders. 'It's all right, Eddie. Come back to the bar and have a drink. A stiff brandy will help.'

'She was here in the room with me, Sheil. Jo. Her face was alive with maggots.' He clutched his stomach and convulsed, vomiting on the floor.

'Charming,' Bennett said quietly to Casey. 'How many has he had anyway?'

Farrant wiped his mouth with the back of his hand. 'I know what I saw. And no, I'm not drunk. Jo was here, in this room.'

'Well she's not now,' Bennett said, his voice more terse than he intended, but fear was getting the upper hand now and he was no longer as controlled as he would have liked. 'Back to the bar. We need to talk this through and make some decisions.'

When they were all seated in the bar with more drinks Bennett began, 'Casey thinks she might be able to work the radio in the boat. We could then call for help.'

'And you're going to send her out there alone?' Eddie Farrant said; his face was still white and he was visibly shaking.

'Of course not. One of us will go with her.'

'I'm not going anywhere,' Casey said. She was sitting on one of the seats, her knees pulled up to her chin, her arms wrapped protectively around her legs. 'I'm sorry, Mike. I've thought about it and I'm not going out there.'

'Can't say I blame you,' Johnson said.

'Shut up, Andrew,' Bennett said. 'Casey, you've got to. You could be our only hope.'

Casey shook her head as tears pressed out from her eyes and trickled down her cheeks. 'I'm sorry.'

'Shit!' Bennett pushed himself to his feet, went across to the bar and poured himself a large glass of Coca-Cola, swallowing in one long gulp. He slammed the glass down on the bar. 'Well that's it,' he said. 'I'm sick of you people. We've got a really serious situation here, and you just fall to pieces. I can't shoulder the responsibility for all this on my own.'

'That's not fair, Mike,' Sheila said. 'And no one's asking you to take responsibility.'

'No, but as the senior member of staff . . .'

'We're not at work now, Bennett,' Farrant said. He'd recovered himself sufficiently for some of his old asperity to reassert itself. 'You can't tell us what to do, and you can't force Casey to go out there if she doesn't want to.'

'Well, what would you suggest, Eddie?' Bennett said, pouring himself another Coke. 'Come on, let's hear your brilliant plan to get us out of this bloody mess.'

Farrant's eyes narrowed. 'You sail, don't you? I've heard you spouting off about it to anyone who would listen after one of your weekends out on the ocean.'

'Kilvington Reservoir is hardly the ocean,' Bennett said. He knew he'd exaggerated the part he played on his weekend sailing trips.

'You still have experience of boats. Which is more than I can say for the rest of us. You could take the launch back to the mainland and get help.' Farrant knew he was laying down a challenge.

'He could also pilot the boat and take us all off the island,' Sheila said. Desperation echoed in her voice. She was as scared as any of them.

'Piss off, Sheila,' Andrew Johnson said. 'You're mad if you think I'd put my life in *his* hands. No, thank you very much. I'd rather stay here and take my chances.'

Bennett was silent for a moment. He stared down into the bottom of his glass and saw all the old familiar demons lurking there. For Coke substitute whisky, bottles of it. He tipped the remainder of the drink down the sink. 'Andrew's right . . . for once,' he said. 'I'm not sure that I can handle the launch. Having you all along for the ride would only put me on edge. Best I try this alone, then I've only got my own neck to worry about.'

'Or to save,' Farrant said. There was a thin edge of insult in his tone.

Bennett glared at him.

'Shut up, Eddie,' Sheila said. 'I agree with you, Mike. Better that the rest of us stay here together. Nothing can happen to us if we're all watching out for each other.'

CHAPTER EIGHT

It was barely nine in the morning when Robert Carter lit his fifth cigarette, threw the cold remnants of his coffee onto the grass and sat back in his canvas garden chair. The inevitable suspension from duties that followed his assault on Crozier had given him three days at home so far and the days seemed destined to merge into weeks. Crozier was not a man for forgiveness; certainly not where Carter was concerned. Carter smiled; it had been worth it though. The satisfaction from the actual blow was one thing, but the look of surprise on the man's face was priceless.

The weather had been kind and Carter had spent most of his enforced rest in the garden. The view down to the lake was spectacular, and there were hardly any tourists yet in this part of the Lake District so distractions were few.

He had worried over and over in his mind about the events that had led to Sian's disappearance but couldn't reach a conclusion. There seemed no explanation, logical or paranormal, to comfortably fit her complete loss from the world. The results from the car interior didn't even reveal any DNA traces from her. It was as if she hadn't existed. Only Carter knew she did exist, was a living, breathing, warm and loving girl, and it was his fault she was gone.

His fault and therefore his task to find her.

He picked up the laptop from the small glass-topped table and checked that he was still online. Wireless Internet was great but reception was not always as reliable as he would have chosen. The page he had been reading was still displayed. *The Old Straight Track and Alfred Watkins.*

Carter had always been taught that Alfred Watkins, a Herefordshire businessman, had discovered the concept of ley lines, or Leys, in 1921, and published his findings in his book *The Old Straight Track*. Watkins had been out in the countryside when it struck him that many of the footpaths seemed to pass in a straight line over the hilltops. These hilltops seemed to connect ancient sites of interest and Watkins argued that there was a whole pattern of alignments across the land, not only in his immediate view but much further afield as well.

Watkins suggested these straight tracks or ley lines might be the remnants of prehistoric trading routes. The fact that many of the tracks went up extremely steep hills he left to conjecture and over the years many explanations for these direct lines were examined, until Leys took on a mystical element.

Ley lines seemed to be alignments of ancient sites or holy places that are situated in a straight line and can range to several miles in length. They can be identified by the placed marker sites, or by the remnants of an old track.

Watkins said in his book, '. . . visualize a mound, circular earthwork, or clump of trees, planted on these high points, and in low points in the valley other mounds ringed with water to be seen from a distance. Then great standing stones brought to mark the way at intervals . . .'

Carter learned that Watkins told his son, 'The whole thing came to me in a flash.' Carter guessed this was a simple way of saying his thoughts and ideas coalesced simultaneously in a moment of inspiration but over the years the 'flash' began to be interpreted as having a magical meaning. Watkins believed the lines dated back to pre-Roman times.

From the Internet Carter found earlier references to Leys. In 1870, again in Herefordshire, William Henry Black gave a talk called *Boundaries and Landmarks* to the British Archaeological Association where he suggested, 'Monuments exist marking grand geometrical lines which cover the whole of Western Europe.' Of course this might have been where the idea first embedded in Watkins's mind, as he was a keen archaeologist, but for Carter the idea that ley lines might span the whole of Europe was fascinating.

He lit another cigarette and looked out over the treetops to the expanse of lake. Rods of sunlight cut through the thin gray cloud bouncing from the surface of the water as if smiles in a mirror.

Scrolling through related pages he found references to later ideas about Leys. Two British dowsers from the British Museum linked ley lines with underground streams and magnetic currents. Claims were that crossings of negative water lines and positive magnetic lines made a site holy, with many of these double lines on sacred sites.

Two German Nazi researchers, Wilhelm Tuedt and Josef Heinsch also claimed Teutonic peoples added to the construction of a network of astronomical Holy lines or

Heilige Linien, which could be mapped against sacred sites throughout Europe. One example given was the rock formation in central Germany called Die Externsteine.

Later writers mentioned China and the whole landscape being in touch with the earth due to the laws of feng shui. It is thought that ancient civilizations believed the harmony of their people was dependent upon the harmony of the earth. To preserve this union they built their structures and monuments according to ley lines. Apart from China there was evidence in Greece, the civilizations of the Aztecs, the Mayans, the Incas, and even close to home in England and Scotland. Most schoolchildren knew about Stonehenge, though most were less familiar with the larger Avebury.

He stubbed out his cigarette and walked back to his cottage to brew some fresh coffee and make a sandwich.

Seated at the battered pine table he listened to the coffee machine performing its magic. It was the only sound in the house. He lived alone, and always had. There were plenty of women he shared his life with from time to time but none that stayed around long enough to move in. None that he wanted to open up to, with whom to share his innermost thoughts. Given his psychic ability he knew that if he ever did find someone to share his life with they would have to be special.

He poured out the coffee. There had been a woman, once, one that might have been special. He had let her go. She was married and he didn't want any relationship they might have to end with pain. That was what he told himself.

Back at the garden table he bit into his toasted cheese and tomato sandwich. The research about ley lines had a point. He was agonizing over Sian. He was looking for links between the house they had investigated and recent similar occurrences.

Ley lines were one part of the possible link but what he had been pondering was what similarities there might be between the actual places. He had his files on the other chair. The house he was familiar with was the most recent, and not one he needed any notes to recall. The others were spaced out a few months apart. One was a small factory outlet in an industrial park; another was a multistory car park; and then there was a small retreat that consisted of a number of terraced houses knocked through into one dwelling.

There was no instantly recognizable link, so Carter went back to the first file and started again. What did the factory do? Did it make things, assemble things, what? After wading through reams of paper Carter found the answer: religious artifacts. Okay, that was a start. How did that link to the car park? There was no obvious clue in its purpose so he looked at the location on a map. It was in a residential area, houses all around, a row of local shops, and a church.

The next file was the ordinary house from a few days ago. Again there was nothing about the house itself to provide any clues. The location was as ordinary as the house; nothing there seemed liable to produce a link. The Flemings were ordinary in every way so far as he could tell; hardworking, clean living, even churchgoers. He checked again, though he knew the answer. Sian was a regular churchgoer as well, a strict Catholic girl.

With mounting anticipation Carter pulled over the last file: the retreat. The file indicated it had originally been a row of terraced houses built for the workers at a mill that produced cotton at the turn of the twentieth century. In the 1990s it had been cleverly converted into a single dwelling, long and narrow though it was organized to accommodate up to fifteen priests. The retreat was a house for Jesuit priests to stay in and meditate.

CHAPTER NINE

Michael Bennett reached the top of the incline and stopped running. A stitch was creasing his side, and his legs felt like lead. The run yesterday morning had exhausted him and he had very little left. The plan to drive the Land Rover to the jetty had foundered at the first hurdle. Three of them had tried to get it to start and all had failed. The engine wasn't even turning over. Going by foot was the only option. And now it was late in the day and the light was beginning to leach from the sky. Another couple of hours and it would be dark, and that would be a disaster. He had to find the jetty in daylight; he'd have no chance come nightfall.

Leaning forward to catch his breath he looked about him and groaned. He'd climbed the hill in the hope it would give him a view across the island, but now he was at the top he realized it wasn't high enough—nowhere near high enough. He took the compass from the side pocket of his backpack, flipped open its waterproof cap and held it out in front of him.

That couldn't be right!

The compass needle was swinging backwards and forwards, unable to decide which way was north. Slowly it started to spin in lazy revolutions, which confounded him further.

It was hours since he'd left the others and set off, and he was no closer to finding the jetty and the boat. He didn't want to let them down. As he'd left the Manse he'd looked at their faces and seen a host of emotions painted on them, ranging from derision to hope, from hope to abject terror.

The women, Sheila and Casey, seemed to have a kind of blind faith in him, believing that he would somehow find a way back to safety. He remembered Scart's words on the boat on the crossing over. *Group Leader.* That was a joke. Before coming to this godforsaken island he had never actually led anything in his entire life. And with that arbitrary decision had come a responsibility, and the fact that he didn't want such an onus on him was neither here nor there.

He moved his weight to the left, intending to carry on—what other course was left to him?—but as his foot came down it hit a half-buried, moss-covered rock and twisted over on itself. The pain lanced up his leg as far as his groin; white-hot, excruciating. He cried out and crashed to the ground, lying there panting from his exertions, humiliated by his ineptitude and very frightened.

He thought he could hear movement through the trees and undergrowth behind him, and he could imagine a pursuer closing the gap between them. When he looked back he could see nothing, no sign of anyone or anything. But the panic had taken hold of him now, and with a groan of resignation he made himself stand.

The pain, when he put weight on his twisted ankle, brought tears to his eyes. Oh God, if only he'd listened to his wife. Diane had told him bluntly—and quite cruelly—that this management exercise was beyond his physical capabilities. 'Michael, you're forty-eight; too old and too out of condition for a week gallivanting around some remote Scottish island.' And he'd argued with her, trying to make her see that he had no option. If he wanted to survive against the junior managers, the young Turks, the predators regarding his senior position with hungry eyes, then he had to compete with them on equal terms. Only, where were they now? Cowering in the shadows of the Manse, sending him out to seek help from . . . from God knew where. The island was deserted. The only hope left to him was to reach the jetty and the launch that had brought them across from the mainland. With any luck he'd be able to get the radio working and be able to summon help. And then he wouldn't have to test his seafaring skills on the choppy waters of the North Sea.

He limped on, keeping an eye on the fading light. Five minutes later it started to rain; a thin sleety drizzle that blew into his eyes.

This was hopeless. He'd never find the jetty now.

And then he saw it; not more than four hundred yards away. The boat was still there, tied to one of the stanchions, rising and falling on the swell. His heart leapt and he started at a hobbling run, trying to ignore the pain from his injured ankle that knifed up his leg with each stride, until the separate shafts of agony converged, becoming one long, scintillating scream.

He was so focused on the speck of hope in the distance that he didn't notice the gully. Only when his foot hit empty air and he found himself pitching forward did he realize he'd made a terrible mistake. The ground fell away and he rolled and bumped down the incline, sharp stones and clumps of thistles raking his skin, drawing blood, creating new hotspots of pain on his already pain-wracked body. As he rolled to the bottom of the gully the deep undergrowth of bracken and heather swallowed him.

Shaken and disoriented he tried to push himself upright, but a new pain surged through him. It was ten times worse than anything he had experienced so far, and so intense he blacked out for a few seconds. When he came to and shook his head to clear his thoughts he realized with numb surprise that he'd broken his leg.

With a sob he shrugged off his backpack and tried to pull himself upright, but the pain was too much. He collapsed back onto the springy, moist ground and started to cry; fat, wet tears pushing out from his tightly closed eyelids. Tears of pain, frustration and utter hopelessness. For the first time in many years he found himself praying to a God he hoped still had Kulsay on the radar.

There was movement in the bracken beside him. He opened his eyes, seeing the white, flaccid skin of the hand that was holding back the undergrowth, exposing him. He looked from the hand to the white, dead eyes staring impassively down at him, and started to scream. And kept on screaming until the hand reached into his mouth and ripped out his tongue.

In the cellar, Eddie Farrant listened. The noise of the helicopter was increasing, becoming more like a roar of thunder, and the noise brought him with relief back to reality. He didn't want to think about Jo Madley; her disappearance and horrific reappearance. He didn't want to think about what had happened to Andrew, Sheila and Casey. To relive those memories would only bring him closer to the madness that was lurking in the shadows of his mind. He didn't want to think about what might have happened to Bennett after he'd left them all in the bar.

Instead he burrowed still deeper into the sacks so that anyone—or anything—that entered the cellar would not find him.

And then something grabbed hold of his leg.

He cried out and threw off the sacks. A pale-skinned hand was jutting out from the floor and long bony fingers curled themselves around his ankle. He watched with disbelief as his foot was dragged into the hard earth floor of the cellar.

'Get off me!' he yelled, but as the words left his lips another hand burst from the floor and grabbed his other leg. He started to struggle, twisting his body, trying to pull his legs away, but they had already sunk into the floor to his knees.

'Oh Christ!' he whispered as another hand emerged and caught hold of his arm and more fingers wrapped themselves around his throat. Kicking and screaming he was being pulled into the ground. His breath was forced from his lungs as the earth closed around him. *It hurts*, he thought numbly. *Jesus Christ it hurts!*

Within seconds the only evidence of Eddie Farrant ever being in the cellar were a few urine-sodden sacks and an empty Mars wrapper.

The cold hit John Harrison like a physical blow as he jumped from the doors of the helicopter to the ground. The north wind cut through his thick denim jacket like an ice spear, making him shiver and turn up his collar. He thought for a moment about the group and the conditions they must have suffered. Soft office types whose ideas of hardship were defined by the coffee machine packing up or the failure to find a parking space. He imagined them thrust into this pitiless, almost alien world and having to give up the comforts and order of their daily existence. It was small wonder they'd got themselves into trouble.

From the ground the Manse looked even more impressive, and even more forbidding. The granite walls were pitted and eroded by years of buffeting by salt-laden winds and the windows, whilst freshly painted and in a good state of repair, looked like nothing more than black, sightless eyes, staring out unseeing over the wind-scorched shrubs and inadequate grasses that comprised the garden.

Still no one had come to greet him and the feeling of abandonment that hung over the place like a wet cloth unsettled him. He tried the handle of an oak door set into the granite wall.

Locked.

He swore softly. He looked through one of the windows at what was obviously the dining room, a long refectory table, set for a meal with white china and bone-handled cutlery on a pristine white tablecloth. But there was no sign of any diners.

He made his way around to the front of the house. Had he bothered to look back at the helicopter he would have seen the wheels slowly sinking, inch by inch into the solid earth. By the time he reached the polished oak front door of the Manse, only an inch of rubber was visible above the surface. Minutes later the tires disappeared completely from view and the body of the machine started to be eaten by the ground.

The front door was wide open. Harrison hesitated before entering. 'Hello! Is anyone there?' He waited just outside the door for a response, but the house was silent. He reached into his jacket and pulled out a Browning automatic, comforted by the weight of the gun in his hand. Then he took a tentative step inside, listening carefully, alert to any sign of danger. Still the feeling persisted that this was a bad place to be. His instincts were screaming at him to get back to the helicopter and get the hell off the island. But he'd been paid to do a job and he'd do that job to the best of his ability.

He checked the downstairs rooms quickly. All empty. No signs of life; a long smear of dried blood on the floor in the doorway of the dining room confirming his belief that there was something seriously wrong here.

He pulled his cell phone from his pocket and checked the screen. No network. *Damn!* He was on his own. As he moved to the bottom of the stairs he thought he heard something. He froze. There it was again, coming from one of the upper floors. A soft whimpering sound. A child crying? But there were no children on the island. He knew that much from the dossier given to him by the KDC. 'Hello!' he called again. 'Is there anyone up there?' The whimpering stopped for a moment, as if in response, then started again, slightly louder, slightly more desperate.

He took a breath and started to climb the stairs, the gun stuck out in front of him like a talisman. As he climbed he heard the whimpering grow louder, until he reached the landing on the first floor, when it stopped completely.

'Where are you?' he called. 'I'm here to help.'

'Thank God. I thought you'd never get here.' A female voice, quiet and alone.

Harrison spun round at the sound of the voice. Two paces away stood a young woman. Dark haired, pretty, dressed in sweatpants and tee shirt. 'Are you going to shoot me?' she said, staring at the gun pointing at her face. Harrison looked from her to the barrel of the Browning, and slowly lowered it; but not completely. His instincts were yelling at him again. There was something about her that didn't hang right, but he couldn't tell yet what it was.

'I thought the place was empty,' he said.

'It is . . . apart from me.' She smiled.

'And you are?'

'All alone,' she said dreamily.

'No. Your name. What's your name?'

'Casey,' she said. 'Casey Faraday.'

'Ah.' He remembered her from the dossier. She was one of the Waincraft group. Casey Faraday. Twenty-nine. Married. Degree in computing from Loughborough University. 'What happened to the others?' he said.

'They left me here. They went to get help.' She was speaking as if her voice was a recording being played back at slightly the wrong speed.

'Help? From where? I've just flown over the island. There's nothing here . . . apart from a few sheep, and I doubt they'd be much good for anything.'

She smiled at him. 'Why are you here?' she said.

'I told you. I'm here to help. A rescue mission. The KDC sent me to airlift you off the island.'

She continued to smile but there was vacancy in her eyes. Nothing behind the smile; nothing much of anything at all. 'What happened here, Casey?' he said.

She turned and walked away from him. 'Bad things,' she said. 'Very bad things.'

He started to follow her. 'Care to tell me about it?'

Her pace quickened. She shook her head. She reached a room and ducked inside.

'Wait!' he called after her but the door slammed in his face. He stood there for a moment, indecisive. Then he grabbed the handle and pushed it open.

The room was empty.

He flicked on the light. He was in a bedroom. Clothes were strewn over the bed and hanging from the back of a chair. 'Casey?' he called. But there was no one there. He was standing with his back to the only door. The window was closed and there was nowhere for anybody to hide. Yet he'd seen her come in here.

He was about to turn and leave when he heard a small peal of laughter. 'Damn it! This isn't a game. Where are you?'

'In the walls . . . in the air . . . I'm everywhere.'

He heard the voice, close to his ear, but couldn't tell where it was coming from. 'Okay. Please yourself. You play if you want to, but don't waste my time.'

A small draught tickled the back of his neck. He spun round, raising the gun, waving it in front of him. There was nothing there behind him, but the door was now closed. 'What the hell . . .' He grabbed hold of the handle and yanked it down, at the same time pulling at the door, but it refused to budge. The laughter again, feminine, ex-citable. *Under the bed, stupid! He hadn't checked under the bed!* He got down onto his hands and knees, and lifted the counterpane. A suitcase and a pair of hiking boots. Nothing more. Damn! He was convinced . . .

The blow came from nowhere, from out of the air. Something smashed down on the back of his neck, sending him sprawling onto his face. Dust from the carpet stuck to his lips. He wiped them with the back of his hand and rolled over onto his back. The pain in his neck was excruciating, sending hot spikes of agony up into his skull. He groaned and stared up at the ceiling.

'You shouldn't have come here.'

A male voice this time, but whether he'd actually heard it or whether it sounded only in his head he couldn't tell. He used the bed to pull himself into a sitting position and looked about the room once more. It was still empty, but there was something different. The air seemed charged, pregnant with menace. The blow to the back of his neck had made him drop the gun. It lay on the carpet a yard away. He reached for it but it spun away from him as if it had been kicked out of his reach. And then it rose into the air, spinning slowly end over end. Finally it stopped, the barrel pointing at the bridge of his nose, and gradually the trigger was pulled back. He could see it move, as if an invisible finger was depressing it.

He threw himself backwards a split-second before the gun fired. His head cracked against the floor but the bullet missed him and punched a hole in the small pine cupboard by the side of the bed. He kicked out and caught the gun with the toe of his boot, sending it flying through the air. It hit the wall and clattered to the floor.

Harrison sprang to his feet, ignoring the pain in his head, and ran to the door. He yanked at it again and this time it opened, the sudden release making him stagger backwards. He regained his balance and ran from the room and along the landing to the stairs. There was only one thought in his head now. He had to get back to the helicopter and get the hell off this island. Casey Faraday and anyone else in this stinking place could look out for themselves.

'Wait!'

He was halfway down the stairs. He stopped and turned to look back at the landing. Casey Faraday was standing at the top of the stairs. She was naked.

'What is this?' Harrison said, furious now. In some way her nakedness only fuelled his anger. 'Cover yourself up,' he said, his strict Baptist upbringing resurfacing. 'Now!'

Casey started to descend the stairs but, although he could see her drawing closer, he could not see her legs moving. It was as if she was gliding down towards him. And she seemed to be bathed in a shimmering light that was throwing her in and out of focus.

He rubbed at his eyes, trying to see her clearly, but even as he watched her she was starting to change.

Her breasts were sinking back into her chest, the small bush of pubic hair dissolving. The features of her face were smoothing out, becoming bland, anodyne, and the hair was starting to fall from her scalp, leaving a shiny bald dome in its place. Her eyes had rolled back into her head until only the whites were showing, but the gaze was fixed upon him.

He shuffled backwards, finding the next stair, stepping down. He wanted to turn away from her, wanted to run, but the white orbs in the expressionless face held him, and sapped his will.

It was no longer Casey Faraday descending the stairs towards him, but a featureless, sexless creature, white, impossibly thin. Even the ears had disappeared, leaving only smooth skin behind.

He misjudged his next step. His foot caught the edge of the riser and twisted painfully. He cried out and started to fall, but long, thin arms embraced him and held him. The mouth in the blank face was lipless and white, but it opened in a red shriek and buried itself in his neck. Skin and muscle tore, blood poured out of his severed artery and splashed down the leather of his jacket.

I'm going to die, he thought. And ten seconds later he did.

CHAPTER TEN

Jane Talbot squinted slightly in the bright lights of the office. Cold, hard and brittle; those were the words she used to describe the chrome and white décor and the antiseptic, almost futuristic look of the desk, the chairs and other office furniture. It was also the epithet she used to describe her boss, Simon Crozier. She sat on a white leather and chrome chair, designed for elegance rather than comfort, facing Crozier across a glass-topped desk. The desk was another design conceit—smoked glass supported by a chrome-plated tubular steel frame, and Crozier kept the desk clutter to a minimum. There were two white telephones, a small laptop computer and a black leather file, positioned at right angles to the edge of the desk, and nothing more. The glass was polished to within an inch of its life and nothing, not even a thumbprint or a flake of dandruff marred its pristine surface.

How different, she thought, to the desk in her office at home with its clunky, antediluvian computer that hissed and wheezed and made hard work of all but the most simple word processing tasks; the piles of unkempt, dog-eared paperwork that never seemed to reduce in size no matter how many hours she put in trying to clear them; the cracked plastic telephone with the answer phone that refused to record messages; and Amy's headless teddy bear, that was renting space on the desktop while it waited for emergency surgery. There was nothing pristine about the surface of *her* desk, marked as it was with sticky rings from a succession of coffee cups, and the dark brown burns from neglected cigarettes that had tumbled from the permanently overflowing ashtray.

Simon Crozier leaned back in his plush leather chair and stared at her over the top of his half rims. 'I'm sorry to drag you in on your day off, Jane. I hope you had nothing important planned.'

'It's okay. Gemma's at school and David's at home today, so he can take care of Amy,' she said with a smile, but actually it wasn't okay—it wasn't okay at all. David had purposely taken the day off so they could be together. They'd arranged to drop Amy off with Jane's mother and then come up to town.

The plan was to go to the Tate Gallery to see the Turner exhibition, and then to go on to Clerkenwell for something to eat at one of their favorite restaurants. Jane's mother had agreed to pick up Gemma from school and have the girls overnight, to give them some much needed time together. It was so long since it had been just the two of them for any length of time that tiny cracks were beginning to show in the marriage. Nothing too serious, not divorce material yet, but given time and left unchecked, the cracks would turn into fissures and then into bloody great canyons that would be impossible to bridge. She'd seen it happen to other couples, friends of theirs whose romance had turned sour and whose marriages had become battlegrounds on which to mount a daily fight to the death. She didn't want things to get to that pitch, so she'd planned a quiet day together, to help heal the cracks, and to soothe the real, or imagined, grievances and slights that two busy working people with hectic lives and two delightful but demanding daughters, allow to mar an otherwise solid marriage.

None of which mattered to Simon Crozier, who lost patience with people when they let their lives outside the Department get in the way of their work. He was a large man in his early fifties, with iron-gray hair cut close to his skull. His eyes were deep brown and penetrating and his hawk nose gave him a predatory aspect that was reflected in his manner. Simon Crozier was not a man to suffer fools gladly and made no pretence that he did.

The atmosphere created by his austere office and his fierce manner was almost like being in church, Jane realized. As a strict Catholic, and bringing her children up within the faith, she found her own church comforting. Crozier's office was religious in appearance but held little comfort.

He leaned further back in his chair and crossed his legs. 'Kulsay Island,' he said. 'What do you know about it?' There was something about his appearance today that was different from usual, but Jane couldn't quite decide yet what it was.

Jane thought for a moment. The name was ringing bells in her mind but it took her a few moments to retrieve the information. 'It was in the news a few weeks ago,' she said finally. 'It's an island off the east coast of Scotland. There was a helicopter crash. Wasn't it something to do with an adventure holiday going horribly wrong?'

'Yes . . .' Crozier said. '. . . And no. It wasn't an adventure holiday but one of those Outward Bound courses that misguided company directors like to send their middle-management people on. Take a handful of highly stressed, out of condition, soft living people and dump them in some extreme conditions to see how they cope and interact; that kind of rubbish. There *was* a helicopter but it didn't exactly crash.'

'But I remember seeing it on the news. Footage of the Navy searching for the wreckage,' Jane said.

'Yes, but that was all part of the cover-up. An elaborate fiction to satisfy the families of those poor souls who went missing. It was a smokescreen, designed to hide what really happened.'

Jane was intrigued. She ran her fingers through her cropped brown hair. 'So what *really* happened?'

Crozier leaned back in his chair and steepled his fingers. 'Ah, now that's where it gets interesting. Nobody really knows. Six people in the management group, the helicopter pilot, and the entire staff of nine from the island. Sixteen people, disappeared without a trace. The Ministry of Defense sent a team out to Kulsay to search the island and they found nothing. Not even the helicopter, and that was the most extraordinary thing. They know the helicopter landed there from the last communication from the pilot, a man named Harrison, ex–U.S. Air Force, very experienced. He contacted them just as he was coming in to land. But there were no further communications, nothing to say that he collected his passengers and took off again.'

'So what does the Ministry think happened? Come to think of it, why were the MOD involved in the first place?' There was a huge bruise on Crozier's lower jaw, that was what was different about him.

'The missing people worked for Waincraft Software, and Waincraft are fairly tied in with the Ministry. They provide the software for various missile systems and defense projects of a highly sensitive nature. The MOD is not speculating. There were some half-hearted rumors of a Middle Eastern conspiracy, but I think that was just pie in the sky; if no other explanation fits, blame Al-Qaeda. You know the thinking. But I think the truth is that they really haven't got a clue what happened on Kulsay.' He sat forward in his chair, opened the black file on his desk and took out a sheaf of paper. He slid it across the desk to her. 'These are the personnel files of those who disappeared.'

Jane flicked through the pages, staring for a few moments at each of the small photographs attached to each individual file. Six average-looking people, captured in that flat, rabbit-caught-in-the-headlights style of all passport photos.

'Do we have the files on the island's staff, or the pilot?'

'Any day now. They were all employed by the Kulsay Development Corporation, the owners of the island. They've promised me " every assistance." They are a division of The Anderson Corporation, one of the U.S.'s Top Ten companies. International as well as national. Into every sector you can think of.'

'So have we been assigned to investigate? And what happened to your face?'

'The Minister thinks what happened might fall into our sphere of operations.' He totally ignored the remark about his face. Since being hit by Carter he had suffered a couple of loose teeth, some bruising, but mainly a lot of damaged pride. He wasn't a physical man, and had never been in a fight in his life. In fact that was the first time he had ever been hit by anyone.

'I see,' Jane said. 'So they've exhausted all rational explanations.'

'It would appear so. And there's something else. There was another incident like this. Remarkably similar in fact.'

'On Kulsay?'

He nodded.

Alarm flashed in her eyes, but it was quickly extinguished. She knew Crozier well enough to know that he didn't make unsubstantiated remarks. He was a very careful man. 'You're really sweetening the cake, Simon,' she said. 'Have you got any details?'

'I haven't got them to hand, but I can lend you Martin Impey for the rest of the day. He's been researching it for the last twenty-four hours. I'm sure, by now, he'll be able to give you chapter and verse. You know how thorough he is when he gets his teeth into something like this.'

'A dog with a bone,' Jane said. She knew Martin well and had worked with him many times in the past. A painstaking and tireless researcher, he was the Department's fount of all knowledge.

Crozier was watching Jane's face carefully. He was confident that despite any initial doubts she might have, she would take the assignment. She was one of the Department's greatest assets. She'd earned a master's degree in psychology at Cambridge and was the owner of an astute and incisive mind. Intellectually, Jane could wipe the floor with the majority of the Department—in fact with most of the people he knew, himself included. Crozier's only reservation about her was her tendency to let domesticity come between herself and her work. He'd known David, her husband, for years, and was indirectly responsible for bringing the two of them together, but he felt now that David was the worst thing that could have happened to her. Being with David had softened her and dampened much of the fire that had previously enlivened her work.

She laid the files on the desk and sat back in her chair. 'I don't know,' she said. 'When would you need a commitment from me?'

'I want to proceed on this as quickly as possible, so I need an answer today.' He was slightly surprised she might consider his request as something to consider. In his world a request was the same as a demand.

She raised her eyebrows but said nothing. What David was going to say was uppermost in her thoughts.

Crozier pressed on. 'Would you like me to call Martin in?'

She nodded and he stretched out his hand, hitting a key on his laptop. 'When you're ready, Martin.' he said.

Somewhere within the microchips of the machine his words were transformed to a printed message and flashed directly onto the screen of Martin Impey's computer in an office down the hall.

A few moments later the door to Crozier's office opened and he entered the room. He was thirty-eight, five years older than Jane, and had been with the Department for the best part of ten years. He was a small, energetic man who reminded Jane of a Jack Russell Terrier. Fiercely intelligent and possessed of a cutting wit that more than compensated for his lack of physical stature, he was one of the most popular members of the Department. His brown eyes always seemed to be smiling, as if he had looked at the world and decided it was one huge joke, but today he seemed unusually somber.

'Martin, how's the work on Kulsay Island coming on?'

'Hello, Jane. How are you?' Martin said, ignoring Crozier's question, but managing not to seem rude in doing so.

'Fine, Martin. And you?' Jane stood and shook his hand.

'Good. I'm good. David okay?' They might have been at a cocktail party and both were aware that Crozier was firing daggers at them with his eyes.

'He was, last time I checked. And Emilie?'

Crozier held up his hands. 'Enough! You can catch up on small talk later. Martin, I asked you a question.'

Martin winked at Jane. 'Finished, Simon. Actually I finished a couple of hours ago, in as much as you can *finish* something like this. There are dozens of question marks, a score of anomalies and a couple of things that make absolutely no sense at all. Would you like me to bring you up to speed?'

'You can fill me in later, but for now, take Jane back to your office and run her through everything you've found out.' Crozier turned to Jane. 'When you've finished down there, perhaps you'll come back and give me your decision.'

Jane got to her feet. 'Very well,' she said. 'By the way what *did* happen to your face?'

'Emilie's pregnant,' Martin whispered in her ear as they walked to the door.

Jane clutched his sleeve. 'Martin, that's brilliant news.' She, like most of the Department, was aware that they had been trying for a child for the best part of eight years. 'How far along is she?'

'Three months. Early days yet, but fingers crossed.' He grinned at her.

'Close the door behind you,' Crozier said.

Martin turned and threw him a mock-salute.

As the door closed behind them Simon Crozier slid the folders back into the file, then sat back in his seat and frowned. He had a bad feeling about this case. A very bad feeling.

Martin scrolled down the screen. 'This is Kulsay Island,' he said as a picture of a barren, rocky coastline appeared on the screen.

'Looks pretty bleak,' Jane said.

'From the reports I've read on the place it sounds like a hellhole. The island is about six miles across from north to south, about three east to west. The south end was once populated, mostly crofters. It was quite a thriving community at one time. There were a couple of pubs and one church. Population was about three hundred according to the 1931 census. But it's the north end of the island where the incident took place, and that really is inhospitable.'

Jane stopped him. 'Backtrack a little. Crozier said some kind of mass disappearance happened before. When was that?'

Martin frowned. 'I know what he's referring to, but the circumstances were different.'

'How different?' She crossed and uncrossed her legs. This promised to be a long session so she had better get herself comfortable.

He called up a menu, opened another page and started to read it, paraphrasing it for Jane's benefit. 'Round about sixty years ago a man called McMullen took a boat out to the island. He had a meeting planned with some of the crofters regarding the sale of their wool. Apparently when he got there the crofters had gone. In fact he couldn't find anyone on the island at all. Kulsay was completely deserted. He poked around for a few hours, entered some of the houses, the pub and the church, but there was no sign of the locals. It was as if the whole population had upped sticks and left en masse. Drinks had been left unfinished in the bar of the pub, and in several of the cottages, radios were still on and meals were served up but half eaten. And interestingly enough the entire canine population of the island had gone as well.'

'Is that significant?' Jane had heard of people disappearing before, even small groups of people, and everyone had heard the story of the Marie Celeste. But she had never heard of a whole community leaving not a trace and no clues before.

'Only in as much that there were almost as many dogs on the island as there were people. Sheep farmers rely on their dogs and value them highly. Makes sense that if they were going to leave the island they'd take their dogs with them.'

'So it was a mass exodus?' Thoughts and ideas were running through her mind and she knew that whatever the assignment was that Crozier offered her, the chances were very high that she would take it.

'You'd think, but if it was then I'm buggered if I can find out where they went. There's no record of three hundred people plus dogs pulling into any harbors on the mainland. Everything I've read suggests that the entire population disappeared without actually going anywhere.'

Jane made notes on the large pad beside her. 'Listen, what happened to Simon's face?'

Martin smiled. 'Haven't you heard?'

She shook her head. 'Come on, what's the gossip?'

'Not gossip, actual fact. Trudy went into his office and he was still on the floor.'

'On the floor?'

'Robert Carter was in the process of storming out. He'd punched out Simon and knocked him flat.'

'No!' Jane could barely believe that Carter had hit Crozier. No wonder he hadn't been around for a while. The reason had stayed quiet. Not that she was surprised; it was well known through the Department that the two men loathed one another.

Martin laughed. 'That would have wiped the arrogant smile from Crozier's face. But the hardest part for him would be if anyone found out. And someone did find out—me. I just need to bide my time until I let him know . . .'

'Oh, Simon's not all bad. Even he has his good points.'

Martin moved his attention back to the computer. 'Any more questions?'

'Loads. Surely there must have been some sort of inquiry?'

'There was, but the results were inconclusive. There were no witnesses, no evidence. After a while the incident was swept under the carpet and simply forgotten about.'

Jane scribbled some more notes. It didn't make any

kind of sense. 'What about the media? I can't believe that such a sensational story would simply be ignored.'

'There were the usual fluff pieces, but the stories were never given much credence. On a par with today's tales of UFO sightings and crop circles. There was nobody to corroborate the stories so eventually they just petered out. Remember this was sixty years ago. The press was a fairly toothless beast back then. Not like now.'

'And the crofters' families?' She had written down a few random questions as they occurred to her and was ticking them off as they spoke.

'No one came forward.' Martin knew the material by heart; he had a photographic memory, with no need of notes or briefings.

'You're kidding.' Jane found that hard to believe, surely someone questioned three hundred people just evaporating into thin air.

'Seems rather odd, doesn't it?' The same misgivings had occurred to Martin when he first read the reports. There was something strange about the whole episode. Not just where had they all gone, but why?

'Perhaps they knew something. Some reason for the disappearance.' Jane was letting her brain work through possible scenarios. Her conclusion would eventually be the same as Martin's. They hadn't chosen to leave the island.

Martin shrugged. 'If they did, then they weren't shouting it from the rooftops. No one ever heard from them, apart from their immediate neighbors on the mainland.' He looked at Jane, and inclined his head. 'Then there are the other disappearances more recently.'

Jane sighed. The sixty-year-old mystery would have to remain unsolved for the moment. 'Okay, let's come up-to-date.'

He tapped a few keys on the computer. 'So, what do you want to know?' he said as a new file opened with the most recent documents about Kulsay Island. The Waincraft management team.

'Everything,' Jane said.

CHAPTER ELEVEN

The Society of Jesus, or Societas Iesu, is an order of the Catholic Church that directly serves the Pope. Its members are known as Jesuits, although are often called Soldiers of Christ or foot soldiers of the Pope. It is the largest religious order of men in the Catholic Church and over two-thirds of them are priests. They mainly work overseas on education as well as missionary work, involved in human rights and social justice.

Carter had done a Google search. *Catholic* had naturally thrown up thousands of results but refining the terms of inquiry narrowed the number of references. Surfing through the initial pages he found plenty of relevant mention of the work of the Jesuits. None of it displayed any clue of anything remotely sinister about a seemingly benign group of God-fearing men.

He watched as a heron flew gracefully over the lake, soaring and swooping as the wind currents pursued. A fresh packet of cigarettes lay on the table but he resisted. He closed his eyes and tried to formulate his thoughts into some coherent order. The sites, the possible supernatural occurrences, the people involved.

The files revisited yielded what he suspected. The first house was near a church, a Catholic church; the Flemings were practicing Catholics; Sian was Catholic, and the Jesuits were as close to the Pope as anyone could be.

The Roman Catholic Church seemed to be the link. Why?

In 1534 Ignatius, later Saint Ignatius of Loyola, and other students at the University of Paris formed a group they called the Company of Jesus. They swore to perform religious duties wherever they could and in 1537 traveled to Rome to seek approval from Pope Paul III. They were accepted and ordained as priests and set about working for the Pope in Europe, founding schools, converting people to Catholicism and helping stem the tide of the Protestant faith. In 1540 the name changed to the Society of Jesus.

Later Jesuits traveled more widely, settling in Japan, Tibet, South America, India and Russia. They became very powerful and this led to suppression by the ruling governments. Gradually though the order grew, as did the Church itself, and their influence was felt worldwide.

Carter opened the packet of cigarettes, lit one and drew down the smoke in anger. He was no nearer a solution that might find Sian. He remained convinced she was alive somewhere, being held against her will. She *had* to be alive, she just had to be.

The water on the lake, even at this distance, was obviously rippling. He watched the trees; swaying in an encroaching breeze. The weather was changing. He guessed he had about another hour before it would rain. He set himself that hour to complete his research, and then a late lunch.

He scrolled down a few pages, looking for something that might give a less flattering view of the Jesuits. *Controversies*— what was this?

Being an influential body, the Jesuits attracted enemies. Catholic and Protestant critics accused them of being involved in secret missions for the Pope. Conspiracy theories grew about their participation in an oath taken by senior members to allow and justify any action taken to safeguard the papal leader and the faith. This included infiltration of other religions. In many languages the word *Jesuit* acquired the meaning of devious. Recent popes have spoken against the order and, incorrectly, rumors have spread that the Jesuits are against much of the Catholic direction including abortion, priestly celibacy and homosexuality.

A Superior General leads the Society of Jesus, with General Curia headquarters in Rome in a historic complex of buildings including the Church of the Gesu, the Jesuit Mother Church.

Carter closed the laptop and lit another cigarette. The bushes at the end of his garden were gently breathing in the enveloping wind, giving the impression of living, moving creatures.

He knew full well that his house was built on a ley line; it was one of the reasons for buying it. He enjoyed the forces, real or imagined, that pulsed beneath his feet. Now he had a connection of Leys, and Jesuits. But what did either of them mean to each other? And what help were they to Sian?

There had to be more but it was eluding him. Usually his investigations found a link between the event and the history of the site. Either that or the participant had a secret that had somehow caused the manifestation in whatever form it took. This time, and he realized in the most recent preceding cases, the link they had assumed to be the solution was something else.

He needed to dig deeper, and if that meant using the power of his mind then he would have to risk it.

CHAPTER TWELVE

'Can I pick my own team?' Jane said.

She had been with Martin Impey for most of the day. Now the light was fading from the sky and she was back with her decision.

'Of course,' Crozier said. 'With one proviso.' He spoke the words as though through gritted teeth.

'And that would be?' She was studying his face. He wouldn't meet her eyes and she wondered what he was leading up to.

He shifted uncomfortably in his seat and cleared his throat.

It's going to be good, she thought. This is something he doesn't want to say but has no choice. If someone as senior as Crozier was being made to do something, then the orders had to come from a very important and high up source.

'I want Robert Carter to go with you.' He turned his chair around so that it was facing the windows. It was as if he had been in the confessional and wanted anonymity.

'Robert's not been around for a while, has he?' she said, feeling the blood rushing to her cheeks. There was history between her and Carter that she didn't want to remember while her husband was waiting for her at home.

'There was a disciplinary matter.' Crozier was still looking away from her. Jane could imagine the look of pain and anger that must be clouding his face. She couldn't reveal that she knew from Martin what the *matter* involved. 'Carter is under suspension at present.'

Jane felt uncomfortable talking to the back of Crozier's

head but she had little choice. 'I didn't know that. So he can't be part of the team?'

Unexpectedly Crozier spun his chair back so that his legs were under the desk. His face was darkened with frustrated anger. He sat forward and rested his arms on the desk. 'You know what I think of Carter. The man's unstable, and the methods he uses are dubious, and sometimes downright dangerous. I've clashed more with him over the years than any other member of the Department. I don't like him, never have. But I'm also aware that he's the most gifted *sensitive* I've ever worked with, and I think we need his involvement in this assignment.'

'So you're removing the suspension?'

There were no files, no paper on the desk, but Crozier fiddled with his fingers as though there were. 'No, I'm not, you are.'

'Me?' Jane didn't have the seniority to remove disciplinary suspensions.

'Who better?' Crozier was smiling now and that worried Jane even more.

'You?' She leaned forward so that her hands were on the edge of the desk. She sensed Crozier's concerned look that she might smudge the pristine surface. 'You have the seniority, I don't.'

Crozier smiled. 'Do you honestly think he'll listen to anything I've got to say?'

Jane frowned. The animosity between the two men was the stuff of legend within the Department. And now with the suspension . . . "No, probably not. But you make it sound as if Robert needs persuading to come back. Surely if he's been disciplined he'll be only too glad to . . .'

Crozier shook his head as though he was saddened at Carter's plight.

'He won't do it. You saw how he was after he lost Sian Davies. He won't come back. Phone calls have already been made. His exact words—no, I'll paraphrase—he said something like, 'Suspend me, retire me, fire me—all the same. I've finished with it all.' Yes, he was a mess after Sian Davies disappeared. Blamed himself, and quite rightly too in my opinion. But that doesn't alter the fact that he's the best there is working in his specific area of expertise.'

Crozier stood abruptly and walked across to the window, staring down at the cars passing by on Whitehall. 'Look, Jane, I'll level with you,' he said, not shifting his gaze from the traffic below. 'For a long time this Department has been a thorn in the side of the Whitehall mandarins. Every year it gets more difficult persuading them to support us. This year the budget has been slashed by forty percent. If we are to continue, we have to keep the Minister on our side.'

She nodded her head slowly as realization dawned. 'And it's the Minister who's insisting on Robert's inclusion in this?'

'He thinks it was a mistake to let him go.' Crozier was speaking quietly now; the secret was about to be revealed.

'But we didn't, did we? I thought you said he was suspended.' Jane's words hung in the air, like incense in a church.

Crozier said nothing but continued to stare out of the window.

'Or was he persuaded to go?' she said, interpreting Crozier's silence.

'Let's just say I didn't try to dissuade him when he said he was considering leaving the Department.' Crozier had placed one hand, palm first, onto the window, and as he moved it Jane could see the imprint of it on the glass.

Jane took a breath. 'I see.' She had personal reasons for finding the thought of working with Robert uncomfortable, but she was realistic enough to know that he was the best person for this assignment. Not only that, but she knew Crozier had used his dislike of Carter to get rid of him.

'Don't be angry, Jane. I think the same now as I thought then. Carter is a maverick and as such, a liability. I think the Department's better off without him. But my hand is being forced on this.' God how he hated letting her know that he was being told what to do, and against his better judgment.

It was as if Jane was reading his thoughts. 'So how do you feel about losing your autonomy, about the Minister laying down conditions . . . and is this the only condition, or will there be more later?' Jane knew Crozier would be extremely uncomfortable admitting any form of weakness, and to him being made to reemploy Carter was a weakness.

Crozier shrugged. 'If there are, then we'll just have to bite the bullet. As I say, we need the money. As for future operations . . . well, we'll just have to wait and see.'

'And if I do manage to get Robert to reconsider and to join us on this, which of us will be running the show?' She needed to know where she stood professionally, but also with Carter.

Crozier turned to face her. 'You, of course. I told the Minister that the only way I'd have Carter back is as a special consultant, for this one assignment only.' He puffed back his shoulders as if reaffirming his authority. Once the job was done he envisaged Carter slinking back to lick his wounds at that Lake District cottage of his.

Jane considered this for a moment. 'What's the contingency plan should I fail to convince him?' she said.

'There isn't one. We're snookered.' The Minister had made it crystal clear that the terms of the contract were binding.

She sighed. 'Okay. I'll drive up and see Robert in the morning. But I can guess what his answer will be.'

'Just do your best, Jane. If he'll listen to anyone, he'll listen to you.' He went back to his desk and sat down. Once back inside his comfort zone his demeanor changed. Suddenly he was all business again. 'Right. What about the rest of your team?'

'I'd want Kirby Grant. Is Raj Kumar back from Teheran yet?'

'Three days ago.'

'Then him too. Raj and Kirby work well together.'

'Okay. Neither of them are assigned to anything urgent so they should both be available.'

'And I want John McKinley too,' Jane threw in quickly.

'But won't that create a conflict if Carter comes on board? The two are virtually interchangeable. Similar abilities.' Carter and McKinley were both powerful psychics.

'Exactly. That's why I want him there.' Jane hardened her voice; she was ready if some bargaining was needed.

'In case Carter screws up?' There was almost a hint of hope in his voice.

'A safety net.' Nothing more than that, but she knew it *was* more than that. They were going into the unknown and two minds like these would be better than one. She was also aware that Carter had been out of action for a couple of months and they would all need to be ready and alert.

'All right, but there's one other thing I must stress. This is strictly voluntary. Everyone has an opt-out clause, including you. If, once you've slept on it, you decide you want no part of it, then it won't reflect on your record.'

Jane hid a smile behind her hand. She could almost smell the bullshit. Officially it might not affect her record, but forevermore she would be compromised by the case she'd decided not to take. Crozier could use it against her like a lever and it would make her future with the Department very uncomfortable. Calling it a voluntary operation assuaged his conscience should anything go wrong, nothing more. 'I'll make that clear to them,' she said.

'Very well then. Gather your team and brief them, then go out to the island and take the place apart—stone by stone if necessary. Call me in a day or so, once you've spoken with Carter.'

Jane took the elevator down to street level. In her mind she was already rehearsing how she would break the news to David.

CHAPTER THIRTEEN

As she let herself into her house she knew immediately that something was wrong. There was an atmosphere of melancholy that was almost palpable. It insinuated itself under her skin, making her shiver. She dropped her bag on the hall table, took one step towards the lounge, and saw the small suitcase left casually at the bottom of the stairs. This was not a good sign.

She found David in the lounge, sitting in front of the television, his jacket on, a glass of whisky in his hand. He looked up at her as she entered, then his gaze reverted to the ten o'clock news playing out the day's events on the screen.

'Hi,' she said, with a lightness she didn't feel.

'Hi.' He didn't even look at her.

'How are the girls?' She was still standing in the doorway to the room, uncertain whether she was waiting for an invitation, or just a sign that she was welcome.

'At your mother's.' The item on the news was about the Pope's planned visit to the old Eastern Bloc countries in the spring.

'I thought you might be having them.'

'You thought wrong. They'd been looking forward to

seeing her. I didn't want to disappoint them.' A slight hesitation. 'There have been enough disappointments today.'

She moved to the sideboard and poured herself a scotch. 'I think we need to talk,' she said. 'I saw the suitcase in the hall. Going somewhere?'

He didn't take his eyes from the screen. The newscaster was now reporting a suicide bomb attack in Israel. The words washed over her. At that moment there were more important issues to deal with—at least in *her* life.

'I spoke to Graham Turner earlier. He has a room he wants to rent out. I thought I'd take it for a while.' He sounded like a petulant schoolboy. *He doesn't want this,* Jane thought. *I can still keep us together.*

'So it's not a permanent arrangement?'

He shrugged.

She crashed down into an armchair and took a long pull on her drink, wincing as the neat spirit burned its way down her throat. 'When did you decide to leave?' she said.

'About five minutes after you left this morning.'

'And you didn't think to talk it over with me first. We'd arranged to go out today. Talk, relax, sort things out.'

The news had moved on. Football results.

'Can you turn that bloody thing off?' she said. His lack of engagement with her was casting doubts on her earlier belief that she could retrieve things.

His hand reached out for the remote and he stroked a button. The screen went black. He looked at her, but the look was dispassionate, staring at her as if she were a total stranger. 'No,' he said quietly. 'I didn't. Think to talk it over with you first, that is. Besides, you weren't here.'

A wave of despair flooded over her. 'I'm really sorry. Crozier insisted I attend an all-dayer. You know what my job entails.' She couldn't let eight years of marriage end.

Not here tonight. Not like this. 'What about Gemma and Amy? They need their father.'

'They need their mother too, but that fact seems to escape your notice whenever it's convenient.' His tone had taken on a cold analytical embrace.

'That's not fair,' she snapped at him. 'It's my job. I need to work.'

His voice remained infuriatingly level. 'No, you don't. We don't *need* your salary. You *choose* to work, and you *choose* to neglect the girls.'

Despair gave way to anger. 'I don't neglect them!' She took another sip of her drink, measuring her next words carefully. 'Is there someone else?'

He laughed, a hard, brittle sound. 'You know me better than that. Anyway, would you blame me if there were? Our sex life's not exactly setting the world alight is it?'

She couldn't answer that. It was true. She couldn't remember that last time they'd made love. Though that had been on the aborted agenda today, at least in her mind.

He stood up and set his glass down on the sideboard. 'I'd better be going. Graham's expecting me.'

'Stay. Just for tonight. We can talk. We need to talk.' She tried to keep the pleading note out of her voice and failed miserably. 'I love you, David. You know that.'

Yet here she was, sitting at home, numb with shock, as her husband, a stranger, a dab of shaving foam behind his ear, told her their life together was over. There was no one else involved, but it appeared she had lost control of the marriage; perhaps she had fallen asleep at the wheel for a few seconds, lost her bearings. The occurrence was apparently quite common, according to many of their friends, whose own marriages had needed several air bags for survival.

The hard look in his eyes softened slightly. 'Look,' he said. 'I have a bag packed. Pack one for yourself and we'll drive out to the airport and pick up a flight to Barcelona, or Paris. Your mother can have the kids a few days. She won't mind. Just the two of us. An anonymous hotel, good food, soft beds, plenty of sex.'

She stared at the glass in her hand, swirling the liquid around. When she spoke it was little more than a whisper. 'I can't,' she said. 'I have to go up to Scotland for a few days.'

His shoulders dropped, just as the smile dropped from his face. 'And you know what the sad part is?' he said. 'I'm not even surprised.' They both stood, looking at one another as if for the first time. Jane leaned forwards and wiped the shaving foam away with her finger. He left the room and a few moments later she heard the front door close and his car revving to life.

'Shit!' she said and poured herself another drink.

It seemed to take ages for her mother to answer the phone. 'Hi,' Jane said. 'It's me.'

Her mother sounded cross. 'Jane, it's very late. The girls are asleep.'

'I should hope so,' Jane said, keeping her voice light. 'Listen, mum, could you do me a huge favor? I need you to look after Gemma and Amy for a few days. I have to go away.'

'But what about your nanny, that Annalise girl? That's *her* job.' She could sound annoyed, accusing and pleading all at the same time.

'Yes, but she doesn't live in. I'd need you to come here and stay, so you can take care of them after Annalise goes home.' Jane tried to stay as casual and normal as possible.

'Can't you pay her extra to stay on?' It was obvious her mother was going to fight hard to do what Jane wanted.

'No, mum, I can't. She has a life too. It wouldn't be fair.' Wouldn't be fair, and she wouldn't give the same love and attention the children's grandmother would.

'So where are you and David going?' At last Jane heard a hint of acceptance.

'It's work, and David's not going with me.'

'But I thought . . . well, if David's not going with you, what's wrong with him taking care of them in the evenings. I'd say yes, Jane, you know I would, I love having the girls, but I've got a lot on at the . . . .'

'David's left me.'

There was a long pause, then, 'Oh, Jane!' her mother said in her best, *what a disappointment you are* tone of voice. She'd heard that same tone so many times in her life it almost didn't affect her anymore. Almost.

Her mother sniffed. She was crying. 'But why? When?' A devout Catholic who didn't accept divorce, she was already preparing her list of accusations about whose fault it was.

'Look, mum, I don't want to go into details now. He's only just left and I'm feeling a little shell-shocked. Just do this one favor for me and I promise we'll talk about it for as long as you like when I get back.'

'Well, I haven't got a choice, have I?' her mother said, sniffing back the tears and injecting a little venom into her voice. 'I don't have to tell you how disappointed I am, do I?'

'No, you don't. But you're probably not nearly as disappointed as I am.' Sarcasm would be lost on her but it felt good to give a little anger back.

'Is there any hope for the marriage?' The question was coached in an *all hope is gone* kind of way. What she was saying is will *he* take *you* back under *any* circumstances?

'Oh yes, there's always hope,' Jane said, far more encouragingly than she felt. But she was not sure she believed it. Even though her mother had brought her up to obey the Ten Commandments, sometimes lies were a necessary evil.

CHAPTER FOURTEEN

The woman who sat across the desk from Simon Crozier was young, in her late twenties, early thirties at the most. She was dressed in a navy business suit, her dark hair cut into a long bob, with heavy fringe. As the morning sun poured through the window of her office in Regent Street, it played on her hair, picking out the auburn highlights and making it shine. Jessica Anderson was Chief Executive Officer of the Kulsay Development Corporation and it was a role she loved, despite the problems of the last two months.

'So Jane Talbot's agreed to take the assignment,' she said in a clipped Boston accent. Her U.S. education had been of the highest quality. Everything her billionaire father could afford.

'Yes.' Crozier shifted in his seat, slightly uncomfortable to be seated on the wrong side of the desk in an unfamiliar office. He crossed his legs and then uncrossed them, unable to settle.

Jessica Anderson smiled with satisfaction. 'Good, that's good. And Robert Carter?'

'Jane is going to see him this morning, to persuade him.'

The smile slipped from her face and a concerned frown creased her brow. 'Yes, good. But will she be successful? I thought you said the Minister would only go ahead with the investigation if Carter's part of the team.' Her anxiousness was part of her youthful inexperience but also intrigued Crozier. Why was Carter so important to these American businesspeople? And to the Minister?

Crozier sighed. 'He wants Carter as part of the team, but I'm sure his position is flexible. He wants an answer to this mystery, as we all do. And, as I've told you before, Jane Talbot is the best investigator we have. She's more than capable of running this assignment. I would have thought that, from your point of view, you need to get this matter sorted out, by whatever means.' He hadn't been entirely honest with Jane. Sometimes he wondered if he had forever lost the capacity to be honest with anyone, even himself. The Minister *had* insisted Carter be part of the team for Kulsay, but he had hinted his hands were being twisted somewhat. Putting everything together in his mind, Crozier had concluded the Andersons were pulling the strings.

'We do, but we'd also prefer to have Robert Carter on the team. My people put together a dossier on him.' She tapped the gray folder on the desk in front of her with a perfectly manicured index finger. 'He really is a remarkable man.'

'He's also stubborn, cantankerous and a bloody nuisance,' Crozier said, a cold smile playing on his lips.

'You don't like him, do you, Simon?' Jessica wasn't smiling at all.

'My personal feelings are neither here nor there. Though I'll admit I don't much care for his methods. He's a maverick; insubordinate and reckless. The fiasco that led to Sian Davies's disappearance was down to him. If he'd followed proper procedure it might never have happened. At least he had the good grace to resign over it.'

'Resignation would have been good for you, maybe, but for the Department?' She skewered him with a look. 'That's if it had been a resignation. My dossier suggests suspension . . .'

Crozier shifted in his seat again. 'The Department can manage without him. John McKinley's taken over many of Carter's cases, and made significant progress. He's really very good. All he needs is a chance to flex his muscles.'

She opened the gray folder and flicked through a few pages, ignoring Crozier for a moment. Finally she said, 'You may not like Robert Carter's methods, Simon, but he does get results, which is why we want him on Kulsay.' *Was that an admission?* Crozier wondered. *Is she going to reveal what's behind this interest in Carter?*

'You should read McKinley's file. It's just as impressive as Carter's.' He continued to prod and probe.

'I've read it and I agree, but that's not the point. We want Carter. Do you think Talbot will be able to persuade him?'

Crozier shrugged. 'I really can't say. But if *she* can't, given their history, then no one can.'

Jessica Anderson smiled. 'I see. They have a history. It's always useful to be aware of these things.' She snapped the file shut. There was nothing in the dossier she had been shown that mentioned a romance between Talbot and Carter. 'When will you know?'

'Jane has promised to call me after their meeting. I'll let you know then.'

'Then I'll wait to hear from you.' The meeting was over.

Once outside in the street Simon Crozier took a deep lungful of London air. The night was humid. Along Regent Street cars were bumper to bumper, their exhausts blowing out clouds of pollution that gathered in a haze above the city. He pulled a handkerchief from his pocket and wiped the sweat from his brow, then waved the handkerchief in the air to hail a taxi. 'Beaumont Place,' he said to the driver, took a seat in the back of the cab and opened his briefcase. For the duration of the fifteen-minute ride back to his apartment he read through Martin Impey's file on Jessica Anderson and the KDC, refamiliarizing himself with the details.

Jessica Anderson seemed to be a very sharp, very confident businesswoman, a woman who appeared to know her own mind and had a very clear idea of what she wanted out of life and what she expected others to provide; but when he dug a little deeper into the file a wider picture of the dynamic within the KDC and within Jessica's family itself began to emerge.

The money behind the KDC came from Jessica's father, the financier Carl Anderson. Anderson owned large swathes of land in North America, but had made his fortune as a venture capitalist, financing various companies and creaming off the profits. He was a major player on the New York Stock Exchange, and it was obvious he was grooming his daughter to follow in his footsteps. As far as Crozier could see the KDC was the first of his projects in which Jessica had been involved. Her father had given her sufficient leeway and let her develop it, making her the company's figurehead, but so far it had been a financial and PR disaster.

Anderson had a reputation for being a ruthless operator, and Crozier couldn't imagine him letting the Kulsay situation drift for long before instigating some kind of damage limitation plan. He wouldn't let his family name and his own reputation be tarnished, and if that meant relieving Jessica of her position as CEO, Crozier was in no doubt the man would do it. So Jessica was a woman with a lot to prove and Crozier didn't envy her.

Which still didn't explain the interest in Carter, and the insistence on his involvement.

As the taxi pulled up outside the apartment block in Beaumont Place, Crozier snapped the file shut and slipped it back into his briefcase. He paid the cabbie and let himself into the block, taking the elevator up to the fourth floor where his apartment was situated. With its view over the Thames and desirable postcode, the apartment cost him a small fortune each month, but he wouldn't choose to live anywhere else. He opened the door onto the balcony and looked out over the water. There were cars on the nearby Tower Bridge, nose to tail, making snail-like progress across the river. A pleasure boat, lit up like a Christmas tree, was meandering its way west, music from an onboard disco wafting up to him on a thermal of torpid air. Further down the river a police launch was cruising past a line of houseboats, a regular patrol to reassure the boats' inhabitants.

He went back inside and poured himself a large brandy and brought it back to the balcony. He slumped down on a steel-mesh chair and lifted his feet onto the balcony railing. As he took his first sip of Courvoisier the telephone rang.

'Crozier,' he said. He hoped it might be one of his regular companions, inviting him out for dinner and afterwards some mutually pleasurable entertainment.

'Simon? It's Jane.' The female voice quashed his rising anticipation.

'Jane,' he said, trying to keep the surprise and disappointment out of his voice. She'd never called him at home before. 'What can I do for you?' Surely she hadn't contacted Carter already.

There was a long pause at the other end of the line. Finally she said, 'I'm very drunk.'

'That's nice. Celebrating?' He looked at his watch. Once this conversation was dealt with he'd call a friend and make the arrangements for the night.

Another pause.

'Celebrating. . . . yes . . . We didn't, you know . . . Rob and me . . . we didn't . . . the affair was not like . . .'

'Jane, is everything all right?' Despite his instinct to stay detached he was concerned about such an important person in the Department acting in this way.

'I know you think we did . . . everyone thinks we did . . . but we didn't.' Her voice was clear, though palpably slurred.

'If you say so.' He knew from CCTV footage he had been secretly shown how far Carter and Talbot had or had not proceeded in the denied affair.

'David's gone . . . left me.' The sound of liquid being poured into a glass accompanied these words.

A flicker of hope toyed with his thoughts. A fully concentrated Jane Talbot would be a major coup in obtaining ongoing funding. 'I'm sorry to hear that. Is there anything I can do?' He glanced at his watch.

He thought he heard a sob on the other end of the line but the mouthpiece was hurriedly covered.

'Jane?' An unfamiliar feeling of genuine concern had permeated his emotions. He was never any good with weeping women. Never any good with women at all in all honesty, which is why he preferred the company of men in all aspects of his life.

'No, nothing you can do . . . nothing anyone can do . . . bloody job! Bloody, bloody job! Good night, Simon.'

'Would you like me to come ov . . .'

There was a click and a buzz as the phone on the other end of the line was disconnected. Crozier switched off the phone, took a long, thoughtful sip of his brandy, shook his head and stared out at the night. Before Jane met David she would have ripped out her own tongue before making a phone call like that, especially to him. Now they had split perhaps the Jane of old would resurface. He found himself hoping the rift was permanent.

Then he pulled out his little black book and dialed who was currently his favorite male companion.

Jane put down the phone, staggered across to the sideboard and poured another vodka, splashing in a small amount of tonic to fill the glass. *Big mistake,* she thought. *Phoning Simon. Big mistake.* A large mirror was screwed to the wall above the sideboard. She stared at her reflection. She barely recognized the woman who stared back at her. The eyes were bloodshot and bleary, the hair disheveled, the skin pale and insipid, throwing into contrast her flushed cheeks. 'You look like shit,' she said to her reflection. 'No wonder he left you.' And then she started to cry. Sinking to her knees, she watched the tears wash down her cheeks. It was a mess, an awful, unnecessary mess! The glass slipped from her fingers, spilling the vodka onto the beige carpet. She didn't care. She didn't care about anything anymore. Without any warning whatsoever she vomited, her stomach going into spasm, retching and retching until there was nothing to bring up but sour air.

Almost instantly she was sober, or at least, less drunk than she had been. She hauled herself upright and stumbled up the stairs to the bathroom.

An icy jet of water hit her body and made her gasp, but she gripped the showerhead and directed it into her face, feeling it prickle on her closed eyelids. She stood like that for fifteen minutes, letting the spray blast away the remainder of her drunken self-pity. Finally she added some hot water to the mix and soaped her body and shampooed her hair.

By the time she was drying herself on the pale blue bath sheet she was feeling a little more human.

The clock on her bedside table told her it was nearly midnight. She picked up the phone and hit redial.

'Crozier.' The phone took a few rings before it was answered.

'Simon. You're still up. Good. It's Jane.'

'Oh.' There was some whispering, and Jane realized Crozier was with someone.

'It's all right, before you hang up, I'm sober now. I just

wanted to apologize for before. Ringing you like that.
Very unprofessional.'

'Are you okay now?' There was an edge of sleepiness to
his voice.

'Oh Christ, did I wake you. I'm sorry.'

'Jane,' Crozier said patiently. 'If you're okay now, just
go to bed. You'll need a good night's sleep if you're going
to tackle Carter. You'll need your wits about you.'

'Yes,' she said. 'You're right. And sorry again.'

She hung up the phone and pulled back the duvet, sliding
her legs over the crisp cotton sheet, spreading herself across
the king-sized bed, reveling in the space. There were advan-
tages to being on her own. Minutes later she was asleep.

CHAPTER FIFTEEN

The lake was a still sheet of glass, broken only by the occasional stream of bubbles from the fish that swam beneath
the surface. Robert Carter sat on an old wooden jetty, his
legs dangling over the edge, his boots inches above the
water. A fishing rod was propped on a wire stand to the
left of him, to the right a bait box, its plastic tray filled
with hooks, spools of line, spherical lead weights and a
polythene container with hundreds of ivory-colored maggots, writhing and wriggling on a bed of sawdust. Hanging from one of the jetty's stanchions was a keep net,
mostly submerged, containing half a dozen perch swimming listlessly in circles: the day's catch.

He sat, smoking a cigarette, watching the fluorescent or-
ange float bobbing gently twenty yards away, waiting for a
fish to strike. The day was the best summer had to offer; a
clear blue sky, streaked with thin wisps of cirrus; a gentle

breeze tempering the heat of the sun before it could become oppressive. High above him in the trees, jays, thrushes and blackbirds serenaded him with their summer songs and once in a while a kingfisher swooped low over the water looking for its next meal.

The Lake District of England was a beautiful natural wonderland of lake and forest. The different lakes, Ulleswater, Derwent, all had their own unique attraction, and the entire area was a magnet for tourists all through the year.

'Hello, Rob.'

He hadn't heard her approach. He didn't look round. 'Jane,' he said. 'You're the last person I expected.' He always knew someone would come for him. Knew there would be at least one more job that only he was right for. His research had given him a pretty good idea what that job would entail.

Jane moved the bait box to one side and sat down next to him. 'Do you mind?' She settled herself on the bank and looked out over the calm water.

'Feel free.' He flicked the cigarette into the lake and emptied his lungs of smoke. 'So what brings you all the way up here?'

'A fool's errand, I suspect.' There was a sigh in her voice. She had thought about what she was going to say, tried to plan little speeches, but now she was here, in this beautiful setting, and she had to admit to herself, now she was with Robert, none of her preparations seemed to matter much.

He took another cigarette from the pack and lit it.

'You still smoke too much,' she said, though she had a smile in her voice.

'Sorry, did you want one?' He offered her the pack.

She took one and leaned in so he could light it with his gold Dunhill lighter. The lighter had been a gift, from her to him. She was surprised he still carried it. 'Thanks,' she said, breathing smoke out through her nose. 'You realize we'll probably both die of cancer.'

'Probably.' He was surprised they had sent Jane.

'Doesn't it bother you?' She sucked down the smoke and suppressed a small cough as it caught in her throat.

'Dying, or cancer?' His gaze was fixed on the float; he was still avoiding making eye contact. It was starting to unsettle her.

'Either. Both.' She had known this wasn't going to be easy.

He shrugged. 'Not really. So, what are you doing here?'

She took a breath and came straight to the point. 'Simon needs your help on an investigation.'

'Then why isn't he asking me himself?'

'He thinks I might have more success.' All the practiced phrases she had rehearsed in the car were abandoned. Now she was with him she instinctively knew that only honesty would work. She owed him that much.

'Do you think you'll succeed?' He turned and looked at her for the first time.

'No, I don't. I think it's a bad idea, but Simon wants you in on this one, or more specifically, the Minister wants you involved. Simon's worried that if he doesn't give him what he wants, the Department will lose his support in Whitehall, and that could be the end of it.'

'And that concerns me how?'

'Come on, Rob, I know you better than that. Once upon a time the Department meant everything to you. It was your life.'

Carter took a drag of his cigarette and shook his head. 'It was, and then when I screwed up I was dropped like a stone. I owe Crozier, or the Department, nothing.'

'He thought that might be your reaction.' She was surprised at the depth of his bitterness.

'Then he was right. I'm not coming back.' It sounded final.

She sighed. This was going exactly as she had expected. She tried a different tack. 'Don't you want to know what it is we're investigating?'

He finally turned to look at her. 'I've a feeling you're going to tell me.' He smiled at her for the first time and she was pleased.

She briefed him quickly. Kulsay, the disappearances, the mystery. 'Still not interested?'

'No, Jane, I'm not.' He pointed to the keep net. 'Look there.'

Jane looked. 'What am I supposed to see, apart from a few poor fish that've been dragged away from their simple lives by a hook and line.'

He smiled at the implied criticism. 'Watch them swimming round and around. You'd think they were quite content. Then occasionally one of them will swim deliberately into the net. Do you know why?'

Jane shrugged, not sure where this was going.

'They're looking for a way out, for a gap in the mesh. Well, after all this time, I've found my gap and now I'm in open water, swimming free, and I have no desire to jump back into the net again.'

She nodded her head slowly and ground out her cigarette on the jetty. 'A bit dramatic for you, but I get the point. I think I'm wasting my time here. I'd better go.'

He laid a hand on her arm as she began to stand up. 'Stay a while,' he said. 'It's been a long time since we talked. How are David and the girls?'

She sat back down, pulled a stem from one of the reeds growing at the side of the jetty and twisted it in her fingers. 'The girls are fine. Becoming more beautiful and more of a handful every day.' She lapsed into silence, staring down at the reed stem twined through her fingers. She'd twisted it around her wedding ring, hiding it from view.

'And David?'

'I really don't know,' she said, very quietly. 'He's left me.'

He looked at her sharply. 'That's very sad. I thought you two would be together forever.' •

She laughed bitterly. 'Oh, don't write us off yet. It's early days. He only left last night and, to be honest, it's knocked me sideways. I really wasn't expecting it. I knew things had been a little sticky lately, but . . .'

Carter said nothing but slid an arm around her shoulder. She shrugged it off brusquely. 'Don't!'

He let his arm drop. 'Sorry.'

'No, *I'm* sorry. That was very rude of me. It's just that I'm a bit raw at the moment and very edgy. I cried three times on the way up here, and I don't have to tell you how out of character that is for me.'

'Hard as nails, you,' he said with a smile.

'It's a facade. Inside I'm marshmallow.'

'Yes,' he said. 'I know. Do you want to talk about it?'

She shook her head. 'Not really, it's one of those things we have to work out for ourselves.'

He stood. 'Come on; let's go back to the house. I'll make you a coffee.' He reached down and released the cord tying the keep net to the jetty, letting the fish swim free. Then they walked back through the wood that surrounded Carter's small picturesque cottage. The path was well used.

In the kitchen he boiled the kettle while Jane sat at the long pine table. 'You shouldn't blame yourself, you know,' she said as she watched him move from the sink to the range cooker.

'For what?'

'For what happened to Sian.'

He joined her at the table, pulling out a wheel-backed chair and sitting down heavily.

'I don't know what happened to Sian,' he said. 'Nobody does.'

'She might have just taken off. If the manifestations in the house were as frightening as you described in your report, no one would have blamed her for making herself scarce.'

'True, but I don't think that's what happened. According to the official version, don't forget, there were no *manifestations*. No one's had any contact from her since that day. Not her family, not her friends.'

'What's your theory?'

'I haven't got one.' He sounded as if he had exhausted every possible avenue.

'No one's heard anything from her at all?' Jane knew people disappeared all the time. It was a recurring nightmare that one of her children went missing and she spent the rest of her life searching for them. She would never be able to accept a loss like that.

He shook his head. 'Besides, the car was locked. She couldn't have left the car and locked it after her. I had the key.'

The kettle started to whistle.

'What *really* happened the day Sian disappeared?' she said as he put two steaming mugs of coffee down on the table.

'You know what I know. You read my report,' he said defensively.

'Yes, that's right, I did. Now I'd like you to fill in the gaps. In the report you said you blacked out for a "considerable length of time."'

'I did. Over four hours.' He took a mouthful of coffee and swallowed.

'And nothing happened in that time?' She tried not to sound doubtful.

'How would I know? I was unconscious.' He made no attempt not to sound defensive.

Her eyes narrowed. She looked at him closely. Okay, she knew he had been suspended, but his reaction to Sian disappearing seemed out of proportion to her. He and Sian had worked together a while but there was no logical reason why Carter should seem so devastated. He avoided her gaze by staring down into his mug, swilling the liquid around the cup and watching the light reflecting on its surface.

'No. You're bullshitting me, and I've known you too long to be taken in by it,' Jane said.

This was the Jane Talbot of old; perceptive, intuitive and dogged. It's what made her such a damned good investigator. She wasn't going to let him off the hook.

He sighed. 'Okay,' he said, finally meeting her eyes. 'I'll tell you everything I remember.'

By the time he'd finished, the coffee had grown cold. Jane went across to the sink to fill the kettle again.

'I think I can understand the symbol of the operating theatre in your vision.' Jane said. 'It's a place of uncertainty, of the unknown, of possible danger. But why should your subconscious be placing *such* significance on something as mundane as having your tonsils out?' she said, putting the kettle on the range to boil.

He looked at her bleakly. 'It's quite simple really. That was the day I died.'

'What? What are you talking about?' Jane said.

Carter took a breath. 'I've had this power, gift, whatever you want to call it, for as long as I can remember. Up to the age of seven it was undefined and fairly random, just the odd flash of precognition, nothing very clear. I was a fairly sickly child; all the usual ailments—measles, chickenpox, mumps—but I suffered quite badly from throat infections. So much so that our doctor recommended I have my tonsils out.

'I was too young to realize what was really happening, but a few days before the operation I started getting very clear visions. I knew with absolute clarity that if I went in for surgery there was a good chance I wouldn't survive it. As I said, the odd flash of precognition. I told my parents, but of course they didn't understand. I was only seven years old after all. They knew I was prone to *flights of fancy*, as my mother liked to call them. So the operation went ahead.

'The procedure was routine. The surgeon operating had performed hundreds of tonsillectomies; he could have probably operated them with his eyes closed. But this time it went wrong. In the final stage of the operation, complications developed with the anesthetic. My heart failed and for several minutes they had to fight to revive me. For those minutes I was clinically dead. They brought me round, of course, but things were never quite the same again.'

'In what way?' Jane said. He had never told her this before.

'It was as if my powers shifted up a notch. The precognition intensified; I started displaying signs of telekinesis, and I also started to see and hear people who were supposed to be dead. The visions were very clear, and sometimes very frightening.' As he pulled out a cigarette and lit it, Jane noticed his hands were shaking. He blew a plume of smoke up at the ceiling. 'My mother was something of a crank. She belonged to a Spiritualist church and used to go to regular meetings. When she realized what was happening to me, she called in the church elders, who confirmed that her son really was something very special. After that she embraced my new powers with something like an evangelical zeal. Suddenly she had something of value to offer her church; a currency that she could use to raise her standing, so she started to take me along to the meetings.

'Not long after that the circus began. Slowly at first; she'd get me to give clairvoyant readings to the other members of the church and, though I say so myself, I was pretty damned accurate.

'But it was my father who saw the potential for making money out of it. He'd always been something of a wheeler and dealer, always on the lookout for a way to make a buck. He was like that up to the day he died, and I think even then, with death staring him in the face, he was still looking for some kind of angle on it; some way to turn it to his advantage. Well, to him I was like the proverbial goose laying golden eggs. And the next ten years were a blur of séances, readings, palmistry . . . you name it, all organized by him. Thanks to me they lived very well for a decade. The money poured in and I became something of a celebrity. TV talk shows, radio interviews. Little Bobby Hinton, the psychic wonder.' He didn't try to disguise the bitterness in his voice.

'Hinton?' Jane said.

'Carter's my mother's maiden name. I adopted it when I decided I'd had enough of living under a microscope. I grew to hate being treated like a performing seal. I knew instinctively that I'd been given this ability for a higher reason and I was sure it was not to be prostituted.' He paused. 'Christ, that sounds pompous, but that was genuinely how I felt.

'When I hit seventeen I left home. My father was very ill by then, and I knew he wasn't going to last much longer. Mother had been uncomfortable with the commercial side of things for a long time—it didn't sit well with her religious beliefs—but she was too afraid of my father to say anything. He was a bully, and he had a terrible temper.

When I told her I wanted to leave home she was upset, but supported my decision. It was tough for her, knowing that her husband only had a short time to live, but she put her feelings on the back burner for my benefit. I'll always be grateful for that.

'I left home, changed my name, and set about finding ways to use my gift to help others rather than turning a profit.'

'So what happened next?' Jane said, probing deeper. In the years since they'd first met she'd never known him to open up like this. She was seeing a completely different side to Robert Carter; a softer, more vulnerable side. It made a refreshing change.

'I'd had enough of England so I went to America. I'd heard about a research center in Kansas dedicated to exploring psychic phenomena in a totally scientific way. It was an antidote to all the Spiritualist mumbo jumbo. When I arrived I met others with powers similar to my own, and I had a chance to talk about them, to explore ways to use them. For the first time in a decade I stopped feeling like a freak, a sideshow turn. The three years I spent out there were the happiest time of my life.

'I'd heard of Simon Crozier, and was aware he'd recently taken over for Sir George Logan at Department Eighteen. Walt Whitney, the director of the Institute, was a friend of Crozier's and put my name forward as a possible candidate for the new regime. The picture Whitney painted was very attractive so I flew back to England to meet with Crozier. I can't say I liked him—still don't—but the idea of the place intrigued me enough and I found the invitation hard to resist. It was everything I'd been looking for. I knew there were only a handful of people in the world who had the same kind of psychic range as me, and so did Simon Crozier. Of course, by inviting me to join the Department, he was pandering to my ego and I let him. But for a long time, working there, I felt I was doing something worthwhile with my life.'

'Until Sian disappeared.' Jane began to understand why it had hit him so hard.

'Yes.' He ground out his cigarette.

'And as I said before, you can't blame yourself for that.'

Carter swallowed the dregs of cold coffee. The bitterness of the coffee was mirrored in his words. 'That's the problem, you see. I can and I do, because I *knew* something terrible was going to happen that day. Just as clearly as I knew I was going to die on the operating table when I was seven years old. I knew even before I entered the house that there was something awful waiting just over the threshold. Something that would change my life forever. But I thought that whatever was going to happen would happen to *me*. I just didn't foresee it happening to Sian. I should never have taken her along. I should have gone alone.'

Jane said nothing. She got to her feet abruptly and walked to the door.

'Going?' Carter said. 'You're probably as disillusioned with me as I am with myself.'

'It's a long drive back to London.' She paused, her hand on the latch. 'Yes, I'm going, but no, I'm not disillusioned with you. Quite the reverse. I shouldn't have come here. It wasn't fair. And it wasn't fair of Simon to ask me.'

'When do you leave for Scotland?'

'There's a briefing first thing Thursday morning, then we're flying up to Aberdeen.'

'I see.' He lit yet another cigarette. 'Why did you and David split up?'

The question jolted her. 'I can't even begin to get into that one,' she said.

'It was the job, wasn't it?'

She hesitated, and then nodded her head sharply.

'Yes,' he said. 'It has a habit of ruining lives. Take care, Jane.'

'Thanks,' she said, and let herself out of the house. As she walked to the car, a single tear seeped out from her eye and rolled down her cheek. She wiped it away impatiently with the back of her hand and got in behind the wheel, then drove away from the cottage without looking back.

She'd gone no more that five miles when her cell phone rang.

She punched a button. There was a brief silence, then Carter said, 'Where are you?'

'About a mile from the motorway. Why?'

'Can you come back?'

'Why?' But she was already looking for a place to turn round.

'There's something you should see.'

The door opened at her first knock. 'Well?' she said.

'Come on through to the kitchen. I want to show you something.' It was as if he was resigned to show her something he had been reluctant to share.

Spread out on the kitchen table was a map of the British Isles. He'd marked four stars on it with red pen. 'The stars are the sites of my last four investigations.' He took a ruler and laid it over the stars. They formed an arrow-straight line.

'Interesting,' she said. 'Ley lines?' Jane was as familiar with the ancient passages as she was with her own history.

'It certainly looks that way.' With a pencil he drew a line all the way down to Weymouth on the coast. 'I wouldn't mind betting there's been more activity along that line. The incidents have been gradually moving south.'

'I haven't heard of anything,' Jane said.

'Maybe, but the Department only gets to hear about a fraction of these occurrences. After you left I looked at the map again. A straight line from Redditch all the way down to Warminster.'

'Which was where Sian disappeared.'

'Exactly. And what happened to the management team on Kulsay Island?'

A frown creased her forehead. 'They disappeared.'

They disappeared! Vanished without a trace, except for the blood.

It was suddenly *so* obvious. She picked up the pen and drew a line north. It traveled through the Midlands, through Newcastle upon Tyne, and then out into the North Sea. She followed the line and drew another star.

'Kulsay,' she said. Though she didn't yet know what it meant.

'Kulsay.'

'So Sian's disappearance could be connected to what's happening on the island.'

'It's possible.' He wasn't yet ready to share the rest of his conclusions with her. He wasn't yet ready to show her the other map. The one where he had overlaid all the ley lines that connected known supernatural incidents during the past fifty years. The map that showed the straight lines from Kulsay, all the way to Rome, and the Vatican City.

'And you still won't join the investigation?' Jane opened her hands to him in a helpless gesture.

'I don't have a choice now, do I?'

CHAPTER SIXTEEN

Jane's mother, Brenda, sat simmering in an armchair, ostensibly reading the Sunday newspaper, but taking in very few of the words. Every time the paper rustled Jane glanced across, ready for the next caustic comment that would surely follow.

Jane was ironing Gemma's school uniform, attempting normality despite the strained atmosphere. The girls were playing in the garden, seemingly unconcerned that their grandmother had been looking after them for the past few days, and they hadn't seen their daddy. He had telephoned though; awkward 'What have you been doing?' conversations usually associated with occasionally seen aunts.

'Cup of coffee?' Jane asked her mother.

The newspaper was immediately lowered. 'I'll get it.'

Jane had switched off the iron. David should be here quite soon. 'No, you're fine. Read your paper.'

Brenda put the paper on the small table that held her small glass of sherry. 'I can't take any of it in. Some government scandal about peerages, rising crime rates; the whole country is fading fast.'

Oh God, Jane thought. *Not the 'like was it in my day' rant. Not today.* It was difficult enough shepherding her feelings about seeing her husband again, without her mother giving her a hard time. *Harder* time she should say, because since she'd arrived Brenda had wasted no opportunity to let her know what she had done wrong, *must* have done wrong to let a good man go.

In the kitchen Jane was cut off from conversation, unless her mother chose to follow her, which this time she didn't. Waiting for the kettle to boil she watched the girls in the garden. Their innocence was so precious and yet she knew that in a few short years they would begin to be embroiled in the responsibilities and pressures that affected everyone.

Stop it, Jane. She remonstrated with herself. *Let the children have their special few years of bliss, let them be children for as long as they can.* She smiled as she heard their laughter, sweet and high and boundless.

Telling the girls that David was going away for a few days seemed dishonest but was possibly all that was happening. Both Jane and David had spent time away on business so absence wasn't unusual. What she would say if the days became weeks, became months, became permanent, she didn't care to think.

It wouldn't come to that, she told herself. *I'll get this Scottish trip out of the way and then I'll take some time off; I'm owed some leave. We can all go away, David and the girls, perhaps Spain, somewhere hot where we can relax and rebuild what we had. Once I get back from Kulsay everything will be all right again.*

The doorbell rang. Before she had a chance to get more than halfway into the hall the front door was opened and Brenda was welcoming David with luxurious warmth. 'David, it is good to see you. How have you been?'

David looked well. Jane couldn't see straightaway what it was but he seemed different. He looked over Brenda's shoulder as she hugged him and raised his eyes in greeting to Jane. She smiled back and waited for her mother to release him.

Gradually he wrestled his way out of her grip and walked uncertainly to Jane. 'Hello, Jane.' He kissed her cheek and she felt as if her heart had been ripped from her chest. The kiss of strangers, affectionate but lacking any passion.

Then she saw what was different about him. New clothes. Smart gray trousers with front pleat, pink shirt, a color that under no circumstances would he wear for her, and casual laceless shoes. *He's got someone else,* she thought, and it seemed so obvious that tears welled in her eyes.

David misread the emotion and stepped away from her.

'You've bought some new things,' Jane said quietly.

David made a deprecating gesture. 'Most of my stuff is still here. I'll have to take it soon.' He glanced at his watch. 'Not today though.'

Brenda bustled into the kitchen. 'I'll pour the coffee.'

'The girls are in the garden,' Jane said. 'We've got half an hour yet before church. I'll bring the coffee outside.'

David went out to see his daughters, and Jane heard the excited squeals and shouts when they saw him. Whatever happened between Jane and David, he would always be their father. Jane determined to make that her main priority. Despite that pledge her mind was racing; *someone else, someone else . . .*

The day was bright and clear with that warning tint to the sky, that hint that this is a day to savor before the storms come running after you.

Jane took the tray with the coffee cups out into the garden and placed it on the round green trestle table she and David had picked last summer, when things were good. Before the storms came running. Brenda stayed inside, believing the two needed to sort themselves out without her interference. Not that she didn't believe she couldn't bring them back together; a few stern words, especially with her daughter, wouldn't do any harm at all in her opinion.

David looked across at Jane, said a few words to the girls and sat down at the table, leaning forward to lift up his cup. It was then Jane noticed the other thing about him that had changed. He had taken off his wedding ring.

'Girls,' she called. 'Gemma, Amy. Run inside and wash

your hands, please. We have to go to church in five minutes.' She held up her hand with the fingers spread so they could count them and make the association.

'Is Daddy coming?' Amy asked.

Jane nodded and David smiled.

The two girls ran into the house hooraying and cheering.

Jane ignored her coffee. 'Bit soon to remove the ring, isn't it?'

David began to feign ignorance but realized it was pointless. 'We'll need to talk.'

A shiver ran through her that she tried to suppress. This was the end, she knew that now. She stood from her chair and walked back into the house.

Once they were in David's car the girls carried on a nonstop chatter that under other circumstances Jane would have enjoyed. Her thoughts were a turmoil of anger, sadness and fear.

The car park at the back of St Joseph's Roman Catholic Church was always full at least twenty minutes before Mass began, so everyone knew to arrive early. David managed to get the last but one space and reversed into it.

Jane had been brought up in the Catholic faith by her mother and had continued it into adulthood, though she didn't believe she was quite as fanatical as her mother. She said hello to a few people as the family made their way along the aisle to an empty pew. She genuflected to the altar, showed the girls what to do and they all sat, David on the other side of the two girls. He wasn't a Catholic but had no difficulty with helping Gemma and Amy be brought up in the religion.

As people settled themselves, waiting for the priest to enter, Jane kneeled and said a silent prayer to her God. She prayed for the girls to survive her marriage split, for David to find happiness and for her to have the courage to see it through.

She sat back on her seat and the priest entered, walking along the aisle, Bible in hand, accompanied by the lay preacher, and two young altar servers. One of them was swinging the incense, waves of which filled the air, anointing the congregation, pungent and cloying.

Once on the altar the priest raised his hands in the air. He made the sign of the cross and the congregation did the same. 'May the Lord be with you.' As one everyone replied, 'And also with you.'

Prayers followed, hymns, and all Jane could think of was what she would do when David had gone; when he was with another woman. The problem was that having thoughts like that in church made her guilty. David called it the *religion of the guilty* and she had to acknowledge she knew what he meant.

Our father who art in Heaven
Hallowed be thy name

Movement to her left caught her attention and she looked across to the statue of Lord Jesus. Blood seeped from the nails through his palms and feet.

Thy kingdom come
Thy will be done

She turned to the people behind her but apart from glancing at her they were intent on the prayer. David was oblivious to her, probably already thinking about whoever he was meeting afterwards. Jane looked at the statue again. Jesus had pulled Himself free of the cross and was poised to jump to the floor.

On earth as it is in Heaven
Give us this day our daily bread

His eyes seemed to pour into Jane's as He walked in front of the altar. No one else seemed able to see Him. Everyone continued with their attention on the priest. The figure of Jesus was changing as He walked towards her. The benign smile was fading, being replaced by a reptilian anger that made her think of flicking tongues and dry, flaking scales.

And forgive us our trespasses
As we forgive those who trespass against us

Within a few feet of her Jesus was no more. The figure that approached her was barely recognizable as human. It was more of the beast, but Jane was the only one who could see it.

Lead us not into temptation
But deliver us from evil

Standing next to her, pressing a dark claw into her arm, she could smell the raw meat stench of its breath, feel the rough texture of the skin as it rubbed itself against her. Its eyes were fetid pools of hopelessness, alive with mocking fury.

For thine is the kingdom
The Power and the Glory
Forever and ever
Amen

The massed voices spoke aloud 'Amen' and Jane involuntarily joined them. With that the vision disappeared as if it had never been there. She looked up at the cross and Jesus was back where He belonged.

The priest began to prepare the sacrament, holding up the Lamb of God, pouring the wine, laying out the basket of symbolic bread.

People began turning to one another to offer the hand of peace, 'Peace Be With You,' 'Peace Be With You.' Jane turned behind her and it seemed like a thousand hands thrust forward, clutching at hers. She drew back her hand and the middle-aged man looked hurt at the insult, pausing before offering peace elsewhere.

Jane bent down to Gemma and smiled the best she could at her dear daughter, 'Peace Be With You.' A voice that wasn't hers but came from Gemma's mouth said, 'Fuck off you boring old cow. Daddy wouldn't have left if it hadn't been for you.' Jane flinched and in her normal voice Gemma said, 'What's the matter, Mummy? You have to say, "Peace Be With You." Don't you remember?'

People began to file forward for the Communion. Some would only take it from the priest himself but Jane was happy for she and the girls to accept the lay preacher. When it was their turn Jane let the girls go first, shepherding them along before they could start to ask questions of the poor man as they often did.

When it was her turn Jane opened her mouth for the wafer to be placed on her tongue. The man suddenly put his fingers into her mouth and took tight hold of her tongue. 'Deliver us from evil, Jane. Deliver us.' His fingers were gone and Jane felt the wafer in her mouth.

Back in her place she knelt to pray. Her mind was a rainbow pattern of thoughts and emotions, uncertain what was happening and how much of it was real. Real or hallucinatory, she wondered what was causing it.

As Mass drew to a close she became aware of a darkening in the church. The light through the windows started to dim. The candles flickered as if caught in a breeze. Flower displays drooped with dead petals floating to the floor.

She was vaguely conscious of the priest concluding, 'Mass is over. Go in Peace.'

People were filing past her, some smiling at her, recognizing her from the primary school, or from the nursery.

David was readying the girls, collecting their drawings together, placing their pencils in the Barbie Doll pencil case.

One of Gemma's drawings caught Jane's attention. She picked it up from the pile. 'What's this?' It was a large domed shape, and she could swear it was a good likeness of the images she had seen of Kulsay Island. Was that what this was all about? Gemma laughed, 'It's a hippo, silly. I can't say the full name . . . hippopolemus . . . but it's my hippo.'

David was looking at his watch. Family time was over. *She* was waiting and Jane imagined a glamorous blonde, with dark lingerie and boundless energy.

The church had returned to normal. A place of worship with no threats beyond eternal damnation and endless confession.

As he opened the car doors in the car park David said, 'I'll drop you home. Then I do have to get off.'

Jane pulled her seat belt across her chest. 'Of course, David, come back and visit us again soon, won't you?'

CHAPTER SEVENTEEN

The fine weather broke on Wednesday night. Storm clouds blew in from the east and drenched the capital in a torrential downpour. It was still raining on Thursday morning, hammering against the windows of the briefing room.

There were five people in the room, including Jane Talbot and Robert Carter. Carter was sitting at the back, away from the others, and they in turn were tactfully allowing him space to settle back into the routine of his working life. Jane stood at the front of the room. She had given dozens of briefings in the past, but couldn't shake off the feeling that this one was different.

Raj Kumar glanced across at the rivers of rain rushing down the windows. 'Did you order this specially, Jane?' He had become accustomed to the harsh climate of Afghanistan recently, and the moderate and unpredictable British weather was still confusing.

The others laughed, except for Carter who was reading through the thick file given to him by Martin Impey before the meeting started. He had been received with friendly affection by everyone in the building, from the people in reception to his colleagues in this room. He hadn't yet seen Crozier but he was ready for that occurrence. John McKinley had shaken his hand but kept flashing glances in his direction, obviously uncertain why he was here.

'Doesn't bode well.' This from McKinley, who was a tall black American whose large frame seemed uncomfortable, curled in his seat. His deep voice resonated like the bass lines in a complex jazz composition.

'It's only a drop of rain, John,' Kirby Grant said. 'It won't hurt you.'

'Try telling that to my sciatica,' McKinley said. 'Give me sunshine any day.'

Conversation stopped as the door opened and Simon Crozier stepped into the room, accompanied by Jessica Anderson. He introduced her. 'Jessica is here to represent the Kulsay Development Corporation,' he said to the room. 'She'd like a few words with you before you leave.' Inevitably his eyes met Carter's; it was the first time they had been in the same room since Jane reported her success with him. Carter raised his eyebrows in an ironic gesture of welcome, which made Crozier look away. He turned to Jessica Anderson. 'Jessica, over to you.'

'Thank you, Simon,' she said, and stepped forward. 'I'll keep this brief. I know you want to get on with the job. I'd just like to say that we of the Kulsay Development Corporation would like to thank you in advance for your help in trying to solve this dreadful mystery. The poor wretches who disappeared from Kulsay may still be alive . . . they may of course be dead, but we pray that isn't the case. We have every confidence that you will get to the bottom of this one way or another.

'As I speak, the Manse on Kulsay is being readied for your stay. You'll find that every possible convenience has been provided, as well as a freezer full of food. Each of you will be issued cell phones. We've installed a signal amplifier recently, so you shouldn't have any trouble with them, but as a safeguard we've also installed a radio transmitter with direct links to the KDC and to the Department. If you feel it is necessary, make contact and a helicopter will be sent from Aberdeen to airlift you off.'

Raj cleared his throat. 'I seem to remember that scenario. Didn't you lose a helicopter the last time?' His dark eyes were hooded, cloaking the intelligence that swam behind them.

For a split second Jessica Anderson glared at him, then her face relaxed and she let a smile curl her lips again. 'I don't believe that lightning strikes twice in the same place,' she said.

'Fingers crossed,' Kirby said, and her ready smile lightened the meaning.

Sensing the tension that had suddenly enveloped the room Crozier smiled and said, 'Jane, for Jessica's benefit perhaps you'd like to introduce the team.'

She was taken aback, not least by Crozier's overtly courteous manner. 'Oh, okay, fine,' she said. 'From the left then. Raj Kumar and Kirby Grant.'

'Sound and Vision,' they said, almost in unison.

Jane smiled. 'It's their job to record any phenomena we witness on the island, both visually and aurally.'

Kumar was a tall, slim Indian, early thirties, a very private man, with nervous, fluttering fingers, long black hair and a wispy goatee.

'I take the photos,' Raj said. 'Kirby records the screams.'

'Is that an attempt at humor?' Jessica said, clearly unimpressed.

'A very poor one,' Kirby said quickly, shooting Kumar a look. She had been watching Jessica and her appraisal of the team had reminded her of farmers back when she lived with her parents. They ran a farm, and the monthly cattle market attracted people who viewed the animals with a similar dispassionate stare.

'This is John McKinley,' Jane continued, walking across and laying a hand on the tall man's shoulder. 'John's just come back from India where he was overseeing an investigation into a case of apparent demonic possession.'

'A crock,' McKinley said. 'But the weather was better there.'

'If you've read the file you will have seen that not only is John a leading parapsychologist, but also one of the most gifted *sensitives* in the country, if not the world.'

'I also play a mean game of pool and make an excellent fourth at bridge,' McKinley said with a sardonic smile.

The expression on Jessica Anderson's face didn't change. Jane moved quickly on. Jessica Anderson was not a woman that people would immediately warm to. Clearly she must have been aware of that fact, though it didn't seem to bother her.

'Kirby Grant,' Jane said, standing behind a girl who looked no more than nineteen, but was actually in her mid-twenties. Small and slight with olive skin and a shock of wayward coal black hair. 'Kirby records all our findings and tries to put them into a semblance of order.'

'I'm also the catering manager,' Kirby said, deadpan.

'Ah yes,' Jane said. 'Kirby is a culinary wizard. She keeps us fed and watered, performing small gastronomic miracles with the most basic ingredients.' She spoke with a humorous flourish but trailed off when there was no reaction from the American.

Jane moved to the back of the room. 'Robert Carter,' she said.

'You don't need to introduce Mr. Carter,' Jessica said. 'I'm fully aware of his talents.' She walked across the room, hand extended. 'I'm indebted to you, Mr. Carter, for agreeing to come on this mission. Mission . . . is that the right word? I'm sure if anyone can get to the bottom of this it will be you. If there's anything you need, anything at all, don't hesitate to contact us. I'm sure we'll be able to accommodate you.'

Carter shook her hand and glanced across at Jane. She looked annoyed. 'Thank you, Ms. Anderson, but Jane is leading this assignment. She'll be the one making contact.'

Jessica Anderson leaned into him. 'Very gallant,' she said softly, so the others couldn't hear her, then let his hand drop and turned back to Jane.

She couldn't fail to hear Carter's murmured, 'Bitch.'

'And that's it,' Jane said. 'The team.'

'And of course yourself,' Jessica said.

'Jane Talbot,' Jane said. She wasn't going to give any further information just to see if it irritated Jessica Anderson. Jane realized all her details were on file, and knew the American would have already seen them.

As if confirming this Jessica said, 'I've read a lot about you, Jane. Your file is impressive.'

'I'm flattered.' Jane knew she was being made aware of the pecking order. Jessica was in charge.

'Flattery doesn't come into it,' Jessica said. 'I know from experience how hard it is for a woman to advance in what is essentially a man's world.'

'I wouldn't say . . .'

'Please, no false modesty,' Jessica said, holding up her hand, effectively dismissing Jane, then turned to Crozier. 'A word, Simon,' she said brusquely and walked from the room, Crozier hurrying to catch up with her, making no pretence that he had a choice in the matter.

'Do you think we passed the audition?' Raj said. His smile suggested he didn't really care.

'I wouldn't like to say,' Jane said.

'A problem, Jessica?' Crozier said once they were outside in the corridor.

She wheeled on him. 'Why is McKinley going?' she said, coming straight to the point.

'Because he's good,' Crozier said.

'Yes, but not as good as Carter. I really don't see the need for his inclusion.'

'And that's where we disagree, Jessica,' Crozier said easily.

'We did as you and the Minister wanted and got Carter to come along, but Jane Talbot insisted on McKinley's inclusion, and I agree with her. As far as we're concerned, Carter's damaged goods. He always was unpredictable, but he got results. The way things stand now I can't guarantee he'll get the job done. We want McKinley there to catch the ball if Carter drops it.'

Jessica Anderson considered this for a moment, then shook her head. 'I'm sorry, Simon. I'm not buying it. In all honesty, I'm not that happy with the team as a whole. They're not really what we had in mind.'

'Who were you expecting, Ghostbusters?' He said it with a rare smile but there was disguised venom in the words. He had spent most of the day with her and if she voiced one more supercilious opinion, or patronized one more 'quaint' English tradition he suspected he would replace Carter on suspension.

Jessica glared at him. 'Don't waste your humor on me, Simon. You seem to have forgotten who's paying for all this.'

Crozier took a step back. 'What do you mean?'

'Didn't the Minister tell you? The KDC are footing the bill for this investigation. Very remiss of him. He really should have mentioned it.' The lipstick on her mouth twitched slightly in what was probably the memory of a smile.

Color had drained from Crozier's face. 'Yes, he damned well should have done. I would never have agreed to . . .'

'Yes you would, Simon. From what I've been told, the Department's future is currently hanging in the balance. You need a good result on this case in order to guarantee your survival . . . at least for the time being. So let's skip the righteous indignation. We're all whores at the end of the day. We all have our price. And I'm not going to pay for something I'm not happy with.'

Crozier looked her steadily in the eyes, noticing how unnaturally blue they were. 'Whores? You might have spent time on your back getting to where you are today, but don't judge everyone's morals by your own.'

There wasn't a flicker of emotion on her face. 'No, Simon, from what I've heard, "on your back" isn't your preference at all. When you get fucked it's usually in a completely different position.'

Crozier walked a few steps away, determined not to display any anger. He hated himself for being in this situation. Perhaps spending more time at his house in France was going to be a good idea. Not full retirement, just a slowing down, spending less time amongst the sharks and the predators with whom he worked every day.

'Jessica, I told you, I thought I was clear. Jane Talbot would put a team together to investigate Kulsay for you and that's what she's done. And in my opinion it's probably the best team she could have assembled. What Jane didn't say in her introductions is that every person on her team is a *sensitive*.'

'Psychic you mean.'

'That's not a term I use. Conjures up images of séances and ouija boards—both useful tools in our line of work, but only the tip of a very large iceberg. Each member of the team has a special gift as well as their more practical talents. As well as being a skilled sound engineer, Kirby Grant is also a first rate dowser. A number of high-profile companies use her because she's ninety-nine percent accurate, whether it's water or oil, or even precious metals. And she is also one of the best physical mediums I've ever come across. Raj Kumar is an excellent photographer and an expert in all visual media, and he's also a gifted clairvoyant.'

'And Talbot?'

Crozier hesitated. 'No. Jane has no gifts. But she is our control. It's imperative to have someone on the team impervious to any psychic influence. Jane fulfills that role. She is also a brilliant psychologist and is able to dissemble the output from the others and rationalize it.'

Jessica Anderson's eyes narrowed. She nodded her head slowly. 'Okay, I'll give you the benefit of the doubt. But I expect results, Simon, and I expect them quickly. If Talbot's team falls short of the task and doesn't deliver, I'll demand your balls on a plate,' she said.

'I have every confidence that they'll find the answers you're looking for. I doubt my balls would be much use to you. From what *I've* heard you prefer your partners without any at all.'

'Let's cut the crap, Simon. This team had better deliver. I shudder to think how much all this is going to cost me.'

Crozier suspected that Jessica Anderson knew down to the last cent how much the investigation was going to cost, but he didn't say so. It would be counterproductive to antagonize her further. 'Is there anything else you'd like to say to them?' he said.

She checked her watch. 'No, I've a flight to catch at Heathrow. I've a reception to attend in Boston.'

'Reception?' Crozier said.

'Well, a party really,' she said. 'Tomorrow's my birthday.'

'Then I wish you many happy returns,' he said, and his complete and utter lack of sincerity was said with a skill practiced many times over.

'Oh, I don't think you do, Simon. I think you'd prefer it if I never returned at all.' She smiled. 'Keep me up to speed,' she said. '*Ciao.*'

For once in his life Simon Crozier wished he were straight. He'd never met anyone like Jessica Anderson before. And then again, he wished to God he never had.

Jane stopped pacing the room as the door opened and Crozier came back in. 'Problems?' she said.

'You could say that.' He put his arm around her waist and led her to the far corner of the room. 'A word in private,' he said in her ear.

'You realize this compromises our position?' Jane said as Crozier dropped the bombshell *sotto voce*. The independence of the Department was the key to its success. To perform an investigation for a company or corporation could easily leave them open to charges of bias. It was like those surveys that seem to prove eating meat with your left hand increases the chances of cancer, and you worry about it, until you read that the survey is conducted by an organization with a vested, usually financial interest, in the results.

'I know,' he said. 'I'm going to phone the Minister and demand an explanation.'

She looked at him steadily. 'He can explain all he likes, but it doesn't change the position. We've lost our autonomy.'

'I wouldn't say that, Jane. Once you're on the island I don't see how the KDC can interfere.'

'Oh, wake up, Simon! I've only just met her, but I can see that if Jessica Anderson takes it into her mind to interfere, nothing on God's earth is going to stop her. I'm sorry. I don't think I can work under these conditions.'

'Please, Jane. Bend, just a little.' God, how he was beginning to hate the role he was in; reduced to begging.

She chewed her bottom lip as she thought about it. Finally she said, 'Okay. I'll take the team to Kulsay, but I'll be relying on you to keep that woman off my back so I can do my job. If you don't, then I won't hesitate to halt the investigation and bring everybody home. Understood?'

'Fair enough,' Crozier said. He had no intention of complying. Jessica Anderson was not going to feature in his life if he could help it.

'Right. I'll tell the others once you go.' She started to think about what she was going to say to the team.

'That's your call,' he said, and turned to the room. 'Right, everybody, gather round. Final arrangements. There's a hotel booked in Peterhead for tonight, and we've arranged for a boat to take you across to Kulsay in the morning. There you'll be met by a representative from the KDC to transport you and your equipment to the Manse. Any questions? No? There is just one other thing, but I'll let Jane brief you on that. I'll just wish you all good luck, and let's hope we get a result.'

Once he'd left the room the others looked at Jane questioningly.

'Well?' John McKinley said.

Jane sighed. 'Jessica Anderson is our paymaster. The KDC is funding the investigation.' The comment was met with a stunned silence. 'Seems like you all share my reservations.' She kept her tone as light as possible. The role of a leader as far as she was concerned was to achieve the task, and to do that she needed to take the others along with her.

'It's not the best news I've heard today,' McKinley said.

'No, but that's the way the land lies, so I suppose we'd better make the best of it. Has anybody got anything else?'

Carter looked at the others and then spoke. 'From what I've learned from these files,' he hefted the buff-colored folders in the air, 'once we get onto the island we'll have no time to worry about who is or isn't funding the investigation. There is going to be some serious work to be done. I've had time recently—a well-earned rest for those who haven't heard the reason—to check some details of recent investigations. There are things that link Kulsay with a much wider picture. I still need to finish digging into it but if what I suspect is happening, then autonomy of finances isn't going to worry anyone.'

Nobody spoke. They were still taking in what Jane had told them, and wondering if it really mattered, once the job began. Now Carter was confirming that view but giving them even more to be concerned about.

Jane saw the anxious faces and decided action was the best cure. 'Okay, we'll meet in the car park in . . .' She checked her watch. 'Fifty minutes.'

Without a further word they rose from their seats and filed out of the room, until only Jane and McKinley remained. Jane gathered her papers and slipped them into her briefcase.

McKinley unfolded himself from his seat. 'Tell me, Jane, is there any point in me coming along?'

Jane frowned. 'I'm not sure what you mean.' She knew exactly what he was going to say.

'You didn't tell me that Carter was on the team. Don't you think I'm up to the task?'

'That's not the case at all, John. I have every faith in your abilities. Robert's coming along because it was a pre-condition of the Minister that he be included.'

'And you don't believe in the Jonah principle?'

'What do you mean?' She genuinely didn't understand the reference.

McKinley shrugged. 'Some people are born unlucky, and some spread that bad luck to those around them . . . as Sian Davies found.'

Jane felt the blood rushing to her cheeks. 'Look, John, let's get one thing clear,' she said. 'Any problems you may have with Robert, you leave them here. If you can't do that then tell me now, because it's not too late to drop you from the team. I don't want to do that because I think your contribution to this investigation will be vital, but I won't stand by and watch the whole thing unravel because of personal resentments. Understood?'

'Understood,' he said with as easy smile. 'And I'll consider my knuckles well and truly rapped. But I figure we'll all have to watch each other's backs, and I hate to think that one of us will have his head so far up his own ass that he won't be able to do that.'

'I trust Robert,' Jane said. 'He won't let us down.'

'If you say so, Jane. You're the boss,' he said and left the room.

'Yes,' Jane said quietly to herself. 'Yes, I am.' She shook her head and suddenly wished she wasn't.

CHAPTER EIGHTEEN

The flight to Aberdeen was uneventful. A Land Cruiser had been hired to carry them and their equipment on to Peterhead. McKinley drove, glancing in his mirror occasionally at Carter who sat in the back, talking to no one, his head buried in more thick files, keeping his distance from the rest of the team for the moment.

They reached Peterhead a little after three in the afternoon, and set about finding the hotel. The directions they'd been given were inadequate and it was running close to four thirty before they finally found it.

The Cleeves Hotel stood well back from the road as if embarrassed to show itself. It was an ugly modern structure, built in the late 1980s but looked in dire need of renovation. Paint peeled from the window frames and the brickwork was stained with damp.

'Looks like Crozier blew the budget when he found this place,' John McKinley said with a smile as they walked into the lobby.

'It's not as if he knew,' Jane said, still anxious to avoid

any reason for friction, but disliked the defensive echo in her words.

'I just checked the tariff,' Raj said as he joined them at the desk. 'That must have given him a clue if nothing else. This must be one of the cheapest hotels in Scotland.'

'It's only for one night,' Jane said. 'Let's make the best of it.' She approached the reception desk.

A plump receptionist stared at her dead-eyed. 'Yes?'

'You have rooms booked, in the name of Talbot.'

The girl checked the screen on her computer. 'Yes.' She reached under the desk and produced a clutch of key cards. 'You're all on the second floor. Rooms 201 through 203. Lift's at the end of the passageway.'

'Can we book a meal?' Jane said to the receptionist.

The girl took a while staring at her watch. 'The kitchens don't open until six.'

'Good. Then we've got time to rest up first?'

'Last serving is at nine, sharp,' the plump girl said. She was wearing a name tag over her ample left breast. *Fiona Whyte*.

'Well, thank you, Fiona,' Jane said to her. 'We'll bear that in mind.'

The girl gave her a look as if to say, *whatever*.

Jane turned to the others and said quietly, 'And they said good service was a thing of the past,' and then, louder. 'Kirby, you're with me. Raj, here's your key, you and Robert, and John, you're on your own.'

'It's because I'm black isn't it?' he said with a grin.

'No, it's because you're the biggest and the single room has a bigger bed.'

'Fair enough. I snore as well.'

'Good,' Jane said, and went back to the desk. 'We'll book a meal for seven.'

Fiona Whyte sighed and tapped in something on the computer. 'Table for five,' she said. 'Seven o'clock.'

'Thank you again, Fiona,' Jane said with a smile. 'Does the bar stay open all day?'

Fiona shook her head. 'Opens at five thirty,' she said.

'Right. Good.' She rejoined the others. 'We'll meet in the bar at six,' she said. 'Everybody okay with that?'

There was a murmur of agreement.

'Robert? You happy with that?'

'Yeah, no problem,' he said, picking up his bag and heading off down the corridor to the elevator. He knew he hadn't contributed much to the team banter yet but there was a nagging premonition in his head, and the closer they had gotten to the hotel the stronger it had become. The problem was that he couldn't pinpoint the source of his concern.

'He's going to be fun,' Kirby said in Jane's ear.

'Don't you start,' she said. 'Besides, it's only for one night. Once we get to the Manse on the island we'll be too busy for personality clashes, moody silences or anything vaguely human.'

Kirby chased a leathery steak listlessly around her plate.

'Not enjoying your meal?' McKinley said to her.

'I ordered it rare. This has been cremated.'

'Send it back.' He had no patience with poor service, and even less with people who were too polite to complain about it.

'No. I'm going to take it home and have it mounted; hang it on the wall. A trophy of my first and last trip to the Cleeves Hotel.'

After coffee they retired to their rooms.

Raj Kumar sat on the bed surrounded by cameras and lenses. His lank, long hair was tied back in a ponytail, which accentuated his wispy goatee. With a puffer-brush he cleaned dust from a telephoto lens. There were three cameras on the bed. He had others stowed away with the rest of his equipment, but these three rarely left his side. They were his babies and he cherished them; spending many hours cleaning and servicing them. There was a Hasselblad with a digital back and two Canon SLRs, workhorses; one loaded with regular film, the other containing infrared stock. They rewarded his dedication to them by never once letting him down.

Carter was lying on the other bed, reading by the anemic light of a dusty bedside lamp.

'We went out together, you know,' Raj said.

'Sorry?' Carter had heard what he said but needed a moment to control his emotions.

'Sian and me. We went out together.'

Carter put the file down. 'I didn't realize you two . . .'

'Oh, we weren't. At least, not properly. Just a few evenings for drinks and stuff.' Raj was concentrating on his lenses, not looking at Carter. 'She was a good kid.'

'Yes,' Carter said. 'She was.' He wasn't sure what agenda Kumar was setting. The words seemed innocent but Carter guessed there was more to come.

Raj lapsed into silence and Carter picked up the files again and started to read. He could wait for Kumar to make his point; he had all night.

'I wanted to get to know her better,' Raj said, putting the thoroughly cleaned lens back in its case and picking up another from the bed.

With an inward sigh Carter closed the file and laid it on the bed. 'Why didn't you then?'

'There was no point. I could tell it wasn't going anywhere.' Again Carter could tell Raj was skirting round what he really wanted to say.

'Really? Did you try to take it further?' He didn't want intimate details. In truth he was just being polite. All he could think about were the events contained in the files.

'She knew how I felt about her. But there was someone else.'

'Too bad.'

Raj stopped cleaning and turned to look at him. 'She was in love with *you*,' he said.

'Pardon?' Carter hadn't been expecting that.

'Absolutely besotted, she was. She was living in the hope that you might . . . well, you can imagine . . .'

Carter was stunned. 'I had no idea.'

'No, no you probably didn't. The rest of us could see it though. She'd get that dreamy look in her eyes whenever she looked at you. Once I tried to tell her she was wasting her time, but hope is a very powerful emotion. She was convinced that one day you'd notice her. Pathetic really. Silly little cow. I could have made her happy . . . if she'd given me a chance.'

Carter swung his legs to the floor and slipped on his shoes.

'Going somewhere?'

Carter walked to the door. 'I'm going to get some air.'

Raj watched the door close behind him and smiled. 'That was for you, Sian,' he said to the room. 'He knows now. Let's hope he beats himself up over it.'

The night air was warm and sultry, heavy with salt from the sea. The rain had passed over for a while, leaving behind a clear sky, which was turning a deeper shade of blue as the last of the daylight slipped away. Out over the water it was darker, where more storm clouds were slowly massing.

Carter walked through the grounds of the hotel, his mind trying to get to grips with Raj Kumar's revelation. He'd had no idea that Sian Davies felt that way about him. She had never said anything or done anything to show him that might be the case. Or maybe she had and he'd been too wrapped up in himself to notice. That was the more likely scenario. What was the point of having his gifts, of being psychic, if he couldn't even pick up on the most basic of human emotions?

He found himself standing by a small fountain in the grounds of the hotel. The fountain was a remnant of a previous time, suggesting that a much grander building once stood in the space now blighted by the stained concrete and glass of the Cleeves Hotel. It was a stone-built circle with three cherubs on the top of an ornate plinth, their faces pointing skywards, lips pursed, ready to deliver their spouts of water. But it was a long time since anything had passed their lips and they all wore yellow beards of lichen.

The water in the fountain was weed-choked and murky. A few straggly water lilies were making a brave attempt to survive in the inhospitable surroundings, but it was a battle they were destined to lose. Three frogs had found the occasional gaps in the weed and were lying partly submerged, eyes above the surface, on the lookout for passing bugs, their next meal.

He felt incredibly depressed. What the hell was he doing here? He was out of his depth; if his conclusions were correct they were all out of their depths, of that he was certain. Perhaps it would be best to just pack his bags and go home. He was sure he wouldn't be missed. In fact he was sure the majority would welcome his leaving. Damn it! That's exactly what he would do. He'd go back to the hotel, pick up his things and head back down south.

He sat on the edge of the fountain and lit a cigarette, blowing smoke into the night air. Behind him there was a small splash as one of the frogs ducked beneath the surface, followed by the grinding sound of stone on stone. He glanced behind him. The cherubs had moved; their faces were no longer staring at the stars. Now they were looking down at him; all three faces grinning malevolently. He made to rise, but two arms burst from the cover of the blanket weed. White, clawlike hands grabbed his shoulders and he was dragged backwards, over the edge of the fountain and down into the green, stagnant water.

CHAPTER NINETEEN

The iron gates protecting the Anderson house hissed open on well-oiled hinges. The S-Class Mercedes swept through, tires crunching on the wide gravel drive, and pulled up outside the house. The chauffeur stepped out and opened the back door of the car. Jessica emerged wreathed in a cloud of cigarette smoke and Chanel No 5. She walked briskly up the four stone steps to the front door, which opened as her foot hit the top step. A butler dressed in an immaculate black pinstripe suit, crisp white shirt and navy blue tie stood to one side to allow her to enter.

'Good to have you home, miss,' he said, a flawless English accent exaggerated but natural.

'Good to be back, Foxworth. Terrible flight though. Delayed for two hours at Heathrow and turbulence most of the way.'

He smiled sympathetically.

'Is my father here?'

'He arrived home just before you. I believe he's in the study,' Foxworth said. 'Would you like me to let him know you're home?'

'No, it's okay. I'll surprise him. Can you fix me a sandwich? I haven't eaten since I left New York. You know how I hate in-flight catering.'

'Very well, miss. Turkey or ham?'

'Turkey sounds good.' She glanced back at the chauffeur

who was hauling her suitcases from the trunk of the car. 'Jennings, take the bags straight up to my room, and get Maria to unpack for me. After I've eaten I'm going to crash.'

Jennings, the chauffeur, flicked the peak of his cap and carried on unloading. Like Foxworth he knew when to speak and when to stay silent.

'The study you say?' she said turning to Foxworth.

The butler nodded.

She made her way up the stairs to the first floor where her father had his study. She hesitated for a moment outside the door, then took a breath and opened it.

Carl Anderson sat at a large walnut-veneered desk, tapping away at the keyboard of his laptop. As Jessica entered the room he looked up, stopped typing and stared up at her, a welcome in his eyes. 'You're late,' he said. 'I was getting worried.'

He had now entered his sixtieth year, but he was still a good-looking man. His thick hair had turned silver and was swept away from a smooth, tanned face. He was taller than Jessica by a foot, and his well-muscled, gym-toned body strained the material of the pale blue sports shirt. The fawn slacks were immaculately creased, but they were in sharp contrast to his black loafers, which were scuffed and well worn. He'd deliberately chosen comfort over style, a minor allowance to the advancing years and to his mildly bunioned feet.

'I've asked Foxworth to fix me a sandwich. Have you eaten?' Ever the dutiful and attentive daughter, especially when she wanted something.

'I ate at the tennis club.' He was the master of negotiation, having taught his daughter as much as she could learn at this stage in her business development.

'I rang you there to tell you the flight was delayed.' She pulled up a chair and sat down at the desk opposite him.

'Sorry, I didn't get the call. I was in the middle of a game with Oliver Marchant. Beat the old bastard two sets to one.' He smiled at the memory. 'I trust everything went to plan.'

'They're on their way. They'll arrive on the island in a few hours.'

'Well, let's hope they can sort this mess out. What did you make of Crozier?'

'He has a sharp mind. The man's no fool though he plays the part of one quite well. He needs watching. He wasn't at all pleased with the arrangement we made with the Minister.'

'Too bad. The Minister was quite happy to accept our offer . . . and of course there was also the contribution we made to his party's election fund. He never acknowledged it of course, but I'm sure he found it very generous.'

The door opened and Foxworth entered the room carrying a tray containing a plate of sandwiches, a cafetiere of freshly brewed coffee and two cups. He laid the tray down on the desk. 'Will there be anything else?' he said.

'No, that's fine,' Jessica said. 'Thanks.'

Once he'd left the room she poured coffee into the cups and slid one across the desk to her father.

'Are you sure you don't want a sandwich?'

He shook his head.

She took one from the plate and bit into it, savoring the tender turkey smothered in creamy mayonnaise. 'It's good to eat,' she said as she swallowed the mouthful.

'Evidently,' Anderson said, watching her with an expression of mild amusement.

'I hate England,' she said. 'It's so buttoned down. Everything's so precise, so formal. Everywhere feels constipated.' A vision of Crozier crossed her mind and she quickly tried to dispel it.

'I did warn you, but it was your choice to get involved

with the Kulsay venture. Nobody twisted your arm. I could have given it to Levy or Baxter, and then they'd be suffering now. But you seemed so *insistent*.'

'It appeared to be a golden opportunity,' she said, a trace of bitterness in her voice. She knew what she was doing, *thought* she knew what she was doing. She just wished, for once, her father could show his approval of something she achieved.

'Golden opportunities often hide demons that come up and bite you on the ass when you're not looking.' Anderson had collected a variety of truisms during his business life and enjoyed sharing them with those he was mentoring.

'Then I'll consider myself well and truly bitten,' she said. 'What's been happening here?'

Anderson leaned back in his chair. 'Nothing much. There are a few civil cases pending. The helicopter pilot's family has lodged a negligence suit against us, but Legal don't think it's got legs. The fact that both Harrison and the helicopter disappeared and no wreckage was found doesn't give their lawyers much to work with. What's to say he didn't just fly off somewhere? For all anyone knows he could have flown out to the Caymans or the Bahamas, sold the chopper and is now living a life of luxury. The only other pressing matter is the party tomorrow.'

'Is everything ready?' She was making short work of the sandwiches.

'My secretary's dealing with it, but I understand the caterers and the pianist are booked; thirty-five guests have confirmed.' He leaned forward, resting his elbows on the desk. 'I still think it's impolitic to be going ahead with the party,' he said.

Irritation flared in Jessica's eyes but it was gone in an instant, to be replaced by an easy smile. 'We've got nothing to hide, and nothing to be ashamed of,' she said. 'No one will be looking at what happened on Kulsay and blaming us for it. Hell, hardly any of them will have heard of Scotland, let alone a remote island.'

'Except Harrison's family,' Anderson said. Voicing remorse for an employee was uncharacteristically humane for the notoriously hardhearted Anderson. Jessica wondered whether he was unwell.

'They won't be here,' Jessica said, her voice cold. 'I've told you before; you worry too much about what people think.'

'Now, listen. I've spent forty years building my reputation. I'm not prepared to sit back and see you destroy it. I've given you every advantage; the best schools, a Harvard education, but in some ways you've learned nothing. Your arrogance will be your undoing. You think you're fireproof, but this Kulsay fiasco has proved you're not. You're out of your depth, Jessica. My only decision is whether to throw you a lifeline or let you drown.'

She regarded him coolly, but inside her emotions were writhing. 'We've let it be known that we're doing everything humanly possible to get to the bottom of what happened on the island. If we cancel the party, at such short notice, the media will be all over us. They'll take it as an admission of culpability.'

'They might see it as a demonstration of restraint and humility.'

'We've nothing to hide,' she said again, desperately trying to stand her ground. 'Our hands are clean. The party will show that.'

He shrugged and got to his feet. 'If you say so. But if there's any flack flying around I may not be in a position to protect you.'

'I wouldn't expect you to. I'm a big girl now,' she said.

'Not to me,' he said, laying a hand on her shoulder. 'It's good to have you home.'

She covered his hand with her own. 'It's good to *be* home,' she said. At that moment they were both sincere.

She watched the door close behind him and bit her lip. She was scared; more scared than she'd been in her life. Everything now rested on the collective shoulders of Jane Talbot, Robert Carter and the rest of the team on Kulsay. She prayed they wouldn't let her down.

CHAPTER TWENTY

Carter awoke in a circular stone chamber with rough-hewn walls and a ceiling so high it was lost in the darkness above. His thoughts were hazy. He couldn't remember how he had gotten here. The stone floor was cold, freezing cold, and the chill seeped through his clothes and into his body, taking up residence in his bones and making him shiver.

There was enough light in the chamber for him to see the walls, but he couldn't make out where the light was coming from. There were also soft noises—the muted sound of someone crying.

He manipulated himself up into a sitting position and realized his clothes were sopping wet, as were the stones on the floor around him. It was a small wonder he felt so cold.

He wasn't alone in the chamber. Sitting on the floor, twenty feet away from him was a naked figure; a girl, head bowed, arms wrapped around her legs, face pressed against her knees, crying softly.

'Where are we?' he said to her.

She didn't respond, but sniffed and continued to cry. He got up and moved slowly across the stone floor, not wanting to alarm her. When he was within a few feet of her he saw something that made him pause. On the girl's naked shoulder he saw a tiny tattoo of a rose. He recognized it. 'Sian?' he said.

Still the girl didn't look up. She hugged herself tighter as if trying to hide her nakedness. He put out a hand and stroked the spiky black hair. 'Sian, it's me. It's Robert.'

The girl said something between sobs that sounded like, 'Go away.'

He crouched down beside her and wrapped an arm around her shoulder. She shuddered at his touch but didn't pull away.

'What is this place?' he said.

'Hell,' the girl said, her voice muffled.

'Sian, look at me. It's all right. I'm here now.'

For a moment the girl's body tensed, as if she might spring away from him, then the tension left her body and she leaned into him.

'Look at me,' he said again, cupping his hand under her chin, trying to lift her face.

'No,' she said.

'Please, Sian,' he said, his voice gently insistent.

Slowly the girl raised her head from her knees and turned her face to him.

'Jesus Christ Almighty!' Carter couldn't help the involuntary exclamation.

The face he was looking into belonged to Sian Davies, but there was something horribly wrong with it. Where the eyes should have been there was nothing but empty holes, bloody sockets. The eyes had been ripped out.

He pulled her close, hugging her tightly, as if holding her could repair the damage to her ravaged face. 'Oh Christ, Sian. Who did this to you?'

'*They* did.' She started to cry again, harder this time, her shoulders heaving as the sobs wracked her body.

'Who are *they*?' Carter looked around but couldn't see anyone.

She took a lungful of air, struggling to control her breathing. 'The ones who took me from the car! The ones who brought me here!'

'I don't understand, Sian.'

A shudder passed through her body. He held her tighter.

'Why did they take you?'

'Because of you!' she shouted at him, her voice rising hysterically. 'To make you come here.' She started to sob again, her whole body shaking and heaving. 'They tore out my eyes to stop me from seeing them,' she said softly.

'I'm going to get you out of here,' he said.

'*A noble sentiment,*' a voice said, a male voice, deep and sonorous.

He jerked his head up, looking for the source of the voice, but there was nobody else in the chamber.

'Where are you?' he shouted. 'Show yourself!'

'*As you wish.*' Another voice sounded behind him; higher pitched than the first—almost feminine.

Carter spun round.

Three figures stood by the wall, tall and imposing, cloaked in gray, cowls covering their heads, making it impossible to distinguish features or gender. Carter scanned the wall quickly looking for a doorway, or some gap in the smooth stone; some way the figures could have entered the chamber. He saw nothing.

Carter stood up and took a step towards them. 'What do you want with us?'

Nothing, only silence.

The figures were drifting in and out of focus, shimmering, as if they were standing behind a heat haze.

'Let the girl go.' Carter took another step and was about to move again when the figure to the left raised its arm. He froze midstride, unable to move.

'Why should we?' Three voices merging into one; baritone, tenor and soprano, speaking in a macabre harmony.

'She's done nothing to you.' Carter struggled to move his body but it was useless. He was paralyzed.

'Bring us the others!'

The central figure raised its arm and Carter was hurled backwards through the air. His body hit the wall, the back of his skull cracking against the rough stone. With a groan he slid down the wall to the floor and darkness enveloped him.

Jane switched off the phone and threw it down on the bed just as Kirby emerged from the en suite bathroom wrapped in a white fluffy towel, her dark hair hanging in wet ringlets about her face.

'Problems?' Kirby said, pointing at the phone.

'You heard?'

'It was hard not to.' She sat on the edge of the bed, grabbed another towel and rubbed her dripping hair. 'So, do you want to talk about it?'

'I wouldn't bore you.'

'You won't. Honestly.' Despite her youth there was a sensible maturity about Kirby that Jane had always liked.

'It's just my mother being . . . well, mother. She's looking after the girls for me and never misses an opportunity to tell me what a terrible parent I am.'

'That's not fair,' Kirby said.

'Not according to her. I take it you heard about David and me?'

'Was it supposed to be a secret? Hard to keep, secrets, when you're surrounded by psychics. Actually, Raj told me. Don't ask me how *he* knew though.' Kirby smiled sympathetically. 'It's a shame. I always thought you and David were rock solid.'

'We were . . . once.'

'What happened?' Kirby continued towel drying her hair but was wholly focused on Jane.

'The job happened.'

Kirby reached across to the dressing table, picked up her hair dryer and started blasting her curls. 'Did I ever tell you about Malcolm?' she said over the noise of the dryer.

Jane shook her head.

'We were together for about five years. I didn't tell him about the job at first. For ages he thought I worked in the Civil Service—which I suppose was true in a way. It was only after we'd been together for quite a while—a few months, I think—that I told him what I actually did.'

'How did he take it?' Kirby had never opened up about her private life before.

'He was fascinated. He wanted to know all about it; what cases I was working on—all the details. Looking back on it now, I think his interest bordered on the unhealthy. It became something of an obsession for him. He started spending hours on the Internet, researching psychic phenomena and all the related mumbo jumbo. I suppose he was trying to find out what made me tick.' She switched off the dryer and ran her fingers through her hair, fluffing out the curls. 'The turning point came when I was sent to investigate that house in Bradford. Do you remember the one? The Lockhart family?'

Jane nodded. She had a photographic and retentive memory, and could list all the cases, certainly the recent ones, without reference to any notes.

'If you remember, they had the teenage daughter—a troubled soul—and there was an awful lot of poltergeist activity. Things moving from room to room, clothes ripped to shreds, all manner of noises and smells. Well, everything was fine until we started getting similar activity at home.

Malcolm was a keen golfer and he got home one evening to find that a couple of his clubs had been taken from his bag, twisted into pretzels and dumped on the bed.

'He was angry at first, but gradually, as more and more things happened, he started to get freaked out by it. It was when he started getting messages flashing up on his computer screen—rather bizarre messages, mostly of a pornographic nature—that he turned on me. I could understand that the poltergeist activity was affecting him, but he was also freaked out by me, or rather by my abilities, and had been for a while. He couldn't really deal with the fact that I was psychic; couldn't get his head around it at all. He thought I had the power to read his mind and tell what he was thinking, and that bothered him a lot.'

'And could you? Tell what he was thinking, I mean.'

'Of course I could. But there was nothing paranormal about it. He's a man, for Christ's sake. And Malcolm was not the most complex of the species; not by any stretch of the imagination.'

Jane laughed.

'Anyway, I sorted out the poltergeist thing, but shortly after that he packed his bags and left. He just couldn't handle it . . . me . . . anymore.' She put the dryer down on the bed. 'I guess what I'm trying to say is that these powers we possess, whatever they are, set us apart from the rest of them; the normal ones. We can't help it and, I suppose, neither can they.'

'I'm not sure I'd go that far,' Jane said.

'Think about it. Of the five of us here, who has a stable relationship? None of us. John—single for as long as I've known him. Raj—his partner, Neena, walked out on him three years ago and there's been no significant other since. Me; I've just told you. Since Malcolm there's been no one else, and in all honesty I'm in no hurry to put myself through the wringer again. Now you.'

'John has been alone since his wife died.'

'Christ, I didn't know that,' Kirby said, her hand fluttering at her lips.

'That's okay and anyway you forgot Robert.'

'Well, you know him better than I do, but from what I've heard my theory applies to him as well.'

Jane wondered what she was implying, but let it slide. She didn't really want to delve deeper on the subject of Robert Carter's love life. 'You're forgetting something. I'm not a psychic.'

Kirby's eyes narrowed slightly. 'Are you sure?'

'I think I'd know.'

'Well that's not what I'm getting from you. I've always thought it. Takes one to know one, as they say.'

'No, I'm sorry, Kirby. You've got your wires crossed. I have no psychic ability whatsoever.'

Kirby shrugged. 'If you say so.' In her experience this wasn't something about which a person could be persuaded. It was far too personal.

Outside thunderheads were gathering ominously again, rolling in from the sea; black nimbus clouds, bunching in the sky, heavy with rain. They let loose a flicker of lightning then, a few seconds later, growled ominously.

'Sounds like we're in for a rough night,' Kirby said. 'Let's hope it blows itself out by the morning. I don't fancy a boat trip to the island in a full-blown storm.'

'Couldn't agree more,' Jane said and got up from the bed, crossing to the window to peer out at the night. As she reached the window the hotel grounds were lit up by lightning and, for a split second, the silver flash illuminated the fountain. As was the prone figure lying at its base. 'What the hell . . .'

'What is it?'

Jane pressed her nose to the glass, peering out into the murky, rain-swept night, the rain-chilled window misting with her breath. Impatiently she rubbed the condensation away with the sleeve of her shirt. The lightning flashed again. She saw the fountain again but the figure had gone.

'Jane?' Kirby could tell something was bothering Jane.

She turned away from the window. 'Nothing,' she said. 'I thought I saw something, but I must have imagined it.'

'I think we're all a little jazzed at the moment,' Kirby said. 'After reading the report on the island and knowing we're going to be living there for a while, I don't suppose that's very surprising.'

'I suppose not,' Jane said, but she was distracted now. She was certain there had been someone lying at the base of the fountain. And she was pretty certain she knew who it was.

The grass tasted sweet. Fat raindrops the size of pennies spattered on his back but Carter made no effort to move; he was just relieved to be away from the circular chamber. He felt exhausted and a large bump was swelling on the back of his head where it had cracked against the wall. The experience had drained him. He rolled over onto his back, letting the rain hit his face. A flash of lightning split the sky and a few beats later a peal of thunder rumbled through the night. The intensity of the rain increased.

Gradually his strength returned and he pushed himself into a sitting position. Standing, his legs were weak, threatening to give out from under him. He took a few tentative steps; so far, so good. The hotel seemed miles away but he put one foot in front of the other and by the time the lightning crackled again he'd reached the entrance.

The reception desk was empty, the dining room in darkness. He took the stairs one at a time, using the handrail to haul himself up. He couldn't believe how weak he felt; it was as if he'd left all his strength behind him in the chamber. After what seemed ages he reached his room and unlocked the door. The room was in darkness. He closed the door behind him and stood for a moment, letting his eyes adjust to the gloom. Raj was sleeping. He could hear the steady, rhythmic rise and fall of his breathing.

Creeping across to his own bed he stripped off his sodden clothes and lay down on the soft mattress. He closed his eyes but sleep was hours away. Instead his mind played reruns of his experience in the chamber. He couldn't rid himself of the image of Sian's ruined eyes—the dark empty sockets still managed to look at him accusingly. Lying there in the darkened room he tried to convince himself that what he'd seen was just an illusion, the images planted in his thoughts, but a small, hectoring voice lurked at the back of his mind whispering, *it wasn't an illusion. It was real.* The bump on his head certainly was, and it was aching abominably.

There was something else that evidenced that what had happened was real. Clenched in his left hand were a small gold cross and a broken chain. Sian's.

He suddenly felt very cold. He pulled the duvet up to his chin. It was going to be a long night.

Fiona Whyte watched from the darkened office at the back of the reception desk as a soaking wet Robert Carter entered the hotel and went up to his room. He looked disoriented, unsteady on his feet. Earlier one of the dining room staff overheard a conversation Carter's group was having over their meal. They were departing for Kulsay Island in the morning. Yet another investigation. Fiona had been on duty when the team from the Ministry of Defense had stayed here earlier in the year and they had been downright weird; evasive to the point of rudeness. She knew full well what they were investigating, despite their efforts to keep it secret, and she was pretty sure that *this* group was doing much the same.

Well, good luck to them. She shuddered at the thought of the island. There was nothing on earth that would induce her to set foot on Kulsay. She'd heard the rumors and stories over the years, and preferred to keep her feet firmly on the mainland. But she knew there would be someone who would be intrigued by this latest twist. She picked up the phone and dialed a local number.

The phone was answered on the second ring. 'Bayliss,' a voice said. Whisky and cigarettes gave the voice a sandpaper timbre.

'Hi, Nick. It's Fiona, from Cleeves.'

'Fiona! How're you keeping?' The slurring of the words was barely noticeable.

'I'm good. You know you told me to let you know if there were any more developments regarding Kulsay. Well, something's developed.'

In the cluttered living room of the flat he was renting on the outskirts of town, Nick Bayliss listened carefully to what Fiona Whyte was telling him. When she'd finished he said, 'Interesting. Listen, Fiona, be an angel, get me their names.'

'I'll get the register,' she said. 'Hold on.'

The line was silent for a few moments. Bayliss rummaged through the piles of paperwork lying heaped on the table he was using as a desk. He found an empty legal pad and a pen and waited, poised to write down the names. This was an unexpected but very welcome development. He'd thought the MOD investigation marked the end of official involvement in Kulsay. The book he was writing about the island had stalled since that ended so inconclusively. Maybe this new investigation would kick-start it again. He really needed to finish it. His publisher's deadline was looming and he was fast using up his advance. The small pieces he was writing on psychic phenomena for a few of the trashy tabloids and magazines were keeping him in bread, but there was no jam to sweeten its flavor. He was just a week away from throwing in the towel and heading back to his apartment in London.

'Are you still there?' Fiona came back to the phone.

'Waiting with bated breath,' he said.

'Okay. Jane Talbot, Raj Kumar . . .'

He scribbled the names down as Fiona read them out to him. 'Did you say Robert Carter?' he said when she finished.

'That's right,' she said, and told him what she'd just witnessed.

'Well, it *is* raining rather heavily. If he'd been for a walk he would have got soaked.'

'Maybe,' she said. 'But there was pond weed hanging from his clothes and, as far as I know, *that* doesn't fall out of the sky.'

'Fair point. And you say they're going across to the island tomorrow?' He poured himself another whisky.

'That's what I was told.'

'Is your brother still running the pots?' A plan was hatching in the lower recesses of his brain. The whisky only served to fuel his creativity. The more he drank the better his ideas.

'Of course. Lobsters are still his life . . . poor bugger.' Fiona had a sour opinion of much of life's rich pattern.

'Do you think he'd take me across to Kulsay again?' The island held no fears for Bayliss; that was another consequence of copious amounts of whisky.

'I doubt it, after the last time? Those Ministry people got quite heavy with him. Threatened to revoke his license.'

'But you will ask him?' Overeager, but Fiona wasn't sharp enough to spot it.

There was the slightest hesitation. 'You're a bastard, you know?'

'They were on my case too, you know?' The MOD had

cast a wide net of suspicion in their quest to keep unwelcome questions at bay.

'I'll ask him. Are you coming to see me then?' There was a fragment of hope in her voice, and eagerness of her own.

'Oh, I think so. I'll be there first thing. You'll be on duty, won't you?' It would be easier if she were there to smooth the way with her brother.

'Nick, I'm *always* on duty,' she said, the sourness spreading out like spilt milk.

'Breakfast would be nice.'

'I'll see what I can do.'

He hung up the phone and switched on his computer. Minutes later he was surfing the Internet, running Google searches for the names and writing notes on his pad. He didn't bother to search for Carter. That information was already on his computer's database, filed under Bobby Hinton.

He felt a small knot of excitement beginning to curl in the pit of his stomach. He had a feeling that the next few days were going to be very interesting indeed.

CHAPTER TWENTY-ONE

The early morning air was heavy with the smell of fish as a dozen boats unloaded their cargoes of mackerel and cod on the quayside of the harbor. A watery sun broke through the blanket of gray and glinted off the wet and slippery docks.

'Could be a fine day,' Raj said, looking up at the traces of blue showing through the clouds as he lifted a large cardboard box from the back of the Land Cruiser and carried it down to the waiting motor launch.

'The sea looks calm enough,' McKinley said as he took

the box from him and stowed it on board. The boat rocked gently under his feet and the motion combined with the heavy stench of diesel from the boat's engine was enough to bring on the first stirrings of seasickness. He hated being on the water and was dreading the crossing to the island. He watched as more boxes were unloaded, everyone lending a hand to get the equipment onto the boat as quickly as possible.

This morning there was a real need within the group to get underway as soon as they could. All except McKinley had passed on breakfast, preferring to travel with empty stomachs, but whether this was due to the fear of sickness or the fact that appetites had been dampened by the anticipation of what awaited them on the island Raj wasn't sure. In his case it was a mixture of both. He'd slept badly, the night filled with disturbing dreams; vivid and frightening images had woken him half a dozen times. Now in the daylight the images were hazy and unformed, but the echoes of them were still doing their best to unsettle him.

When the last of the boxes had been loaded everyone climbed aboard. Jane went to talk to the pilot, a large, unshaven man called Jimmy Cowan. Cowan's plaid work shirt was stretched over a prodigious beer belly, straining at the buttons. The sleeves of the shirt were rolled up to the elbows, revealing gaudy tattoos on heavily muscled forearms.

'All loaded and ready to go,' she said as she entered the cockpit. 'How long is the crossing?'

Cowan made some adjustments to the satellite navigation unit to the right of the wheel. 'Hour and a half, give or take,' he said, not looking up from the unit. His accent was thick and the words sounded like nothing more than a guttural growl.

'Right,' Jane said, uncertain that she'd understood him. 'Good.'

Cowan finally looked round at her. 'You're sure about this?' he said.

Easier to understand this time, probably because he was now facing her and she could see the patterns his lips made. 'About what?' she said.

'About going across to the island?'

Jane frowned. 'It's what we're here for. Why?'

Cowan shrugged his huge shoulders. 'Your funeral, lassie,' he said and went back to what he was doing.

Jane resisted the urge to ask him what he meant. She left the cockpit and went back to join the others.

'Not much of a conversationalist, is he?' Kirby said as Jane slid onto the wooden bench beside her.

'Just a little ray of sunshine, that one,' Jane said as the engine started with a deep rumble. Moments later ropes were cast off and they were pulling away from the quayside.

'And so the adventure begins,' McKinley grinned.

Jane looked around at the faces of the others. Anticipation, excitement mingled with apprehension and fear. Only Carter's face was unreadable. He was staring over the side at the gray-green water passing under the launch. He hadn't said two words all morning and his face looked ashen. There were dark half moons under his eyes, giving the impression that he hadn't slept a wink all night.

She moved in next to him. 'Everything all right, Rob?' she said quietly.

'Shouldn't it be?' He glanced at her before turning his attention back to the white-splashed water.

Jane took his arm and squeezed gently. 'You look dreadful. Bad night?'

'I've had better.'

'I thought I saw you. Last night. Out by the fountain.' She weighed the words carefully, almost as if she was reeling in a fish.

'Really?' A bland, noncommittal response, as if they were at a dinner party discussing mortgage rates.

'During the storm,' she prompted. She was used to patience; the girls had taught her that.

'Right.'

'It *was* you, wasn't it?' Her voice became more forceful, demanding he tell her.

'I don't want to talk about it, Jane.'

That was as near an admission as she was going to get. 'Something happened?'

'I said I didn't want to talk about it.'

'I think you should.' She said it with a friendly tone, but he could not mistake the steel beneath.

'Maybe later.'

On the starboard side of the deck Raj groaned and threw up over the rail. McKinley cheered. Kirby's face took on the color of freshly kneaded dough and she hung her head over the side.

There was a change in Carter, that was all too apparent, especially as Jane had known him so well, or thought she did. The story about Sian Davies, her disappearance and how it affected him seemed to be very true. He was much more intense than she remembered, much more withdrawn; like something was churning inside him waiting for release.

She didn't think David knew about the affair, but she had changed during and since, to the extent that he must have suspected something was happening. It wasn't planned, these things rarely are. They saw each other, on and off, for a few months in London, but never stepped over the line; not until Paris. An assignment in Europe that appeared on the face of it to concern the Department. The trip concluded in Paris and a drunken meal in their hotel ended with only one of their rooms being used that night. In the morning expecting embarrassment Jane was astonished to open her eyes and find Robert already awake. They made love again in the glistening dawn and found themselves speaking of feelings far deeper than a mere work trip coupling.

Jane found Carter to be far more sensitive than she expected, and her own emotions hoodwinked her as she told him things about herself and her life that she hadn't even told her husband.

They had three more days in Paris, and two more glorious nights. Room service in this romantic city didn't blink an eye as they delivered to one room one night and the other the next. It was on the last afternoon, as they talked about how they could continue when they returned home that Jane saw the darker side of Robert Carter. In retrospect, as she settled back into some kind of normality with her husband and children, she told herself Carter was just being sensible, was even being a gentleman in allowing her to escape back to reality without any baggage. It hurt all the same.

That afternoon, with bags packed, and clothes scattered around them he told her he cared for her but they should end it now. He didn't use the clichés of not wanting to hurt her, or it being for the best. He was economical with his words, careful but decisive. Apart from working assignments, Jane hadn't seen him since.

From his position on the quayside Nick Bayliss lifted the binoculars and watched the progress of the boat as it negotiated its way out of the harbor. He'd arrived at the hotel a little after seven, had a light breakfast of toast and coffee in Fiona's office, received a brief but satisfying blow job, and then gone down to the harbor to scout out the best position for observing the group as they readied themselves for their trip to Kulsay.

His interest in Kulsay Island began years ago. Raised by his grandparents in a tenement on the east side of Edin-

burgh, his childhood had been colored by wild tales about
Scottish mythology fed to him by his Glasgow-born
grandfather. And the tale about the strange disappearance
of the inhabitants of Kulsay was one of his favorites. His
grandfather imbued and embellished the facts with mystery and intrigue, hinting at dark forces and witchcraft.
They were stories that fired the young Bayliss imagination
and stirred within him an insatiable curiosity about the
unexplained and unexplainable.

The old man's yarns infuriated Bayliss's grandmother
who was a staunch Catholic and thought such tales bordered on blasphemy. She was quick to counter her husband's stories with some of her own; but these took the
form of dire warnings about meddling in occult matters,
designed, he was sure, to steer him away from such a course
and to reinforce the need for strict Christian principals.

His grandfather died when he was eleven and left a void
in his life that he filled with endless visits to the local
library where he devoured any book he could find that
could further perpetuate his grandfather's storytelling
legacy. The books helped ease the loss of the old man and
temper the increasing dominance of the Catholic Church in
his life brought about by his grandmother. He found the
countless masses and enforced trips to confession repres-
sive; they only served to pique his interest in the strange
and unusual.

The older he grew the less hold the Church had over him.
Born with a naturally enquiring mind, and a strong cynicism
inherited directly from his grandfather, Bayliss eventually es-
chewed his grandmother's church and its teachings, preferring to formulate his own beliefs, and Kulsay Island was a
major piece in the philosophical jigsaw he was constructing.

When the Ministry of Defense held their investigation
earlier in the year he'd gone across to the island, hoping to
spy on the team the Ministry sent over there. He'd holed

up in one of the deserted cottages on the south side of the island but he was discovered after a couple of days and kicked off the island without having the chance to learn anything useful. This time he'd be more careful. A small knot of excitement was forming in the pit of his stomach. Soon he would know the truth about Kulsay Island. If his grandfather's stories were even half true, then Robert Carter and his people were in more danger than they could possibly imagine.

As he watched the small launch disappear into the distance he took the binoculars away from his eyes and walked back to the hotel.

CHAPTER TWENTY-TWO

A Land Rover was waiting for them when the launch tied up at the island's jetty. The driver, a young man in jeans and a tie-dyed tee shirt introduced himself as Mark Wallis and dropped a bunch of keys into Jane's hand. 'It's all yours,' he said.

Jane's eyes registered surprise. 'You're not driving us up to the house?'

He shook his head. 'Not in my contract,' Wallis said easily, sweeping a blond bird's wing of hair away from his face. 'Meet you here, hand over the keys. That's all I'm instructed to do.'

'Fair enough. Do you have a map?'

He rummaged in his pocket and pulled out a folded sheet of paper, creased and dog-eared. 'There you go,' he said, handing it to her. 'You'll find the keys to the place on the bunch I've just given you.'

She unfolded the paper. Scribbled on it in pencil was a

rudimentary map, showing the jetty and a torturous route of winding paths and tracks. Red ink arrows gave the directions. 'And we're supposed to find the place using this?' Jane said.

'I did. It's more straightforward than it looks.' Without a further word he threw her a smile and jumped aboard Cowan's boat. Cowan cast off and went back to the wheelhouse. Propellers spun, kicking up a spume of water and the craft edged away from the jetty heading out to sea.

'Well, that's it,' Jane said to Kirby, who was hoisting a large backpack onto her shoulder. 'We're on our own.'

Kirby smiled nervously. 'Better get this in the Land Rover,' she said, jerking her thumb at the backpack, seemingly reluctant to talk.

'Feeling better now?' Jane said, pressing her.

Kirby grimaced. 'Hollow,' she said. 'I mean, just how many times can you throw up in ninety minutes?'

'You'll feel better once we get to the Manse and get the kettle on. I, for one, could murder a cup of tea.' She turned to McKinley who was stowing the last of the gear into the Land Rover. 'John, take this and see if you can make heads or tails of it.' She handed him the map.

He studied it for a moment. 'Magical Mystery Tour,' he said with a grin, then folded the map again and slipped it into his pocket.

John McKinley drove the Land Rover, singing softly to himself—an old Bob Marley song. Kirby sat in the passenger seat, taking the harmony part in her lilting little-girl voice. She held the map out in front of her and paused her harmonizing occasionally to offer directions.

Raj took snapshots of the passing scenery. He framed a shot of some particularly ragged-looking sheep grazing at the side of the road, but didn't take the picture. Instead he put the camera down, closed his eyes and sat back in his seat. He couldn't shake off the sense of gloom that had enveloped him the moment he'd stepped off the boat. He saw his feelings reflected in the eyes of the sheep; a deep melancholy hinting at a darker, deeper despair. He was starting to wish he hadn't come.

Carter had a notebook on his knees and was scribbling sentences in his convoluted spider scrawl, occasionally glancing out at the passing scenery. As he wrote he whistled Mozart tunelessly, the noise providing a jarring counterpoint to McKinley and Kirby's singing.

Jane sat next to him in the backseat of the Land Rover. 'Do you want to talk about it now?' she said quietly.

Closing his book with a sigh, Carter stared out over the bleak landscape. Even with a watery sun spilling its light over the heather and gorse, the place still managed to look depressing. 'Sian's still alive,' he said without looking at her.

She took a breath. 'How do you know?'

'I just do.' His mouth had the stubborn landscape she remembered from the end of the affair.

'I see,' she said, though nothing was further from the truth. How did he know Sian was alive? Where was she?

'I doubt that.'

'I want to help you.' She began to lose her patience with him. If he had material information that affected this investigation, it was his duty to tell her.

'What makes you think I need your help . . . or anybody else's for that matter?'

Reining in her growing annoyance she tried the sympathetic approach. 'What happened last night, when I saw you out by the fountain?'

'Leave it, Jane. I'm not ready to talk about it.' Carter's voice rose and Kirby looked over at Jane, who gave her a 'leave it' signal with her eyes.

'Christ, you're pigheaded,' Jane said.

'No, I'm not. And I'm not being contrary either, but I need to get a few things clear in my own mind first.' At last his tone began to soften and something of the old Robert peered out.

'Well, as soon as you have, come and tell me.' She'd had enough of fencing with him.

'You'll be the first to know,' he said. He didn't patronize her with a smile, but his voice was friendly.

'Make sure I am,' she said, and sat back in her seat, gazing out through the window. He was impossible when he was like this. She'd encountered his stubbornness many times in the past. It didn't get any easier to deal with. She didn't speak to him again until they reached the Manse.

Jane lifted her suitcase onto the bed and started to unpack. Obviously the KDC had spared no expense on the refurbishment of the old house. The decor was modern; the fittings of the bathroom state of the art, but the bedroom had an impersonal, anonymous feel to it. It could have been a room in any of the countless hotels she had stayed at in the past. Smartly furnished and comfortable, luxurious even, but unsympathetic and out of keeping with the traditional ambience of the Manse. At least there were no bloodstains on the floor.

She took a framed photograph of Gemma and Amy from her suitcase, set it down on the bedside cabinet and stared at it for a moment, feeling tears pricking at her eyes. She wanted things to return to the way they were. She wanted her marriage back. Sitting down on the bed she picked up the photograph and traced the outline of the girls' faces with her fingertips. How on earth was she going to break the news to them that Daddy had left and wouldn't be coming back? Amy was too young to really comprehend the news, but Gemma would understand what she was being told. The father of another little girl in her class at school had been killed in a car crash just four months ago and Gemma had shown an almost macabre fascination for the details. She'd talked about it endlessly for three days; asking about Heaven, about funerals, about what it was like to die. 'Will you die, Mummy? Will I die? What happens when you die?' The questions went on forever. And Gemma took the answers she was offered and absorbed them, assimilated them with a pragmatism that only children can summon.

Her enquiring eight-year-old mind wouldn't take the news of a marriage breakup at face value. There would be questions; difficult questions that would require even more difficult answers. It was going to be hell.

A tap at the door brought her back to the present. She replaced the photograph on the cabinet and went across to the door.

Kirby was standing in the hallway, two mugs of tea in her hand, a hesitant smile hovering on her lips. 'Sustenance for the troops,' she said.

'Kirby, you're a lifesaver.'

The girl set the mugs down on the cabinet, sat down on the bed and picked up the photograph. 'Are these your kids?'

Jane nodded. 'Gemma and Amy.'

Kirby smiled. 'They're so pretty. How old are they?'

'Gemma's eight, Amy's five.' God, where did the time go? It seemed like a few hours since she had given birth.

'Gemma looks like you. Does Amy look like her father?' Kirby held the photograph in both hands, as if she was holding the children themselves and didn't want to hurt them.

'No, not really, she takes after my grandmother, all red hair and freckles.'

'She looks like a pickle.'

'Oh, she is, believe me. She's as fiery as Gemma is

placid. She's impetuous, whereas Gemma won't even get out of bed in the morning without exploring all her options first. Chalk and cheese.'

Kirby set the photograph down again. 'You're very lucky.' There was something in her tone that made Jane think she wasn't just being polite.

'You think so?'

'I know so. I was pregnant once. Lost it. Still hurts.' The last two words were said with characteristic lightness but Jane could tell the pain was still heavy.

'I'm sorry. I had no idea.'

'It was a long time ago. Before I started with the Department.' She lifted her legs onto the bed and laid back. 'I often wonder what she would have been like.'

'You knew it was a girl?' Jane was surprised.

'Sacha. Had a name and everything.'

Jane sat down on the bed and took Kirby's hand in hers. There were tears in the younger woman's eyes. She rubbed her other hand across them impatiently.

'Stupid! Bringing all this up now. I don't know what's got into me. Sorry.'

'Don't apologize.'

Kirby leant herself up onto her elbow. 'Sorry,' she said again. 'So what's the plan?'

Jane recognized the need to move away from personal issues and instantly became businesslike. 'The usual, I think. Let Raj and you do your stuff; set all the cameras and wire the place to record anything out of the ordinary, then we'll sit back for twenty-four hours and see if we pick up anything.'

'So you think the house is the focus?' Concentration on a task was often the best way to overcome emotional pain.

Jane stood and moved away from the bed. 'Not necessarily, but it's as good a place as any to start.'

'Are you planning any séances?'

'Not today.' Jane shook her head. 'I want Robert to try one, but I don't think he's in the right state of mind at the moment. Maybe tomorrow. We'll see.'

'I don't like them,' Kirby said, lifting her mug from the cabinet and taking a mouthful of the sweet tea. 'Séances. They freak me out a little.'

'Me too,' Jane admitted, 'but they have their uses. Sometimes they can stir things up a bit.'

'And do we want to stir things up?' Kirby wouldn't admit it to anyone, but she was scared.

'I want to find out what happened here. Not for the Department, certainly not for the KDC, but *I* want to know. I don't like mysteries.' What David had done had upset her more than she could have imagined. It had also given her an anger that needed an outlet. Whatever had happened on this island, solving what had happened was a good way to purge the rage inside her.

'Then you couldn't have picked a worse career.' Kirby looked serious.

'I didn't. It picked me.'

'Really?' Kirby's eyes widened questioningly.

Jane smiled and patted her hand. 'I'll tell you about it sometime. But not now. I'm going to check in with Simon. Let him know we've arrived safely.'

Kirby took that as her cue to leave. She swung her legs to the floor and walked to the door. 'Sorry about the baby stuff. Stupid.'

'Forget it. Please.'

The door closed and Jane picked up the phone.

'Crozier.'

'Simon, it's Jane. We've arrived.'

'Good. How is the place?'

'Seems comfortable enough.'

'Good.' He paused. 'Anything to report yet?'

'Nothing concrete. But there does seem to be some kind of atmosphere about the island itself.'

'Describe. Not a report, just your first impressions.'

'A kind of melancholy. It's already affected Kirby; raising all kinds of ghosts from her past.'

'Can *you* feel it?'

'Slightly.'

'Be careful. You remember Hayden Towers?'

Hayden Towers was an apartment building in North London where the suicide rate was apparently eight times the national average. It was demolished once it was realized the block had been built on the site of a plague pit. It was never established whether the high occurrences of people taking their own lives was directly attributable to the pit, but many thought there was a connection. No one ever built on the site again.

Mass suicide. She considered this for a moment, imagining the members of the Waincraft team throwing themselves into the sea like lemmings. 'It's an interesting possibility. Do you think the explanation could be that simple?' She couldn't keep the skeptical note out of her voice. Anyway hadn't she read recently that lemmings don't actually throw themselves to certain death?

'I'd welcome a simple solution, Jane,' Crozier said.

'So would I,' she said. 'But I'm not optimistic that this thing will be solved that easily. What about the MOD people? Do you know if they were affected by the place?'

'As I told you before, they were giving nothing away. All I know is that a team of three went out to Kulsay, and three returned. I don't even know who they sent.'

'Could you ask around? Call in a few favors. I'd be interested to know their findings. Any feedback at all would be helpful.' For all its depth the report Impey had collated was low on detail about the MOD involvement.

Crozier sighed. 'I'll do my best, Jane, but it's like getting blood out of a stone. I don't hold out much hope. I'm afraid the favors they owed me are all used up.'

'What about the Minister? Could he bring pressure to bear?'

'I doubt it. He's locked into a budgetary conflict with Henderson, the Defense Minister. Apparently they can't stand the sight of each other.' Crozier loved the little snippets of gossip he was privy to, and traded them discreetly in bars and restaurants as a substitute for popularity.

'Do what you can. I'll call you again tomorrow.'

'Fine, but I may not have an answer for you that quickly . . . if ever. Anything else to report?'

Jane hesitated. She had outlined some of her plans to Kirby but she preferred acting on instinct. Once her ideas were shared with Crozier she knew he would consider them set in concrete. 'I'm going to try to persuade Robert to hold a séance tomorrow.'

'Do you think he'll go for it?'

'He may.' She tried to keep her options vague.

'Good luck.' He sounded as sincere as a TV game show host.

'Thanks,' she said. 'I think I'm going to need it.'

She would. They all would. Beneath the house, far beneath the island, there was movement. Stretching far and wide, using powers and secrets long kept dormant, many things were stirring. They had waited a long, long time. Soon the waiting would be over.

CHAPTER TWENTY-THREE

'Okay, everyone, listen up,' Jane began, and waited while attention switched onto her. She had a glass of brandy in one hand and took a tentative sip, hoping she wouldn't choke on its strength.

'Dutch courage, Jane?' Raj joked.

She smiled. 'We may need all our courage for this one. You've all volunteered, and you've got my thanks for that. As volunteers you've had the briefing so you know the position. Missing people, not experts on survival, nothing heard from them now for weeks. Our job is to find them.'

'Dead or alive,' John McKinley murmured.

Jane turned to face him. 'It's not a "missing presumed dead assignment," John. We're here to find them, but if we can't then we have to learn everything we can about what may have happened. People can't just disappear from an island in the twenty-first century.'

She took a sip of her brandy and looked at their faces. No, if she was honest she didn't look at the faces of all of them. Raj was smiling, as usual, and returned her glance with a grin; McKinley gave a curt nod that acknowledged his understanding of the task; with Carter, she avoided eye contact. She looked at a place on his forehead somewhere between the eyes. It was technique she had perfected years ago when she and her father played staring games for fun—look as if you are staring the other in the eyes but avoid direct eye contact. Except Carter knew the method and employed a counterstrategy; he stood up and walked across to her.

Jane involuntarily turned away, then instantly aware

how unprofessional that was, swung back round just as Carter stood next to her. Jane's hand knocked his arm, and for a moment they started to apologize to each other for mutual clumsiness. It was Carter who took her arm, smiled ruefully and shifted his position so that his back was to the others.

It was in her thoughts as they stood together. Everything they had shared and yet here they stood saying sorry about a clumsy greeting, almost like strangers at a train station, muttering sorry while thinking about the menu for the evening meal. Surely, she thought, we are closer than that. Then she realized it wasn't a casual thought, they *had* been close, and her random thought was nearer to hope than she wanted to admit.

'You don't believe all that?' Carter said quietly to her.

It took her a second to adjust to what he was saying; her mind was preoccupied with more sensual matters. 'About what?'

Carter was watching for her reaction. Surely Crozier hadn't kept the facts from her, not if she was being asked to lead the team. But it wouldn't be Crozier's call; Jessica Anderson would have the final say, and she would want Jane to come in unprepared. Not as a simple ploy, not as a maneuver, but so she would argue for his own inclusion in the team. That would be the reason; he wouldn't be allowed to lead a team himself, not directly, not with his maverick reputation, but if the mission was sold subtly enough to Jane she would, despite their personal track record, insist he was included.

When he didn't reply Jane looked away. 'I'm sorry about Sian.'

She heard his intake of breath. 'They're probably all dead anyway,' he said.

Jane knew whom he meant but didn't understand what made him think that. 'Crozier gave me the dossier. Waincraft haven't heard a word from them. There's been no news.'

'Not officially,' Carter said tightly. 'I get my information from a variety of sources, and because of Sian's disappearing act I've been doing some checking; recent missing persons in certain circumstances, possible department links, you know the type of thing.'

Jane understood what he was saying, and she remembered the various whispers and snaps of information that seemed to come his way as if by magic; although it was actually of course from a very sophisticated intelligence network that he set up gradually and slowly so no one was aware of it, and no one could infiltrate it. 'I can't say for certain about all of them, but at least half of the "missing" group is dead.'

He turned and walked out of the room.

She caught up with Carter on the patio. He was sitting at one of the tables, sipping a glass of lager, staring out across the garden. The sun was high in the sky and she could feel its welcome warmth on her face.

'Do you mind if I join you?' she said, pulling up a chair.

He shook his head. 'Something very bad happened here.'

'Here in general, or here specifically?' He handed her an open bottle of beer. He had anticipated she would join him.

'Here, on the patio. There.' He pointed at the ground not two yards from where they sat.

'Do you know what exactly?'

'I can't get a fix on it. Just random impressions.' He turned to look at her. 'We shouldn't be here, Jane. It's too dangerous.' There was serious concern in his face.

'We're here to do a job.' Jane had become used to her role of persuader.

He took another mouthful of lager, swilling the beer

over his tongue before swallowing. It did nothing to take away the coppery taste in his mouth. It was the taste of fear and he was all too familiar with it.

'I want you to hold a séance tomorrow,' she said. The sudden change of immediate subject was designed to deflect any further anxiety.

'Yes, I think I should.' Carter nodded vigorously.

'Pardon?' His quick agreement took her by surprise.

He drank some more beer. 'I think I should. And I'm not going to wait for tomorrow. I'll hold one tonight. After dinner.'

Jane frowned. 'I thought you'd object.'

'Why should I?' Carter said. 'I'm as anxious as you are to know what's going on here.' He swilled the beer around in his glass. 'Have you noticed the gloom hanging over this place? You can almost taste it. There's something here.'

'I was saying as much to Crozier earlier. Kirby seems quite badly affected.'

'So's McKinley. He's even more morose than usual. What about you?'

'It's not too bad, but I'm not completely immune to it.'

'Me neither, but I know how to protect myself. As does McKinley. He hasn't opened up since we got here, and quite honestly I don't blame him. But I'm not sure the others are as prepared as us. Kirby especially—she's like an open nerve. It's like we're sitting in a lion's den, and the lion's watching us, biding its time until it's ready to pounce. It's unnerving.'

'We'll have to watch out for each other,' she said, remembering the conversation with McKinley earlier. 'Crozier raised the possibility that what happened here could be a case of mass suicide.'

'No,' Carter said. 'He's wrong. It's nothing like that. These people didn't choose what happened to them.'

'Can you be sure? Another beer?' She got two more bottles from the bar and waited for his reply.

'Oh, yes, I'm sure. There's something evil on this island, Jane. Something more evil than anything I've encountered before.'

'Very reassuring considering some of the cases you've worked on.'

'And I'll tell you something else.' He pulled two cigarettes from the pack on the table, lit them and handed one across to her. 'It wants something from us.'

'What?'

'I wish I knew,' he said. 'Maybe we'll get some answers tonight. I'll have a word with Kirby and tell her we want to eat early. The longer we have afterwards the better.'

CHAPTER TWENTY-FOUR

'I think you're out of your wee mind, wanting to go over there again. When Fiona rang me I couldn't believe it. Not after what happened the last time. You were lucky they didn't arrest you.' Cameron Whyte closed the engine housing on his boat and wiped his oily hands on a rag.

'But will you take me across, Cameron? That's the question.' Bayliss leaned against the rail, glancing over his shoulder at the wavelets lapping against the hull. A few gulls were circling overhead, crying out to each other and ducking down to the water, searching for food.

'Aye, I'll take you. I'll take you because Fiona asked me to, and that's the only reason.' Whyte threw the rag into a metal bucket and went back to the wheelhouse. Bayliss pushed himself away from the rail and followed him, avoiding the numerous lobster pots littering the deck. Cameron Whyte made a good living as a lobster fisherman. Restaurants as far away as London paid top dollar for the blue crustaceans Whyte and his crew pulled from the waters around this stretch of the coast.

'When?'

'When what?'

'When can you take me?'

'This evening, when I take the pots out.' Whyte looked up at the sky, predicting to himself what the weather conditions would be later. He was generally right most of the time.

'Not before?' Eagerness roared out of every pore of Bayliss's body, making him edgy and more than a little twitchy.

'This evening.' Whyte glared at Bayliss, then turned his eyes to the chart laid out on a table in front of him.

'I was hoping to get onto the island sooner.' He was almost bouncing with anticipation, a remote control figure with the hand controls on maximum.

Whyte looked round at him with amusement. 'Then swim.'

Bayliss held the other man's gaze for a long moment. Finally he relaxed and smiled. 'This evening it is then. I'll be back about five.'

'Make it six.'

'Right. Six it is. See you then.'

He swung himself from the boat and walked back along the quayside. It wasn't the result he wanted, but there was nothing he could do about it. Besides, he'd waited this long for something else to happen on Kulsay; another few hours was neither here nor there.

Raj sat at the computer they'd set up in one of the sitting rooms, making sure the complex arrangement of cameras and microphones he and Kirby had installed so far were working and feeding their signals back. Wireless technology meant Kirby could place equipment in the most obscure locations and record whatever was happening there. It was a far cry from the early days in the Department when they'd had to lay countless yards of cable and double-check every connection. In those days they'd been dependent on main electricity, and a number of times investigations had been hampered by sudden power surges or brownouts. Now everything ran on long lasting rechargeable batteries, so no matter what state the power supply was in, the cameras and microphones continued to record, sending their images and sounds back to the hard drive of the computer.

'How's it going?' Kirby appeared and set a mug of coffee on the desk. She pulled up a chair, peering at the screen.

'Going well, so far,' he said, picking up the mug and taking a long swill of the dark brown liquid. 'Christ, you make good coffee,' he said, wiping his lips with the sleeve of his shirt. 'What's your secret?'

'Cardamom seeds,' she said. 'No secret; just a few in the pot. Gives it an edge, doesn't it?'

'Damned right.' He took another long drink, the heat of the liquid not troubling him at all.

She pulled up a chair and sat down next to him, watching the changing images on the screen as he tested the cameras. 'Where's McKinley?'

'Said he was going up to wire the attic.'

She nodded slowly. 'I wonder if he'll want coffee.' She liked everybody, and enjoyed working with each of them, but McKinley was the most difficult to get to know so she guessed she liked working with him least. She couldn't ever feel totally relaxed with him.

'Couldn't say,' Raj said, shifting his attention back to

the computer and tapping a few keys to bring up a menu.

'What do *you* think happened to the Waincraft people?' Kirby said.

He shrugged. 'That's what we're here to find out.'

'But you must have some idea. You've been on so many of these investigations. You've seen so much.'

'Too much, I think sometimes.' He clicked the mouse and the screen went blank. 'That's downstairs done. Do you want to give me a hand with the rooms upstairs?'

She shook her head. 'I've got food to prepare. Robert wants an early dinner tonight. Apparently he's holding a séance afterwards.'

Raj's eyes narrowed. 'Have you ever sat in on one of Carter's séances?'

'No. What are they like?'

'Unlike any séance you've seen before. For a start four out of the five of us sitting there have some kind of psychic ability. It tends to make things interesting.'

'No table rapping and trumpets?'

'Hardly.' It was difficult to explain to her how unorthodox Carter's methods were compared with most people's. The fact that he did things differently every time made explanation impossible because you couldn't second-guess him.

'I'm disappointed. I was hoping to get in touch with my late Uncle Horace.' It was a lame joke that did nothing to assuage the mounting apprehension she was feeling.

Raj didn't smile, which made her feel worse. 'It's no joking matter, believe me. You'll need to protect yourself. If you're not able to, then I suggest you have a word with Jane, or Carter himself, and give it a miss.'

Kirby bristled. 'I'm not a child. I know how to protect myself.'

'Then make sure you do so. I've seen things get pretty ugly in the past. Carter may be an asshole, but he's an incredibly powerful medium. He sometimes gets some startling results. Did he say where he's holding the séance?'

'In the library.' Why would Raj suddenly express doubts about her ability to see this through?

Raj reached out for the mouse and brought the screen to life. Seconds later he was looking at the library through the lens of the camera. Wall-to-wall books, a low-slung couch covered in faded gold brocade, and a table in the center of the room; round, five feet in diameter. 'Ideal,' he said. 'I dare say he'll want some special cameras set up in there. Infrared, even thermal imaging.' There was an edge of excitement to his voice.

Kirby looked at him curiously. 'You're looking forward to it, despite what you just said.'

'Of course I am. A séance raises challenges that only another photographer would fully appreciate.' He started to scribble notes down on a pad beside him.

Kirby felt as if she'd suddenly become invisible. She sighed. 'I see. You're entering geek mode. I'll leave you to it.' She caught something out of the corner of her eye and looked back at the screen. Something was moving in the library; a small ball of light was bouncing off the walls.

She opened her mouth to speak, to tell Raj about it, when the light-ball hurtled towards the lens of the camera. It happened so fast and so suddenly that she flinched, but she kept her eyes on the screen. In the split second before the light vanished, it changed into a face; white, eyes wide open in terror, mouth stretching into a silent scream.

She must have cried out because Raj grabbed her arm and brought his face to within inches of hers. 'Kirby? What is it?'

She could hear his words, but they seemed to be coming from a very long way away, his mouth working in slow motion to form them.

'Kirby?' Someone was calling her name; she could hear it as if it was behind several sheets of linen.

Gradually everything slipped back to normal. She shook herself. 'It's okay. I'm all right.'

'What happened?' Raj said. 'Why did you cry out?'

'Did I? I wasn't aware . . .' She looked from him to the computer screen. The library was still displayed, but no lights, no face. 'I thought I saw something.'

'Saw what?' He glanced back at the screen.

'Don't know.' She pulled away from him and ran a hand across her face. 'Are you recording this?' she said, pointing to the image of the library.

'I'm recording everything.' Professional pride tinged his voice.

'Can you play back the last couple of minutes?'

He reached out for the mouse and brought up a series of sub-menus. 'Just the last few minutes?'

She nodded. She wasn't sure she wanted to go through with this but in truth she had no choice. Like everyone she had effectively chosen to be here. It was her job to investigate what they found, what they saw, what they heard.

Raj scrolled and clicked a few times. 'Okay. It's rolling.'

She leaned forward, a frown of concentration creasing her forehead. The minutes ticked by.

Nothing.

'Do you want me to repeat it?' It was clear from his tone that he considered that suggestion to be a waste of time.

'Yes.' She must have missed it the first time. The ball of light, the face. It had all been so clear when she saw it.

She watched it through again, willing the light to appear. Even wishing that dreadful face would appear.

'What did you see?' Raj said, studying her closely. She was seriously affected by something she thought she had seen in the computer scrutiny of the library. Trouble was the computer, the cameras and the microphones, had picked up absolutely nothing.

'I thought . . . I saw . . . light. A ball of light.'

'Sorry,' he said. 'Nothing's been recorded.' He kept his voice level, an even tone, so that she couldn't detect any judgment from him. She had made a mistake, and at this level, on an investigation such as this, that was serious.

'Not much point having all this state-of-the-art equipment if it doesn't work,' she said. The attempt at humor died at birth.

'Hey, that's not fair. I didn't see anything. Perhaps you imagined it?'

She looked at him steadily for a moment, a riposte twitching on her lips. Then something went out of her. She maneuvered herself out of the chair. 'You're probably right,' she said. 'This place has got me a little jittery.'

'Yeah, me too,' he said.

'Catch you later,' she said and walked from the room.

He watched her go, then shrugged and went back to his notes.

Back in her room Kirby threw herself down on her bed. Her face felt hot, flushed. She'd just made a complete fool of herself, crying out like that. And in front of Raj, of all people! It would give him the ammunition to ride her about it for weeks. But she was certain she'd seen something in the library. *That face! That screaming face!* She lay back on the pillow and closed her eyes, trying to recapture the image in her mind's eye. Seconds later, she sat up and reached for the file on the bedside table. She opened it, turned to the dossiers on the Waincraft team, and flicked through the pages. When she reached Jo Madley's page she stopped. She took the page over to the window where the light was better.

It was *her*. It was definitely Jo Madley's face she'd seen. She took a few deep breaths, trying to steady her nerves, then went back to the bed and lay down again. Okay. Let's think this through. She closed her eyes and concentrated, bringing the face back into her thoughts and focusing on it. *So where are you?* She thought.

'*Trapped.*'

The answer came immediately. She flicked open her eyes and looked about the room. She was alone.

She closed her eyes again and tried to focus, channeling her mind. *I'm here,* she thought. *I'm open, I'm receptive. Show yourself to me.*

'*Help me!*'

The voice was all about her; everywhere and nowhere.

'Where are you?' She said it aloud this time.

'*Here. Look.*'

She snapped open her eyes. The wall ahead of her was rippling, moving. She blinked, rubbing at her eyes. The floral wallpaper was starting to balloon outwards, as if air was being pumped in behind it. It was starting to take form; a human form. She could make out a head, shoulders, legs; small breasts pushing out from the chest. She could even see the small buds of nipples crowning them.

She got up from the bed and took a few tentative steps towards the wall.

'Are you Jo? Joanne Madley?'

'*Yes.*' The word swirled around her head as if caught by a strong wind.

'How can I help you?'

The figure was perfectly defined by the wallpaper now.

She could make out the features of the face; could see the line of the mouth.

Kirby moved closer, until she was within a yard of the wall.

'Come with me,' the voice said.

The sound of ripping wallpaper was as loud as a thunder crash. Two wallpaper-clad arms burst from the wall and reached out for her; rose petal fingers fluttering, scrabbling at her clothes, trying to get a grip.

Kirby threw herself backwards, lost her balance and fell, her head crashing against the leg of the bed. For a second she blacked out, concussed by the impact of bone against wood. Then her eyes were open and she was drawing quick shallow breaths into her lungs as the spindly fingers closed around her ankles, and she was dragged across the floor to the wall.

She twisted from side to side, fingernails clawing at the carpet, digging in, trying to arrest her terrifying progress. She glanced up at the figure dragging her, but saw nothing but wallpaper, tiny red roses on a cream background, stretched bizarrely across the features of a grinning face. It was Jo Madley's face and she was sheathed entirely in the wall covering; the paper moving as she was moving; rippling, tearing slightly at the joints, making a soft rustling sound. Behind her the wall had opened up into a black cavern, glowing amber in the distance.

Inch by inch Kirby was pulled towards it. She flung out her hand behind her and her fingers closed around the leg of the bed. Using all her strength she hung on grimly; sweating palms slipping; the muscles in her arms screaming with the effort. And then the bed began to slide across the floor as well, and the journey towards the cavern resumed.

She could see figures moving in the dark mouth; gray shrouded figures, emerging from the blackness, coming to receive her.

'No!' she yelled at the top of her lungs. And then the darkness reached out and swallowed her.

Something struck her across the face. Not a hard blow, but it stung and made her eyes water.

'Kirby? Kirby! Wake up!'

Suddenly she was aware of someone else in the room. A familiar voice.

Robert Carter's face swam into view above her. 'Kirby, are you all right?'

She struggled to sit up. There was a crushing pain in her head. Tentatively she touched it, her fingers tracing the outline of a lump at the back of her skull the size of a gull's egg. 'I fell,' she said. 'Must have hit my head.'

There was concern on his face and kindness in his eyes. 'How did you fall?'

Kirby's gaze flicked towards the wall. Smooth, unblemished. 'I'm not sure.'

His eyes narrowed. 'Tell me the truth, Kirby,' he said.

'Nothing to tell.' She got to her feet and walked to the window, resting her forehead against the cooling glass.

'I'm sorry. I don't believe you.'

'Believe what you like.' She could see Carter's reflection in the glass. He was unmoving, staring at her intently.

'I think you should leave the island,' he said.

'You're kidding! On the strength of one stupid accident?'

'But it's not just that, is it? I was talking to Jane earlier. She's under the impression this place is getting to you, and you know Jane, she's very good at reading people.'

'Did she tell you why I was upset?' There was a guarded look in Kirby's eyes.

'No. Do you want to tell me?'

Kirby shook her head.

'That's okay. But you'll have to be careful. The island works on the emotions. Believe me, I know. I felt it the moment we stepped off the boat. What worries me is that some of us won't be able to handle it.'

'You mean *I* won't be able to handle it.' *Christ, first Raj, now Carter.*

'I mean we're *all* vulnerable . . . but some of us are better equipped to protect ourselves than others.'

'I'm fine. I tripped. I fell and banged my head. And I'm sorry if I worried Jane earlier, but you're both reading too much into it. I'm not leaving.'

'I think that's for Jane to decide.' Carter walked across to her and rested his hands on her shoulders. 'Kirby, we're a team. We have to look out for each other. If you've seen something, experienced something, then you owe it to us all to say.'

'Has Raj spoken to you?'

'No, but I heard him talking to McKinley.'

'Jesus! He's probably laughing his bloody socks off by now.'

'He wasn't laughing. He seemed quite concerned. Listen, Kirby. This isn't some high school science project we're involved in here. People have disappeared and are probably dead. I understand if you don't want to talk about whatever happened to you, and if you don't want the others to know. I can identify with that. But when I found you lying on the floor, out cold, I feared the worst. So don't bullshit me. I want to know what it is you think you saw. Because you sure as hell think you saw something, didn't you?'

Kirby chewed her bottom lip, her eyes darting from right to left. 'Okay,' she said softly. Robert Carter led her back to the bed and sat down next to her. 'From the beginning,' he said.

CHAPTER TWENTY-FIVE

Carter found Jane in the library, arranging chairs around the circular table. Raj was also there, on the other side of the room, headphones on, checking the sound levels on an old Revox tape recorder.

Carter pulled Jane to one side and kept his voice low so Raj couldn't hear. 'I think Kirby should leave the island.' Kirby had told him what she had seen; he believed her. His problem was he was convinced Kirby had been very close to being killed and he didn't think she had the strength or the experience to battle what he was almost certain they were going to come up against.

'Really? Why?' Jane said. It was too early in her opinion for anyone to consider leaving, even if there was a means for them to do so.

'Because I don't think it's safe for her to stay.'

'Wise move,' Raj said, glancing round at them. 'This place is going to destroy her.'

Jane spun round to look at him. 'How did you hear . . .'

Raj took off the headphones and pointed to the small button microphone he'd placed in the center of the table.

Jane shook her head. 'Bloody technology!'

'Our job would be a lot more difficult without it,' Raj said.

'Raj, butt out,' Carter said. 'Please.'

Raj shrugged and replaced his headphones.

Jane pulled out a chair and gestured for Carter to sit down. 'Has something happened?'

'According to her, she's been seeing things,' Raj said.

'Raj! Either come over here and join in the conversation properly, or shut up,' Jane said.

Raj waved at her. 'I've finished here for now. I'll leave you to it. I've still got the basement rooms to wire.'

He left them alone.

Jane waited until he'd shut the door behind him. 'Right. Now tell me what's been going on?'

'Well, Raj was right, in a way. Kirby *has* been seeing things. A sphere of light bouncing around in here, for instance. But there's more; a lot more.' He outlined Kirby's account of what she'd experienced since arriving on the island.

'What do you make of it?' Jane said.

'Someone, or something, tried to pull her through the wall. What do *you* make of it?'

'It's too early to say. We need more.' She had no idea what her opinion was. It sounded unbelievable but yet she knew that Carter, and Kirby for that matter, were not prone to exaggeration.

'She was pretty shaken up by the experience,' he said. 'I'm not sure she's safe here.'

'Are you saying she's not up to the job?' Jane bristled, Kirby had been her choice and she had no doubts about the young woman's ability.

'No, that's not what I'm saying at all. I've worked with her before and always found her very competent. But I do think she's very vulnerable, and whatever the forces are that inhabit this house and this island, I think they've recognized that vulnerability.'

'Are you questioning my decision to bring her along?' Jane knew that sounded painfully defensive but she couldn't help herself.

Carter could hear the tension crackling in her voice like a static charge. 'Hey, hold on a minute. Why the paranoia? I'm not questioning your decisions.'

'Well, it wouldn't be the first time, would it?' Jane was digging a hole and had just started with her second spade.

He regarded her coolly. 'I don't really think this is the time for sniping. I'm simply reflecting your own concern, that's all. When we spoke earlier you said you were worried about her. What's changed your mind?'

She returned the cool gaze with one of her own. 'Nothing's changed my mind. I'm still concerned about her. But I need her here, I need you all here. If people start shipping out at the first sign of trouble, then this investigation is going to grind to a halt. And I can't allow that to happen.'

'So the Department comes first? Right?' He realized he wasn't going to persuade her. Her stubborn streak was still one of the qualities he admired in her.

'No, but this investigation is vital if the Department is to survive, and I don't want it to stall before it's even gotten under way. I'll go and have a word with Kirby and assess the situation myself.' She took his hand and felt the hard strength there. 'Thanks, Rob. Let's not fall out.'

He squeezed her hand before he stood. 'Okay, Jane, you do that. But if you let her stay and something happens to her, you're going to have to live with the guilt of that for the rest of your life.'

'That's part and parcel of being in charge, Robert. You, of all people, should know that.' The words were out before she could stop them. 'I'm sorry. That was below the belt.'

He looked at her steadily. 'Yes, it was,' he said, and left the room without another word.

She watched the door close behind him, then glanced about her. 'Shit!' she said.

What was wrong with her? Her people skills had all but disappeared. She was never usually this edgy, but this place was unsettling her. She was convinced there was something here; something watching their every action; something listening to every sound. She could feel it—she could almost touch it. And it had nothing to do with Raj's microphones or the cameras. It was something that existed on a much deeper level. It was like stirring up the bottom of a pond with a stick. Now mud and debris were floating around, clouding the water, pushing understanding just a little bit further out of her grasp. She needed to speak with Kirby. Maybe then she'd get a clearer understanding about what exactly was happening here.

'Robert's worried about you,' Jane said, almost as soon as she found Kirby in her bedroom.

Kirby lay on the bed, eyes closed but not sleeping. She didn't respond.

'Is he right to be?' Jane persisted.

'I'm okay,' Kirby said, her eyes flicking open. It was obvious from her red-rimmed eyes that she had been crying.

'How's your head?' Jane said, deflecting the full frontal attack with a more circuitous route.

Kirby touched her head with her hand. The swelling had subsided a little but there was going to be an unsightly bruise in the morning. 'Sore.'

'Sit up. Let me take a look.' Jane heard her mother's tone come to the fore; it was as if she was tending one of her daughters after a fall in the garden.

Kirby winced as Jane's fingers traced the outline of the lump on the back of her head.

'That's quite a bump,' Jane said.

'I'll live.'

'He thinks you ought to leave the island, you know?' The circuit had brought her back to the central issue.

'He can mind his own business.' Kirby pulled away. Her anger apparent in the lightning flash in her eyes.

'I can't guarantee your safety,' Jane said. She was torn between honoring her responsibility for the safety of her team, and wanting, no needing, Kirby to stay.

'I'm not asking you to. I'm a big girl now. I'm old enough to take the blame for my own actions.'

Jane regarded her for a moment, taking in the stubborn set of her chin and the defiance in her eyes. There would be no persuading her, and Jane knew that any persuasion she tried would be halfhearted. There was a lot of truth in what she had told Carter; Kirby was an integral part of this investigation, but Jane wanted her here for more personal reasons. Having another female presence on the island was important to her; it stopped her from feeling isolated by her sex in what otherwise would be a male-dominated group. She looked upon Kirby more as a younger sister than a work colleague, and having her here to look after compensated a little for being away from Gemma and Amy. 'Fair enough,' she said, taking the girl's hand and squeezing it reassuringly. 'But if anything else happens, anything at all, tell me. Promise me that I'll be the first to know.'

'Promise,' Kirby said, and lay back on the bed. 'There was so much pain in her face.'

Jane was confused. 'Whose?'

'Jo Madley. It was *her* face I saw on the screen.'

Jane immediately recognized the name from the Waincraft file. 'Which means . . .'

Kirby nodded. 'It means she's probably dead. That's why I could see her.'

'Maybe she'll make contact tonight, at the séance. You *are* up for it?'

Kirby sighed. 'I wish everyone would stop treating me like a child. I'll be fine. Honestly.'

'Okay.' Jane said, stroking a stray strand of curly hair away from the girl's eyes. 'I won't say anything else.'

'Good,' Kirby said.

Jane hesitated for a moment before speaking again. Finally she said, 'Kirby, what you were saying earlier . . . about me being psychic . . . how do you know?'

Kirby looked at her, a half smile playing on her lips. 'Jane, everybody's psychic to a certain degree. Everyone's capable of small flashes of precognition. Even if it's just knowing who's on the other end of the line when the phone rings. But some people's psychic ability is stronger than others, and I've always been able to pick up on those people. It gets me . . . here.' She tapped the side of her head. 'Almost like an electric shock, but not unpleasant . . . more a warm tingle, increasing in intensity depending on the strength of their powers. Being around Robert and John, especially at the same time, is almost uncomfortable. With Raj less so.'

'And me?'

'A warm buzz. I'd say you're just a couple of notches behind Robert and John at the moment. But if you opened up to it, and started to use it, you could be more powerful than both of them combined.'

Jane's mouth went dry. She tried to swallow, but couldn't. 'I see,' she said thickly.

'No you don't because you're in denial. For some reason your subconscious is blocking it off. Maybe something happened in your past, something that gave your inner mind some reason to shut the psychic part down. I'm no psychoanalyst, but there's usually a reason for this kind of barrier being erected.'

'So how do I break the barrier down?' She wasn't sure she wanted to.

As if reading her mind, Kirby said, 'You have to want to, that's the important thing . . . and, at the moment, I don't think you do.' Perceptive as well.

'The whole idea scares the shit out of me,' Jane said.

'And I'd like to discover if I was psychic earlier in life and what placed it in a box and threw away the key."

'As I said, you're in denial. I can't help you with that, Jane. That's something you have to sort out for yourself.'

Back in her own room Jane collapsed onto the bed and closed her eyes. *It's not true*, she told herself, but a small voice at the back of her mind, a voice unheard for many years, spoke softly to her and told her she was wrong.

CHAPTER TWENTY-SIX

Jessica Anderson glided through the party guests, sheathed in a red satin dress cut to the bone. Her hair was swept up revealing a swan's neck and showing off the Cartier earrings hanging from her delicate lobes. In her customary business suits she turned heads; dressed as she was tonight she made jaws drop . . . and she knew it. A slight smile played on her lips as she moved through the crowd, acknowledging greetings from old friends and casual business acquaintances alike with a well-practiced response and a flirtatious flash of her tourmaline eyes.

She reached the bar, set up in an alcove near a potted palm, and helped herself to a freshly poured glass of champagne. She looked over the top of the glass at the rest of the room. In the corner her father was deep in conversation with a young blonde actress whose Hollywood star was in ascendancy. She could tell from their body language that they would end up in bed together later. The idea that he took lovers younger than her was something she'd had to accept all her adult life. She still found it distasteful.

She looked away and her gaze alighted on a woman,

draped languorously on the grand piano just to the side of the French doors, watching the handsome young pianist hired for the night, stroking the keys and looking adoringly up at her. Celeste Toland had that effect on men, especially young men. *Not bad for an old broad,* Jessica thought. Celeste Toland was sixty, the same age as Carl Anderson, but looked twenty years younger. Whether her looks were the result of good genes or cosmetic surgery Jessica couldn't say for certain, but she had a pretty good idea. Either way she was a very attractive woman. Tall and slender with a mane of fiery red hair, expertly styled to hover on the line between sophistication and wild abandon. She wasn't conventionally beautiful, her features were too strong for that, but her liquid gray eyes were enticing beacons of seduction and few men could resist their allure, as witnessed by the piano player who was a nudge away from salivating.

Her sexuality was a powerful and dangerous tool. She used it subtly but Jessica wasn't deceived. She knew the other, darker side of the woman. Celeste Toland was a shrewd and cunning manipulator; a predator with a ruthless streak matched only by her own.

Carl Anderson noticed his daughter's presence in the room, peeled away from the starlet and made his way across to Jessica, a smile spreading across his face. 'Jessica, you look stunning,' he said, and kissed her on the cheek.

Jessica looked from her father to the actress, who was helping herself to a glass of champagne from a passing waiter's tray, trying desperately, and failing, to look demure.

'That little slut has only one thing on her mind,' Jessica said. 'You can almost see the dollar signs flashing in her eyes.'

'Yes I know, but she rather amuses me. You'll indulge an old man in his weaknesses, won't you?'

'Don't I always? But do they always have to be so young?'

Anderson shrugged and spread out his hands in a gesture of helplessness.

Jessica glanced across the room again at Celeste Toland, who was peeling herself off the piano, eyes flashing looking for fresh diversions. She caught Jessica's gaze and smiled warmly.

Carl Anderson followed his daughter's gaze. 'I didn't realize that bitch was here,' he said. 'Was she invited?'

Jessica shook her head. 'She came with Paul Forrester; she's his escort for the night. I believe she moves in the same social circle.'

'Yes, she does. She moves through mine too; like a shark on the lookout for an easy meal. I've told Forrester before to tread very carefully with her. She'd have him for a snack before breakfast, if she had a mind to. He obviously thinks he knows better.'

She laid a hand on his arm. 'Don't worry about Forrester, Carl. He's a big boy. I'm sure he can handle the Celeste Tolands of this world.'

Anderson looked doubtful. '*I* can't handle the Celeste Tolands of this world, Jess, so I don't hold out much hope for Forrester. He's a very shrewd banker, but absolutely clueless when it comes to women. That's why he's been divorced three times.'

'Perhaps he brought her here to try to impress you.' Jessica raised her glass to a couple walking by, uncertain quite who they were.

'Sleeping with an old whore like Celeste Toland is not the way to gain a whole lot of credit in my eyes. I can't see why he'd want to impress me anyway.'

Jessica laughed, almost innocent in its delight. 'Then you're obviously unaware of the reputation you have around town. I think a lot of men find the stories of your sexual prowess quite intimidating.'

Anderson frowned. 'I'm not sure I should be talking about my sexual prowess with my daughter,' he said.

'Does it make you uncomfortable?' Jessica teased.

'Frankly, yes, but then you have the same knack as your mother for putting me on the back foot. She was a remarkable woman as well.'

'You miss her, don't you?' The smile had disappeared like ice in the sun.

'Every day, Jess, every day.' The regret in his voice was tangible. He usually hid it so well.

'Go back to your starlet,' she said. 'Enjoy her.'

'I go with your blessing,' he said with a wry smile.

Jessica sipped her drink and stood watching Celeste. She had turned her attention back to the piano player who was coaxing a reflective ballad from the Steinway. Then the woman turned abruptly, locked eyes with Jessica, smiled and raised her champagne glass, mouthing the words, 'Study. Five minutes.'

Jessica inclined her head to show she'd understood, drained her glass and picked up another. Without looking back she left the room.

She was sitting in a leather wing-backed chair, nonchalantly flicking through a copy of *Vogue* when Celeste entered the study. She watched the older woman close the door behind her and turn the key.

'Is that really necessary?' she said.

'A precaution. I wouldn't want us to be disturbed.' Celeste Toland came towards her, moving like water flowing downhill. Jessica put down the magazine and stood to greet her. Celeste's arms enwrapped her body and her lips pressed against Jessica's in a crushing kiss. When the embrace ended she took Jessica's face in her hands and looked deeply into her eyes. 'It's been too long,' she said.

The kiss worked. Jessica's body was tingling. Celeste Toland was one of the very few who could touch her on that level. 'I agree,' she said and kissed her again.

It seemed to last an age, lips bruising, tongues tangling, Celeste's hands on her breasts, kneading, her pelvis thrusting against Jessica's leg like a bitch in heat.

She peeled the dress from Jessica's shoulders and let it drop to the floor, then reached behind her and eased down the zip of her own dress, shrugging herself out of it, letting it fall. She stood before her, naked, then brought her hand up between Jessica's legs and stroked the small bush of pubic hair, savoring the moistness.

And then Celeste laid Jessica down on the rug in front of the fireplace and made love to her.

Jessica stepped into the pool of red silk lying on the floor and pulled it up over her body. 'Zip me,' she said.

'Any news from the island?' Celeste came up behind her and pulled up the zip, inclining her head and brushing Jessica's naked shoulder with her lips, then she crossed to a small cabinet in the corner and poured herself a brandy. 'Can I get you anything?'

'Vodka. Straight.' Jessica stood in front of the large mirror hanging above the fireplace and tidied her hair. 'They've only been on Kulsay for a couple of hours. I'm waiting for Jane Talbot's first report.'

'What's she like, the Talbot woman?'

'Not your type,' Jessica said. 'Not my type either, for that matter. Takes life far too seriously.'

'And you don't?'

'Life's a game, Celeste; an adventure. It doesn't pay to treat it too seriously. I learned that lesson a long time ago.'

'As long as you're not treating the Kulsay project as a game. The Sorority has a great deal invested in this project. As have I, personally. As your sponsor my reputation is indelibly linked with yours. You mess up and my credibility with the other women goes down the toilet.'

Jessica opened her purse and took out a compact and a silver tube of lipstick. Moving closer to the mirror she repaired her makeup. Celeste came up behind her with a glass half filled with vodka and set it down on the mantelpiece.

'Thanks,' Jessica said. 'And you needn't worry. Nor should they. No one's invested more in this in terms of time and effort than me. Kulsay is one project that will be receiving my undivided attention.'

'How do you think Carl will react when he realizes he's been duped?'

'I should imagine that he'll be very disappointed in me. But by then it will be too late, far too late. For the moment though, he thinks he's on top of things, acting as my safety net, and it's better to let him think that way.' Sliding the compact and lipstick back into her bag, she took the glass from the mantelpiece, filled her mouth with the spirit and let it swirl over her tongue. She gave a small shudder as she swallowed. She stared at Celeste's reflection in the mirror. The woman was smiling at her, but the eyes were dead. A very dangerous woman, like the rest of the Sorority. 'I'd better get back, before I'm missed,' Jessica said.

'I'll be in touch soon,' Celeste said, pecking her on the cheek and stroking the downy hairs at the nape of Jessica's neck. 'Very soon.'

Jessica tipped the glass and poured the rest of the vodka down her throat, gave a tight smile and let herself out of the study.

CHAPTER TWENTY-SEVEN

Bayliss stood on the jetty, staring at the departing bow of the lobster boat. He raised his hand to wave, but no one on the craft was looking back at him. Cameron Whyte had said barely two words to him on the crossing, and the small crew of weather-hardened lobstermen had said even less; their surly attitudes leaving him in no doubt that he wasn't welcome on their boat. He shrugged and hefted his rucksack onto his shoulders and made his way inland.

The cottage he'd used as a base last time he was here was one of a group of three, each in varying states of dilapidation. He pushed the door but it didn't give. When he looked closely he could see it had been secured by a row of heavy screws. The MOD had obviously sealed the place after they'd turfed him off the island. He went round to the rear of the cottage, but the same technique had been used on the back door. Idiots! Did they really think that was going to deter him? He found a rock and smashed a window, reached in and unclipped the catch. Seconds later he was inside.

The camp bed he'd used the last time was still against the wall where he'd left it, but the canvas had been slashed several times, making it unusable. He smiled. He must have really pissed them off. The bed didn't matter. Assuming they would have destroyed his original bed, he'd brought one of lightweight aluminum and nylon with him, stowed in his rucksack. He dragged the old bed out of the way and quickly erected the new one. He lay down on it and stared up at the broken ceiling. In the back of his mind he could hear his grandmother's hectoring voice, berating him for coming across to the island; for consorting with the ungodly. 'No good will come of it. You mark my words.'

The salt-sea air had given him a thirst. He rolled over and reached into his rucksack, pulling out a can of beer and flipping the ring-pull. The liquid hissed and bubbled out of the can, spilling over his hand and dripping to the floor. Quickly he closed his lips over the opening and took a long pull. The beer fizzed on his tongue and all the way down his throat. Halfway through the can he belched loudly. From somewhere in the cottage he heard a fluttering of wings. He obviously had company.

Although there were a couple of hours of daylight left in the sky, the cottage was dark, filled with shadows that shifted under his gaze. He shivered and pulled out a blanket, draping it over his legs, letting the fleecy material warm him. For all his bravado Kulsay still had the power to spook him. There was something unwholesome about the place that affected him on a deep, almost subconscious level, making him feel that every action he took, every move he made, was being watched and recorded by hidden eyes.

Setting the can down on the floor he reached into the rucksack again and took out a large, leather-bound journal in which he kept his notes on Kulsay. The notes were copious, detailing the island's history, the events that had happened here, as well as biographical details of the key players in Kulsay's colorful past.

The previous evening he'd added the name of Robert Carter, and the others Carter had brought with him. Only Carter himself had a few paragraphs after his name. The others he'd find out about while he was here. He was one of the few people aware of the Department's existence, and not at all surprised that they had been called upon to investigate the island. Whether they'd have more success than the Ministry of Defense remained to be seen.

'We're ready to start,' Jane said. 'Are you?'

Carter was sitting on the patio smoking a cigarette, staring across at the garden. The sun was starting to die in the sky, its light rendering the trees and shrubs in muted tones. He screwed out the cigarette in the ashtray. 'As ready as I'll ever be. You've never attended one of my séances before, have you?'

'I've never had the pleasure.'

Carter laughed gruffly. 'Some pleasure. I should point out though that I won't be going into a trance or speaking in tongues or any of that mumbo jumbo. I'll simply be opening up and seeing what impressions I get. The point of us all sitting around a table and linking hands is so that I can connect with the others and draw on their powers as well as my own. I expect everyone to open up as fully as me, otherwise there's no point. If someone's blocking, then it will disrupt the flow. I want everyone to open their mind and become as receptive as possible. One skeptic at the table can ruin an entire sitting.'

'I'd hardly describe myself as a skeptic.' Jane was very conscious she was about to get defensive with Carter again. What was it about him that made her so argumentative?

Carter smiled and touched her face. 'What makes you think I was talking about you?'

'Well, weren't you?' She pulled away even though at that moment, right now, she wanted to grab him and kiss him.

He got to his feet, scooped up his packet of cigarettes and slipped them into his pocket. 'Not exclusively but, as you raised it, I'd like to see you rein back the analytical side of your mind until the séance is over.'

'Just go with the flow you mean?'

'Precisely.'

'Deal,' she said.

'I want to have a word with Kirby as well before we get started. If she's too scared to open up fully, then I see no point in her taking part,' Carter said, as they headed towards the French doors.

Jane took hold of his sleeve. 'She won't be in any danger, will she?'

He shook his head. 'As long as she stays linked to the group, and to me, I can protect her.'

The way you protected Sian? The words flashed into her mind but she bit them back before they reached her lips. 'I'll hold you to that,' she said instead.

'Yes,' he said, holding open the door for her to enter. 'I thought you might.'

When they entered the library the others were already seated at the table. Carter took his place at the head whilst Jane slotted herself in between Kirby and McKinley.

Jane leaned in to Kirby. 'Are you certain you want to do this?' she said, her voice barely above a whisper.

Kirby nodded her head but didn't answer.

'It's not compulsory, you know. Robert says that if you can't open up fully then you could spoil the sitting.'

'I'm fine, Jane,' Kirby said. 'Honestly.'

'If we could all link hands . . . when we're all ready,' Carter said, staring at Jane, a question in his eyes.

Jane took McKinley's hand and reached out for Kirby's. The girl gripped Jane's hand fiercely, making her wince. 'We're ready,' Jane said.

'Okay,' Carter said, leaning back in his chair. 'Let's get this show on the road.'

'Do you want me to get the lights?' Raj said.

Carter looked around the room, at all the dark corners,

the shadows potentially lurking. 'No. We'll keep it as bright as possible. I like to see what's happening and I don't like surprises.'

'But I've put infrared film in the camera,' Raj protested. He had assumed the lights would be out.

'You'd better change it then,' Carter said reasonably.

Muttering curses under his breath Raj forced himself out of his seat. There was a small delay while he put regular film in the camera. He then checked the light settings on the video. 'Wish you'd told me earlier,' he said as he resumed his seat.

Carter shrugged.

'I think we're ready now,' Jane said. She checked the time by the long-case clock in the corner. 'First sitting commencing at nine p.m.,' she said for the benefit of the microphone.

'Right,' Carter said. 'Whatever you do, don't break the circle.' He directed the comment at Kirby who glared at him and gripped Jane's hand even tighter.

Jane closed her eyes and started to take deep, even breaths. Gradually the pain in her Kirby-crushed hand receded, to be replaced with a soft tingling sensation. She was getting the same feeling from McKinley. It was like being plugged in to a low voltage battery. Soon she was aware of the silence in the room, broken only by the sound of the others' breathing, and slowly even that faded away until she was focused only on her own heartbeat.

For a long moment her mind became a void; a deep pool of blackness; bottomless and vast. She felt she was teetering on the edge of it and that at any moment she might pitch forward and fall. And then images crept into her mind, filling the void, making the darkness recede. Gemma and Amy playing in the garden; David's face, softly candlelit, gazing at her lovingly across a restaurant table; her fingers tracing erotic patterns on Robert Carter's smooth, well-muscled back; a helicopter slowly sinking, inch by inch, into the ground. She gasped but kept her eyes tightly closed and tried to steady her breathing.

As she settled herself again more images burned their way into her mind. Tiles dropping silently from a bathroom wall; a hand reaching down, fingers forcing their way into her mouth, gripping her tongue; damp and dirty sacks reeking of stale urine smothering her face, making it difficult to breathe.

She tried to push the images away, forcing her mind to concentrate on happier thoughts. The birth of Gemma; her first bath—soft fingers smoothing soap over even softer skin. The indescribable smell of baby. Gemma lying in her cot, staring up in blue-eyed wonder at the Winnie the Pooh mobile hanging from the ceiling above her head; bony white hands gripping her tiny arms and dragging her down through the mattress.

'*No!*' She was on her feet looking about the room wild-eyed. The others were staring at her in puzzlement. Jane stared down at her hands. She had broken the circle.

She took a breath and tried to gather herself, but the image of Gemma being dragged through the mattress was hard to shift.

'Are you okay?' Carter was at her side, his arm sliding around her shoulder.

She gulped and nodded. 'Yes. I think so . . . I . . . I'm sorry I broke the . . .'

'It's okay.' He stroked her back.

'I saw . . .' She was finding it hard to breathe.

'Not now. Don't say anything now.' This wasn't the time for reporting impressions; they needed to draw more out.

'But . . .' She had calmed now, the feel of Carter's hand on her back soothing her, making her heart feel less like a roller coaster coming down the final track.

He put a finger to her lips. 'Do you feel up to trying again?'

She nodded.

'We can leave it until tomorrow,' he said, but she could tell he didn't want to postpone. Neither did she.

'No.' She sat down again. 'Sitting recommencing at . . .' She glanced across at the clock in the corner, and then looked back at Carter in confusion. 'One minute past nine? But how? I don't understand.'

'You only had your eyes closed for a few seconds, Jane. I hadn't even started the séance when you broke the circle.'

'Impossible. It must have been longer than that! Must have been.' She backed away from the table. 'I'm sorry, I can't do this.' She walked out of the room.

John McKinley rose to follow her.

'Leave her,' Kirby said. 'She needs to be on her own.'

'How the hell do you know what she needs?' McKinley said, anger flashing in his eyes.

'I know Jane. She has things she needs to work out.'

'Such as?'

'Such as the fact that out of all us here tonight she is the most powerful psychic.'

'That's rubbish,' McKinley said. 'Jane's always insisted she's *not* psychic. She says it's what gives her objectivity.'

'Kirby's right,' Carter said. 'Jane's powers are incredibly strong, but she's been in denial for years and blocked them out. Self-delusion is a very cunning inhibitor. But she needs to learn to accept what she is and learn to use it to protect herself. If she doesn't this place will rip her apart.'

CHAPTER TWENTY-EIGHT

'Can I come in?' Carter said from the doorway of Jane Talbot's bedroom.

She was lying on the bed, her eyes wet with tears. She sniffed, rubbed a hand across her face and turned her head away from him.

'I'll take that as a yes then?' He sat down on the bed next to her. 'You can't keep running from it, Jane.'

'How long have you known?' Was she the only one who didn't know?

He shrugged. 'Since I first met you.'

'Why have you never said anything before?'

He reached out and stroked her hair. 'It wasn't my place to question you about it. I figured you had your reasons for blocking. I know better than anyone how hard it is to deal with a gift like this.'

She rounded on him. 'It's not a gift; it's a curse! I've spent my life trying to force it out of my mind. Do you realize how difficult that is?'

'I think I can appreciate it. What I don't understand is why you felt you had to.'

She turned away from him again and lapsed into silence, her fingers picking at a loose thread on the counterpane.

He pulled out two cigarettes, lit them and handed one to her.

She sucked smoke greedily into her lungs. 'Thanks.'

'Look, Jane, you need to talk about this.'

She rolled over onto her back. 'I never wanted it. Even when I was very small I realized that I was different from everyone else, and I hated it. I remember playing in the park with some friends. I couldn't have been much more than ten. We were on the swings. There was another little girl there, Melissa. We never really liked her, but she used to hang around with us because no one else would play with her. She was on a swing; Freddie Carpenter was pushing her. I was on a seesaw with another girl bouncing up and down. All of a sudden I felt a piercing pain in my head and everything sort of shifted out of focus. But in my mind's eye I could see Melissa reach the apex of her swing and let go of the chains. I saw her fly through the air and hit the ground, her arm twisted underneath her. Gradually the image cleared. I looked across and Melissa was still on the swing, squealing with delight as Freddie pushed her higher and higher. Then, suddenly, when she was almost level with the the top of the swing she let go. I saw her fly through the air, heard her scream. And then she landed. I can still hear the snap of bone as her arm broke. It was horrible.'

'Horrible, I agree, but not your fault.'

'Wasn't it? I didn't like her, and I was angry that Freddie was paying her so much attention.'

'So, you're saying you made it happen?'

'I don't know. Not for certain. It may just have been a premonition. But it might have been something more. All I know is that I started to block out the feelings, the visions. And I was pretty successful . . . until I hit puberty. I was fourteen when my grandmother died. I killed her.'

Carter stiffened. 'What do you mean?'

Jane rose from the bed, walked across to the wardrobe and stared at her reflection in the full-length mirror. The room behind the reflection shrank away and she was looking at herself in her teens; small and slight; big, dark eyes enhanced by the ultra-short elfin haircut.

'She'd been with us for a few weeks. My grandfather was in hospital and my mother suggested she come and stay with us. Gran didn't drive so she was reliant on my mother to take her to and from the hospital for visiting. We'd never gotten on. She was like my mother in many ways, but more so. More dogmatic, more prudish, more unpleasant. She came home from the hospital one evening and just started in on me, criticizing my clothes, my hair, my schoolwork, my friends . . . She told me I'd never amount to anything, and that I would always be a disappointment to her.' Jane laughed harshly. 'My mother's continued that theme ever since. Anyway, I started to answer back. As I said, I was four-teen and my hormones were in turmoil. She slapped me and I slapped her back. After that I was sent to my room. Christ, I was furious; furious with her and furious with my mother for taking her side. I sat there, seething, angrier than I could ever remember being before. My head was pound-ing, almost pulsating. I think I must have blacked out, be-cause the next thing I remember I was lying facedown on the floor and there was a terrible buzzing in my head, like a fly was rumbling around behind my eyes. I couldn't think straight; I certainly couldn't get up off the floor.

'And then I started having these visions. Flashes, pictures; like watching a DVD on fast-forward. I saw my grand-mother walk from the bathroom and head towards the stairs. At the top she seemed to stumble and trip. And then she fell. She tumbled down the stairs like a rag doll, arms flailing, her head smacking on the wall, on the risers. She landed at the bottom, and I could see from the way her head was positioned that her neck was broken. And I was *so* pleased. Absolutely triumphant, even though I knew it had only happened in my own imagination.

'A few moments later I heard them, my mother and my grandmother, talking outside my room. Mother wanted to come and see if I was all right, but my grandmother wouldn't let her. "Let her stew, Brenda. The little bitch

needs to see the error of her ways. You're too soft on her."
They stopped talking and I listened to the silence for a
while. Then I heard the toilet flush.

'I knew what was about to happen. I could have run out
of the room and intercepted her, but I didn't. I just lay there
on the floor and listened. I wanted to know what would
happen. I remember it made so much noise. First there was
the cry as she tripped and lost her balance, and then there
was this clattering and crunching as she fell down the stairs.
I could picture every sound. I knew when her head hit the
wall, and when her leg caught against the banister and
snapped. Finally the noise stopped and I knew it was over
and that my grandmother was dead.

'My mother *never* got over it. She's been punishing herself ever since for the fact that her mother died whilst in
her care. And she's been punishing me too, for years.'

Carter came up behind her and put a hand on her shoulder. 'Jane, what you're describing is a premonition. There's
nothing in what you've told me that leads me to think that
it could be anything more than that.'

'Even if you're right, and I'm not sure you are, with
this . . . gift, this curse, comes responsibility. I could have
stopped it from happening. I didn't. I just lay there waiting, wishing for it to happen. You were talking to me earlier about guilt. Well I've lived with guilt, Rob, and it's
been informing my life ever since that day. It's the reason I
got into psychology, in order to understand what my mo-
tivations were . . . are. I came to work for the Department
so I could study psychic phenomena firsthand. That guilt
has driven me forward.'

'And at the same time, totally repressed you.'

'Yes.' She said the word quietly and calmly but her body
tremored. When she turned to face him, tears were trick-
ling down her cheeks. Carter wrapped his arms around
her and pulled her close. She let herself be held. She *needed*

to be held. 'Sometimes, it gets too much,' she said, her voice muffled by his shirt.

'Yes,' he said. 'I know.'

'Do you feel up to telling me what you experienced during the séance?' Carter said.

They were sitting on the bed. Jane had dried her tears and was feeling stronger. Although she hated to admit it, just having him by her side was giving her that strength. 'Just random images. Nothing really coherent.'

'Tell me anyway.' He had lit two more cigarettes.

She listed what she had seen in her mind's eye.

'Have you checked that Gemma's all right?' he said when she'd finished.

'First thing I did when I came upstairs. I phoned my mother. Both the girls are fine.'

'Good. The helicopter. You saw it sinking into the earth?'

She closed her eyes and recalled instantly what she had seen. 'Bizarrely, yes.'

He rubbed at the stubble on his chin, thinking.

'Do you think that's significant?' Jane asked.

'I think so, yes. It was never found, the helicopter. No wreckage out at sea; no sign it crashed anywhere. To all intents and purposes it just disappeared, along with the pilot.'

'You think it really happened then? It landed here, then just sunk through solid ground?' She tried to keep the incredulity out of her voice.

Carter nodded. 'It's one scenario.'

'An unlikely one.'

'Unlikely, but not impossible. We have to consider everything that happens as possible, even if it can't be real; not in the normal world anyway.'

Jane sucked on her cigarette and held on to the smoke

in her lungs. Finally she exhaled. 'Do you think it's worth trying another séance?'

Carter shook his head. 'No, I don't think you're up to it.'

She bridled slightly. 'I'll be more prepared next time.'

'I don't think any of us are prepared sufficiently to handle what's happening here.'

'Still, I'd like to try,' she said.

'Okay. It's your call. Let's compromise. After breakfast tomorrow?'

Jane smiled. 'Fine. Can you let the others know?'

'I'll tell them.' He kissed her on the cheek and left the room. She lay back on the bed, took another pull on the cigarette, then ground it out in the ashtray. She picked up her phone and punched in a number.

'Hi, it's me again.' Her voice had changed from her conversation with Carter. She was more reserved now, holding back.

'I've just put the girls to bed, Jane,' her mother said tetchily.

'I just wanted to wish them good night.'

'Phone them in the morning and do it then.'

Jane smiled. Only her mother could conjure up such an absurdity. 'Yes, okay. I'll call tomorrow.'

'Good night, Jane.'

The line went dead.

She dropped the phone on the bed beside her, then stood up and started to peel off her clothes. She felt desperately tired. She crawled under the covers and closed her eyes. Within seconds she was asleep. But it was a fitful sleep filled with nightmarish dreams of snatched children and sinking helicopters.

She awoke feeling wretched with the thought of another attempt at another séance sitting in her stomach like a lead

weight. She showered quickly, skipped breakfast and went
for a walk on the grounds to try to clear her head. By the
time she got back to the Manse the others had already assembled in the library. She took her place at the table.
'Right,' she said. 'Let's start.'

'Are you sure, Jane?' Carter said.

'Let's get it over with,' she said. However she thought
their relationship was developing she couldn't have him
question her in front of the others.

Carter nodded, but was watching her closely. 'Okay.
Everybody link hands.'

Jane joined hands again with Kirby and McKinley, worried they would feel the sweat on her palms.

'Now,' Carter said. 'Everybody breathe deeply, close
your eyes and try to relax.'

Jane took one, long, deep breath and shut her eyes.

At that point the doorbell rang.

John McKinley got to his feet. 'Weren't we supposed to
be the only ones on this island?' he said.

Jane looked puzzled. 'So I was told.'

'Well obviously we're not,' McKinley said and went to
answer the door.

CHAPTER TWENTY-NINE

McKinley came back to the library followed by a young
man, fairly scruffy, looking like he could do with a shave
and a good night's sleep. Kirby's first impression was that
when he was cleaned up he might look a little like Brad
Pitt in the movie *Troy*. Not bad at all.

'This is Nick Bayliss,' McKinley said to the others. His
shrug indicated his bemusement at the casual entrance.

They had all believed access to the island was strictly controlled while they were here.

Jane stood. 'I was led to believe this island was deserted, Mr. Bayliss,' she said, adopting her stern woman-in-charge persona. 'How long have you been on Kulsay?'

Bayliss regarded her with a slightly sardonic smile on his face. 'I could murder a coffee,' he said. The Scottish accent was thick enough to cut with a knife. He dropped his rucksack on the floor.

Jane glanced around at Kirby.

Irritation flashed in Kirby's eyes. She didn't want to miss anything.

'Please,' Jane said, softening her tone. 'We'll fill you in on whatever you miss.'

With a theatrical sigh Kirby rose from her seat. 'I suppose the rest of you want one as well?' she said. As she walked past Bayliss he winked at her. Kirby tucked her chin into her chest and hurried on by. She couldn't help smiling though.

'You didn't answer my question,' Jane said. 'How long have you been on the island?'

'I came over yesterday evening,' he said. 'Do you mind if I sit down? I've been walking for an hour, and the terrain around here doesn't really lend itself to a casual stroll. My feet are killing me.' He flopped down in one of the armchairs by the fireplace and started to unlace his boots.

Jane tapped her foot impatiently. There was something about the self-confident Bayliss that she admired; he irritated and frustrated her, but he was clearly trying to take control of the situation.

Bayliss looked up from his unlacing at the others gathered around the table. 'Sorry, have I interrupted?'

Jane's eyes narrowed. 'No, not at all.' Borderline sarcasm, but kept in check by professional caution.

'Only I thought you may be holding a séance or something. That *is* what the Department is all about, isn't it? Ghoulies and ghosties, and things that go bump in the night?'

Carter leaned forward in his chair. 'Would you mind telling us what the hell you think you're doing here?'

Bayliss pulled off a boot and massaged his toes through the thick wool of his sock. He smiled across at Carter. 'I'm here to help, Mr. Carter,' he said. 'And to answer some of the questions you've obviously been asking yourself.'

Martin Impey sat at his desk collating another ream of paperwork. Sometimes the sheer volume of material he was responsible for was overwhelming. If the public only knew how many paranormal events were occurring every day they'd be shocked and, most likely, terrified. And for every case reported there were ten times that many that went ignored, brushed under the convenient carpet of denial and self-delusion. On his desk at the moment were reports of poltergeist activity in a Birmingham suburb, a suspected demonic possession of a small boy in Surbiton, and half a dozen random sightings of ghosts, as well as reports from two other Department teams that needed to be processed.

Everything on his desk had to be logged onto the computer, cross-referenced and verified. He and his two secretaries faced the daily task of keeping this material under control, and of updating their computers from the many databases from around the world to which they had access. On top of this were the almost daily requests from Simon Crozier and others to provide background information on whatever cases they were working. He picked up a scrap of paper on which were scribbled the words, *The Sorority*. This was a good example.

He'd arrived early this morning, just after six, to play catch-up with his filing. A minute after he got there he was summoned by Simon Crozier. He was convinced the man never slept, yet he always seemed so alert, so unruffled. Martin walked along the corridor to Crozier's office, stuffing the remnants of a bacon sandwich—his breakfast—into his mouth, and clutching a plastic cup filled with hot, sweet tea.

Crozier was sitting behind his desk, tapping away at his laptop, a look of fierce concentration etched into his brow. As Martin closed the door behind him Crozier looked up, noticed the plastic cup in his hand and frowned.

Martin raised the cup. 'Breakfast,' he said.

'Come and sit down,' Crozier said. 'I've a job for you.'

Martin took the seat opposite him and was about to set his cup down on the desk, but Crozier gave an almost imperceptible shake of his head. Martin lowered the cup to the floor, but visions of tipping the tea over the pristine cream carpet prevented him from setting it down. Instead he raised the cup to his lips and drained it, wincing as the scalding liquid burned its way down his throat. Crozier reached down and produced a chrome wastepaper bin from under the desk. Martin dropped the cup in the bin and wiped his lips with the back of his hand. Then he wiped his brow. The hot tea had made him sweat.

Crozier scribbled something on the pad in front of him. Then he folded the page carefully and took a paperknife from a drawer, carefully cutting along the crease. He slid the thin sliver of paper across the desk. 'Mean anything to you?'

Martin picked it up and read the words, *The Sorority*. He shook his head. 'No.'

'What about the name Celeste Toland?'

Martin shook his head again. 'Likewise.'

'Damn!' Crozier said. 'Okay. See what you can dig up on them.'

'But I've got a mountain of paperwork to get through,' Martin said. 'Can't I put one of the girls on it?'

'If I wanted one of the girls doing the job I would have called one of them in. Instead I called you. What does that tell you?'

Martin feigned a second of thought as if considering a quiz question. 'You'd rather I do it myself?'

Crozier gave a perfunctory smile. 'Precisely.'

'And should I know what this is all about?'

'Celeste Toland is a member of a group of fairly high-profile and wealthy women in America who call themselves *The Sorority*. Other than that you know as much as I do. Apart from the fact that this Celeste Toland is, shall we say, rather friendly with Jessica Anderson.'

'And you want to know if this woman and her group have any interest in Kulsay,' Martin said. He preferred to have the terms of reference before he began his researches. It sometimes helped rather than going in with one arm figuratively tied behind his back and a blindfold over his eyes.

'Yes.'

'What makes you think they might?' It was always best to go into a research request from Crozier as well informed as possible.

'I've heard whispers.' Crozier loved to play up the perceived man-about-town image he had of himself.

'Dangerous things, whispers.' Martin found his boss amusing and scary at the same time, but most of all he pitied him on a human level.

'Not when they're from a reliable source.' The way Crozier said it left Martin in no doubt that the subject was at an end.

Martin got to his feet. 'Priority then.'

'Top priority.'

He walked to the door. 'When you say, *rather friendly*, I take it you're speaking euphemistically.'

Crozier smiled. 'I've been led to believe that's the case.' Though he knew precisely how the relationship worked.

'How did you find this out?' Martin tried not to sound incredulous; and certainly didn't want to sound in any way admiring.

'I have a mole in the Anderson court,' Crozier said. 'No one's private life is very private anymore.'

'More's the pity,' Martin said under his breath. The intelligence gathering part of the Department role was still something he felt uncomfortable about.

'Sorry?' Crozier had already turned his attention back to his computer screen.

Martin had the door open. 'I said, "another day in the city." I'll get straight on it.'

'Good. Get back to me the moment you have something I can get my teeth into.'

'Will do.'

'Oh, and Martin . . . this is strictly between you and me. Understood?'

'Understood.' Yet Martin knew this was a brief he didn't fully understand. Why was Crozier interested in a group of American women with too much money and time on their hands? The Anderson connection was the obvious answer, but if so, how did that affect Jane and the others who were already on an investigation, which had the full involvement of the Andersons behind it?

Nick Bayliss had settled himself in the chair by the fireplace; totally relaxed, legs crossed, mug of coffee clenched in his fist.

'We're waiting,' Jane said. Conversation had stalled while they all waited for Kirby to return with the drinks.

'Waiting?' Bayliss was enjoying his moment, the might of the Department waiting for him to speak.

'For you to tell us why you're here,' Raj said. 'As you are well aware.'

Bayliss sipped his coffee, glanced across at Kirby, and winked at her again. 'Great coffee. Cardamom?'

Kirby flushed slightly and nodded.

'Thought so.' He turned back to Jane and the others. 'You're here to find out why those people disappeared. Am I right? Your masters think there might be a paranormal explanation for it.'

'Are you here to tell us there isn't?' Jane said.

'The Ministry of Defense was here two months ago. They thought they were dealing with a mass kidnapping by a foreign power. Idiots! But lucky idiots. They were only here twenty-four hours, then they buggered off again. Had they been here longer they may have discovered firsthand what's really going on.'

'I'm losing patience, Mr. Bayliss,' Jane said. 'Either you tell us why you're here or I'll make a phone call and have you removed.'

'I think you'll find that rather difficult,' Bayliss said with a smile. 'I checked my cell phone before I came here. There's no signal. I suspect yours will be the same.'

'That's ridiculous. I was using mine last night,' Jane said, and pulled her phone from her pocket. The NO NETWORK message on the screen told its own story. 'Everybody, check your phones.'

'Nothing.'

'Dead.'

'No signal.'

Carter walked across to the landline phone and lifted the receiver. No dial tone, just a harsh continuous whistle. He shook his head.

'We've a radio transmitter,' Jane said. Doubt was clouding her mind like a gathering storm.

'I wouldn't waste your time,' Bayliss said. 'That'll be blocked too. It's started.'

McKinley was on his feet. He grabbed Bayliss by the front of his shirt, hauled him out of his seat, coffee slopping over onto the parquet, and brought his face to within inches of the smaller man. 'I've had a bellyful of this, man,' he said. 'Stop pissing us around and tell us what you know.'

'Let him go, John!' Jane said, steel in her voice.

McKinley held onto Bayliss for a few seconds more, and then dropped him back into his seat. Bayliss took a moment to recover. 'They'll use that as well. Any form of negative energy is sustenance to them.'

'To whom?' Jane said, her voice rising.

'The ones controlling what's happening on the island,' Bayliss said. The Scottish accent gave a local flavor and only added to the menace in the words.

The others exchanged looks and glances. It was Raj who gave voice to what the rest of them were thinking. 'What the hell are you talking about?'

Bayliss was watching Carter closely. 'You know, don't you, Mr. Carter? At least you've got a pretty good idea.'

No one spoke.

Carter turned away. He went across to one of the bookcases in the room and stood with his back to the others, blindly scanning the titles. In his mind he was back in the chamber with Sian.

They tore out my eyes.

'Robert?' Jane said. 'What's he talking about?'

'I don't know.' Carter didn't turn to face her. Jane knew instinctively by the way his shoulders were hunched that he was holding back on her.

'He's lying,' Bayliss said, wiping the coffee that had spilled on his legs and hands.

McKinley came up behind Carter, grabbed his shoulder and spun him round. 'Are you?'

'You really need to control your temper, John,' Carter said, his fists clenching.

'Then help us out,' Jane said. 'I'll ask you again. Do you know what he's talking about?'

Carter regarded her for a moment, then said quietly, 'They're the ones who took Sian.'

CHAPTER THIRTY

Jane stared at him for a moment, then stormed across to the door and yanked it open. 'Robert, outside. Now!'

She waited until he'd joined her in the hallway, then closed the door behind them ignoring the quizzical looks from the others, and then she wheeled on Carter. 'No more bullshit, tell me what's going on.'

'Jane, I don't know *what's* going on.'

'Well you seem to know a damned sight more than I do. Is this about what happened at the hotel the other night?' Her voice had a hard edge to it, a bottom of the bottle finality.

'Yes.' It was hard to explain to her what he was still interpreting himself.

'You'd better explain,' she said. 'And make it good. Between you playing your cards too close to your chest, and the Coffee Kid in there with the holes in his socks, I've just about had enough.'

He was silent for a moment, and she could almost see the turmoil in his mind reflected in his eyes. When she spoke again her voice was softer. 'Please, Rob. I need to know.'

He stared at her for a long moment. Finally he sighed. 'Okay,' he said. 'In the vision you had at the start of the séance you saw Gemma being dragged through the mattress of her cot, and you saw the helicopter sinking into the ground.'

She nodded.

He continued. 'The images are the same. Something being pulled from this world, down into another. It ties in with what happened to me at the hotel. I was pulled into the pond. Grabbed and pulled down through the water. I must have blacked out because the next thing I was aware of was waking up in some kind of stone chamber. I can't swear to it, but I had the feeling it was deep underground.'

'And Sian?'

'She was there.' He took a breath, almost a sob. 'Christ, Jane, they'd ripped out her eyes!'

'Do you still think Sian's alive?' Jane said when he'd finished relating the events of that night.

He shook his head. 'I don't know for sure. The whole thing could have been some kind of illusion. But it certainly felt real enough.'

'So what connects Sian's disappearance with what's happening here on the island? There's four hundred miles between the two.'

'You made the connection yourself.' He was lighting a cigarette but Jane held up her hand to refuse the one he offered her.

She thought for a moment. 'The ley line you mean? We haven't actually established that such a ley line exists. There's certainly no record of one. I had Martin Impey check the database and he came up blank. If the Department hasn't got it charted, then it's probably not recorded anywhere.'

Carter blew shrouds of smoke into the air. 'But that doesn't mean there isn't one. You know as well as I do that their location is unreliable, not completely charted.'

'Agreed, but even if there is, I don't see how it moves us forward any. I still can't see how it links Sian to Kulsay.'

'Unless something is using that ley line and others like it to reach out from the island. Think about it, Jane. The population of the island disappeared. The Waincraft team disappeared. Sian disappeared.'

Jane stood and paced. 'But why only take *her*? Why not you as well?'

'I don't know and, believe me, that question nags at me like a toothache. I can only assume it's part of a plan, some grand design.' He waved his hand in the air, ash from the cigarette falling like petals.

'A plan created by whom?' Jane's forehead was as furrowed as a farmer's field at seed planting time.

'Whoever or whatever is controlling things on this island.' Carter savagely ground out his cigarette.

She chewed her lip as she considered this. 'Let's go back to the others. They deserve an explanation. I also want to hear what else Bayliss has got to say for himself.' She paused, her hand on the doorknob. 'How did he know about you?'

'I'm not sure.'

'But he addressed you by name, so he obviously knows who you are. You've never met him before?'

Carter shook his head. 'No. I'd remember. He also knows about the Department, so he's obviously done his homework,' Carter said. 'I think there's a lot he needs to tell us.'

'I agree,' Jane said. 'Let's go back in.'

There was silence in the room as they reentered. Bayliss hadn't moved from his chair; the others were seated at the table, ignoring him and each other. Kirby looked anxiously at them as they came in. 'What's going on?' she said, giving voice to what they were all thinking.

Carter pulled a chair away from the table and set it down in front of Bayliss, a yard away. He took out a cigarette and offered Bayliss the pack. The younger man shook his head.

'Shouldn't there be a spotlight directed at my eyes and electrodes attached to my genitals?' Bayliss said.

Jane smiled ruefully. 'Don't tempt me.'

Carter looked up from lighting his cigarette, squinting slightly as the smoke stung his eyes. 'This isn't an interrogation. We just want some answers from you.'

'I won't split hairs about the semantics of that statement. Anyway I'm happy to tell you anything you want to know.' He smiled across at Kirby and raised his empty coffee mug. 'Any chance?'

Kirby glared at him, but then the glare softened into a faint smile and she came over, took his mug and disappeared back to the kitchen.

'So what are you really doing here?' Carter said.

Bayliss sat back in his seat, totally relaxed. 'Research,' he said. 'For a book I'm writing.'

Carter nodded. 'The subject being what exactly?'

'Kulsay, and places like Kulsay. Sites of great evil.'

'Well Kulsay certainly has an unusual history, but I'd hardly call the island a *site of great evil*,' McKinley said.

'Which just goes to prove that you really have no idea what you've wandered into,' Bayliss said.

'Well, I'm sure you're going to tell us,' Jane said.

Bayliss grinned at her. 'But of course.'

CHAPTER THIRTY-ONE

Bayliss took a swig from his coffee. 'Up until the eighteenth century Kulsay was uninhabited. There had been a few attempts to colonize the place before then but the colonists found conditions too harsh. There may have been other reasons why no one stayed very long on the island even then, but there's nothing documented.

'In 1720 a wealthy Spaniard called Alphonse deMarco arrived in Aberdeen and bought a large house just outside the city, Farley Grange. In the research I've done on him I've seen him described as an alchemist and a necromancer. He might even have been both . . . or neither; the records about him up until then are pretty vague. Either way his arrival certainly stirred up the local population.

'He brought a large entourage across from Spain with him and filled Farley Grange. Before long there was talk of very un-Christian things going on at his house—weird ceremonies, strange rituals, as well as more lurid tales of all sorts of debauchery. To make matters worse he was a very attractive man, with great charisma and charm, and he had no trouble enticing younger, more impressionable members of society to his house for wild parties. Many stayed on after the parties, and after eighteen months it's said that there were more than sixty bodies inhabiting Farley Grange, and indulging in whatever forbidden pleasures deMarco was offering.

'There was an incident in 1724 when a young girl, the daughter of one of the local dignitaries, was found dead in the forest surrounding the Grange. She'd been badly mutilated. Her eyes and tongue had been ripped out. DeMarco was arrested, almost as a matter of course, and he stood trial for her murder. But the case was dismissed when it was proved that deMarco hadn't been in the country when the girl was murdered. He was released and he returned to Farley Grange, but by now public opinion, which had always been set fairly against him, sunk to an all-time low. The local population engaged in what can only be described as a witch hunt. Mysterious fires were started at the Grange and several of his followers were beaten up when they ventured into town. There were no processions of angry villagers holding flaming torches but from what I've read, that would have probably been the next stage.'

Bayliss drained his coffee and set the mug down by the side of his chair. When he looked up again he saw that everyone in the room was sitting, silently, waiting for him to continue. He had them hooked, and he liked that. Storytelling was in his blood; a direct line from his grandfather. The old man would be proud to see him now.

'DeMarco realized he was, to put it mildly, no longer welcome in the area, so he bought Kulsay Island. He had a house built and moved everyone across. Suddenly he had total freedom to indulge his excesses, and the stories that filtered back across to the mainland were even more extreme than those that had preceded them. And, for him, the beauty of it was that there was no one to bring him to book. There are reports of massive cruelties carried out on the island, even human sacrifice. But then all the stories stop. There's no record of anything at all on Kulsay from 1734 through to 1746. Then the records pick up again.

'I had to search for months before I turned up anything else about deMarco, but I finally found an old book in the British library. It's called *Soldiers of God* and was written in the early nineteenth century by Bishop Everard Hislop. Basically it's a history of the Jesuits. I won't bore you with the details prior to 1736, but the chapter that interested me contains a record of that year.

'Apparently stories about deMarco and his followers reached the ears of Pope Benedict XIV. Around that time Benedict was trying to strengthen the moral influence of the papacy, so he decided to intercede in what was happening on Kulsay; his theory being that if he could turn deMarco and his followers back to the path of righteousness it would be seen as a shining example of the power, not only of Christianity, but of the Roman Catholic Church in general.

'He assigned a Scottish bishop, Archibald Prime, to go over to the island and turn these lost sheep back to the way of God. Nothing was heard of Prime for about six months, but then it emerged that, far from turning deMarco and the others back to Christianity, Prime had in fact been turned by deMarco. *Pious* Prime, as he was now called, had wholeheartedly embraced the lifestyle on Kulsay and had been appointed deMarco's lieutenant.

'Of course, the Pope was furious. Benedict himself was highly respected by both Protestants and Catholics alike, and he was seen to be one of the more enlightened pontiffs of the 1700s, but he'd been made to look a fool, and that was a situation he couldn't allow to flourish. So he called in a man commonly known as *The German.*'

'I hate to interrupt,' Carter said. 'But where's all this leading?' He was surprised how much of what Bayliss was saying mirrored the information he had uncovered.

Bayliss frowned. 'You wanted to know what is happening on Kulsay so you can deal with it,' he said. 'Without an understanding of the island's history, you may as well be pissing in the dark. This stuff is important because it explains why the island is as it is.'

'Let him continue, Robert,' Jane said. She was fascinated by what Bayliss had said so far, though she couldn't yet see what events from three hundred years ago had to do with Kulsay today.

Carter shrugged and sat back in his seat.

'Thank you,' Bayliss said. 'Where was I?'

'*The German*,' Kirby said.

'Ah, yes, *The German*. Klaus Meyer, not actually a German at all. He was born in St. Wolfgang in Austria, but his parents moved to Dresden when he was a child. His family was very strictly Catholic and he entered the Seminary when he was in his late teens. He progressed quickly and by the time he was twenty-five he'd joined the Jesuits, and within five years he'd risen to the position of spiritual coadjutor. These are members of the Society of Jesus who take a special vow of obedience to the Pope.

'Benedict sent him on a secret mission to Kulsay, to stop the rot, in whatever way he saw fit, on the strict understanding that, to all intents and purposes, he would be working alone, under the radar so there could be no fallout detrimental to the Vatican. He picked the right man for the job. Meyer was a devout Catholic and a purveyor of what's commonly known today as muscular Christianity. He had a reputation for total ruthlessness, and wasn't shy of violence if he believed that violence would get the Catholic faith across to unbelievers.

'Meyer assembled a small team of mercenaries to go with him to Kulsay. These were men he'd used before and whom he trusted implicitly. They in turn were loyal to him, and him alone.

'The first time he went across to Kulsay he went by himself. He had a meeting with Pious Prime. The two men detested each other on sight.'

'What about deMarco?' Jane said. She was absorbed in the story, sitting forward in her seat as if afraid to miss a single word.

'DeMarco stayed out of the way, at least during the initial meeting. But Meyer made it clear to Prime that he would return to the island, and on his next visit deMarco would meet him face-to-face or suffer, as he put it, dire consequences.'

'And did he?' Jane said. 'Meet with deMarco, I mean.'

Bayliss smiled. 'Oh yes, they met.'

'What happened?'

'He went across to Kulsay with two of his men who were essentially acting as his bodyguards. He not only met deMarco but also six others that he called his High Council. The Council included Pious Prime, which didn't sit well with *The German*. Several years later Meyer's journal was unearthed and in it he claimed that on that day he'd met the Devil's Disciples and Satan himself, in the guise of Alphonse deMarco. From what I remember he wrote, "He pretends to be a man, but in fact he is Lucifer in corporeal form. With God at my side I will send him back to Hades where he belongs."'

'They didn't get on then,' John McKinley said with a wry smile.

Bayliss shook his head. 'Among other things he offered deMarco and the others life everlasting through the grace of God. DeMarco told him he had life everlasting already, and that it had nothing to do with the grace of God. That blasphemy was enough for Meyer. He was a proud man and a fanatical Catholic and was not prepared to sit there and listen to such heresy. He went back to the mainland, gathered the rest of his troops and sent them across to Kulsay with the instructions to eradicate deMarco and his followers.'

'Eradicate them?' Jane said.

'Muscular Christianity, as I said. As far as *The German* was concerned he was ridding the world of heretics and blasphemers. That was justification enough.' Bayliss reached down and lifted his mug, put it to his lips then realized it was empty. Seconds later Kirby was at his side with the coffeepot, refilling the mug, her attitude towards him apparently softening by the moment.

'Did Meyer go back over with his men?' McKinley asked.

'Good God, no,' Bayliss said. 'The man was ruthless but he was no fool. He stayed on the mainland; distancing himself and the Church from imminent slaughter. He remained there for a week, every day expecting to hear that the mission had been successful. He heard nothing. Finally, on the eighth day, he went across to the island.'

'What did he find?' Jane said.

'He went, expecting to find carnage. What he found was even more chilling. Of deMarco and his followers there was no sign at all. They had, to all intents and purposes, vanished into thin air. The house was deserted, as was the rest of the island.'

'And his own men?' Carter said. 'The mercenaries?'

'He found the bodies of two of them. The rest had gone. The first he found at deMarco's house. He was sitting in a chair with his throat cut. He was holding a knife and it appeared he'd taken his own life.'

'And the second?'

Bayliss smiled, but it was humorless, a rictus more than a sign of pleasure. 'Meyer found the other man on the grounds of the house, embedded in a tree.'

'What?' Carter said.

'Just his face, chest and knees were visible. The rest of him was in the tree. Meyer described it in his journal. According to him there was no way of telling where the flesh of the man stopped and the bark of the tree began; they had merged into one.'

Jane and Carter exchanged looks. No one in the room said a word. Bayliss continued.

'Meyer returned to Rome. On the one hand the mission

had been a success. DeMarco and his followers had been neutralized, so they were no longer a thorn in Pope Benedict's side. But the mission raised more questions than it answered. Where had deMarco and his people gone? Would they one day reappear to cause more trouble? What had happened to the rest of the mercenaries? Had they all been killed, or had they joined with deMarco? And as for the man in the tree . . . well that was clearly the work of the Devil. Benedict wasn't a happy man.

'But that's the end of that story. At least, that's as far as my research has taken me. DeMarco and his followers never resurfaced. *The German* was sent home in some disgrace and he never worked for the Pope again. He apparently died a few years later in a small village just outside Dusseldorf, a broken man; haunted by nightmares.'

'So what happened to Kulsay after that?' Jane said.

'Well the Catholics gave the place a wide berth and never set foot on the island again, but thirty years or so later a Presbyterian minister called McLeod led a group of settlers over here. They brought a few thousand sheep with them and turned the island into a fairly thriving farming community. They built the church, held regular services, and McLeod took over deMarco's house and turned it into the Manse. For a number of years the place flourished. Until sixty years ago when the entire population vanished. Then nothing until the island was bought by the KDC.'

'So this is the house deMarco built?' Carter said, looking about the room.

CHAPTER THIRTY-TWO

Bayliss said nothing but nodded slowly.

McKinley gave a low whistle. 'And we're stuck here. Isn't that a pisser.'

Jane stepped in. 'Well, thank you for the history lesson, Mr. Bayliss, but I don't see how it moves us forward. It's just given us a few more mysteries to unravel,' she said.

Bayliss frowned at her. 'You're missing the point I'm trying to make,' he said. 'Before I came here you knew nothing about the island. You had no idea what you were up against. Now you do.'

'DeMarco?' She tried but failed to keep the incredulity out of her voice.

'Exactly.' Bayliss tapped his knee with his coffee mug as if to emphasize the point.

'A man who died over three hundred years ago?'

'I didn't say he died. I said that when Meyer offered him life everlasting through God, he said he already had it.'

'Yes, but obviously he was speaking figuratively.' Jane looked at the others to gauge their reaction.

'Do you know that for certain?' Bayliss said. 'Look, what's been happening on the island isn't just happenstance. I believe there's an intelligence controlling events, and I believe that intelligence is Alphonse deMarco.'

'It's a bit of a stretch,' Kirby said. 'But okay. Let's imagine for a moment that you're right and by some means or other deMarco's found a way to . . . to postpone death, where is he now, and what's his motivation?'

'I believe he's still here on Kulsay. As for his motivation, take your pick. Revenge. Anger. Perhaps he wants to strike back at the Church. I don't know for certain.'

'I'm not convinced,' Jane said. 'I think you're clutching at straws; trying to make the facts fit the circumstances.'

'I disagree,' Raj said. 'I think our friend here is right on the money.'

'Raj?' Jane said. 'Do you want to explain what you mean by that?'

With a sigh Raj set his camera down on the table and stared across at her. He cleared his throat. 'Ever since I arrived on the island I've sensed a presence. At first I thought it was the souls of the poor wretches who died here, but I opened up a little . . . not a lot, but enough to work out that, yes, there are troubled spirits here, but they're just background noise. There's another, much stronger presence. It's controlling everything that happens here, and it's controlling the other spirits on the island. He could be right,' he said, pointing to Bayliss. 'Why shouldn't it be deMarco? I take it the rest of you are protecting yourselves?'

No one said anything, but their collective silence answered his question.

'No, that's okay. You're very wise. As I said, I only opened up a little, after Kirby had her vision. I wanted to know what was going on, so I dropped my defenses; only for a few seconds but, believe me, that was enough.'

'What happened?' Bayliss said.

'I'm clairvoyant,' Raj said. 'I get flashes of precognition; ninety-five percent accurate I'd say.'

'So you saw the future? Is that what you're saying?'

'Yes, with an error rate of about five percent.'

'So come on then.' Bayliss needled him. 'What's our future?'

'You don't want to know.' Raj looked away.

'But I do. And I'm sure the rest of them want to know as well.' He looked about the room and saw from their faces he was right. Except for Kirby, who was shaking her head, a look of something close to terror in her eyes.

Raj looked to Carter, Jane and the others. 'Well? Is he right? You want to know our future?'

'I don't,' Kirby said quickly.

A few seconds later Jane said. 'Go ahead, Raj. I think the rest of us want to know. Sorry, Kirby.'

Kirby's face settled into a frown and she turned her back on the group.

Raj picked up the camera, rolling it over and over in his hands. It was a distraction, taking his mind off of what he was about to say next. He took a breath. 'We haven't got one,' he said quietly.

'What?' McKinley said.

'You heard me, John,' Raj said.

There was an edge of panic to Kirby's voice. 'You're wrong, Raj. You must have made a mistake . . . misinterpreted . . .'

'As I said, there's a five percent chance. All I know is that when I looked forward, when I tried to see what lay ahead, there was nothing. A void. Just a black, gaping hole. We don't have a future.'

'No!' Kirby shouted and stood, looking about the room, wild-eyed.

'Kirby,' Jane said. 'Calm down. You're . . .'

She didn't get a chance to finish her sentence. The window to her right exploded, sending a shower of glass across the room. Kirby cried out as needle-sharp splinters embedded themselves in her face. She threw her hands up to her eyes to protect them.

In front of Raj his camera started to vibrate on the wooden table, then it flew across the room, smashing into the bookcase, lens and body separating, back springing open, a brown snake of film escaping and spiraling across the floor.

Icy wind howled through the shattered window, billowing out the drapes, flapping them around like flags. The table started to rock violently. McKinley and Carter leapt from their seats and backed away from it, watching as the table lifted into the air and sailed across the room. Carter ducked as it flew over his head, crashing into the wall above the fireplace, smashing the large square mirror that hung there. More books launched themselves from the shelves, hurtling across the room, pages flapping like demented birds.

Carter grabbed Jane by the arm. 'Let's get out of here!' he yelled above the noise of the wind. He propelled her towards the door and yanked it open. McKinley and Bayliss followed close behind whilst Carter helped Kirby; she still had her hands to her face.

'Hold on to me,' Carter shouted in her ear. Kirby gripped his arm and Carter made his way across the room to the door, dodging the books that were now spinning in a vortex of wind.

At the door Carter glanced back at Raj. He was standing in the center of the room, arms outstretched, an exultant expression on his face.

Jane bustled past him, back into the room. 'Raj!' she yelled.

Carter caught up with her and pulled her back. 'Leave him!'

She shrugged him off furiously. 'We can't just leave him!' she yelled back at him. She took another step towards Raj, whose head swiveled to look at her. His eyes had rolled back into his head, showing only the whites, and his mouth opened. The sound that issued from his open mouth was louder than the wind, louder than the sound of crashing, splintering furniture. It was a scream, a howl, a roar; deafening in its intensity.

Jane clapped her hands over her eyes. The sound seemed to penetrate her body, vibrating, making her bones ache. She sank to her knees, her legs unable to support her. A heavy leather-bound book detached itself from the vortex and flew at her, hitting her on the temple, knocking her sideways.

Carter gripped McKinley by the arm. 'Help me get her out of there!'

The two men barreled into the room, arms up to protect their faces from flying debris. They grabbed Jane under the arms and hauled her backwards out of the room, slamming the door shut behind them.

CHAPTER THIRTY-THREE

Simon Crozier picked up the phone, punched in the number and held the receiver to his ear.

For a moment there was static, and then a mechanical female voice said, *'The number you are trying to reach is currently unavailable.'*

'Dammit!' he said and slammed the phone down. He looked at his watch. He'd been trying to reach Jane Talbot for the last hour without success. The landline was dead and her cell was either switched off or receiving no signal. He'd tried a few of the others on the island with the same result.

The door to his office opened and Martin Impey entered holding a thin blue file. 'I have the information you wanted,' he said.

'Information?' Crozier was distracted. He was trying to decide whether to give Jane more time or to send a helicopter over to Kulsay to take them off.

'The Sorority,' Martin said, holding the file out in front of him. 'Took some digging up.'

Crozier gathered himself and went back to his desk. 'Take a seat,' he said. 'And show me what you have.'

Martin slid the file across the desk and waited while Crozier flicked it open and scanned through the pages.

'Basically it's a group of high-profile women who've banded together to perform charitable acts; hosting celebrity-studded luncheons, sponsoring music recitals, that kind of thing. I can't really see why you're interested in them. There's nothing there to suggest there's anything more to them than just a group of wealthy do-gooders with too much time on their hands.'

Crozier closed the file, then opened it again and pulled out the list of the Sorority's members. 'Miranda Fry,' he said. 'How do I know that name?'

'Sister-in-law of the last U.S. president. She was a bit of a wild child, then she married Sebastian Fry, head of Nexus Communications, and transformed herself, virtually overnight, into a born-again sophisticate.'

'And Felicity Coleman?'

'Widow of Mark Coleman, the astronaut who died in a plane crash back in the eighties.'

'The other names mean nothing to me, except for Celeste Toland.'

Martin sat forward in his seat. 'Ah, now she's interesting. If only for the fact that she has no history.'

'What do you mean?'

'She came to prominence in the early 1980s when she bought out the Haver Corporation. Bought it lock, stock and barrel. But I can't get a line on her in the runup to that. I found an entry for her in the 1963 yearbook at Priestley High School in Connecticut but after that nothing until twenty years later when she arrived fully formed on Wall Street and started making huge waves in the financial circles of the day.'

'But there must be something to show what she was doing with herself for those twenty years. College? University?'

'I agree, there should be something, but there's nothing documented. Maybe she left high school and went abroad to further her education. If that's the case, then it could take days to pick up her trail.'

'At high school she was listed as Celeste Toland?'

Martin nodded.

'So that means she never married.'

'If what you say about her relationship with Jessica Anderson is correct, then that's hardly surprising, is it?' Martin smiled the way men do when talking about women seemingly beyond them.

Crozier grumbled something under his breath that Martin didn't catch. Then he said, 'Surely there was some press when she bought out Haver? There must have been a curious journalist out there anxious to know who this woman was, where she came from.'

'You'd think so, wouldn't you? But I can find nothing, and I've trawled through every database I can think of. Why are you so interested in her anyway?'

'I'm not . . . not her specifically. But the Sorority interests me greatly, and Jessica Anderson's connection to it. This whole Kulsay Island thing has me rattled. I get the feeling the Department is being used and I don't like that, I don't like that at all.'

'Have you heard from Jane? How are things going over there?'

'I heard from her last night. Nothing today. I'm sure

things are fine.' He drummed his fingertips on the desk-top. 'Do another sweep and see if you can turn up any-thing at all on this Toland woman. Anything at all.'

'But. . . .' Martin started to protest.

Crozier cut him off. 'Just try; there may be something you've missed.'

Martin got ready to leave the room. 'It's your call,' he said. He was annoyed that his habitual thoroughness was being questioned.

Crozier watched the office door close, then picked up the phone again. 'Just answer the bloody thing, Jane,' he said.

'The number you are trying to reach is currently unavailable.'

Crozier sighed and cradled the receiver. It could be nothing more than atmospherics blocking the telephone signals. It might be something altogether more sinister. Ei-ther way it was too early to send in a helicopter to airlift them off the island. Jane Talbot needed time to get to the root of what was happening on Kulsay, and she'd be furi-ous if he overreacted and pulled the plug before she had some answers. He just had to be patient.

But patience had never come easily to him. As a young man he'd been very much like Robert Carter; headstrong, impetuous. He'd been invited to join the Department by the incumbent director, Sir George Logan, but he and Logan had clashed many times over Crozier's methodol-ogy. When the time came for Logan to retire the old man had tried to stop Crozier from succeeding him, but by that time Crozier had made some very influential friends in government and his appointment as Director of the De-partment was little more than a formality.

The directorship tempered his more impulsive tenden-cies, and over the years he'd watched himself turn into a clone of Sir George Logan. It was a fact that irritated him intensely, but the behavioral traits were too embedded now for him to do much about it.

He picked up the phone again and looked at it for a long moment, his fingers itching, anxious to punch in Jane Talbot's number. With an effort of will he stopped himself, placed the receiver back on its cradle and swore savagely.

CHAPTER THIRTY-FOUR

Jane's head was throbbing. Blood trickled from the wound, tracing a crimson line down her cheek. Carter and McKinley were still holding her, but they had lain her down on the floor.

She looked at them blearily. 'Did Raj get out?'

The two men exchanged looks. Jane read the message passed from eye to eye. She struggled to sit up. 'You left him in there,' she said angrily, shrugging her shoulders to free herself.

'All that was Raj's doing,' Carter said, jerking his thumb at the closed door. He could still hear the wind whistling around the room and the splintering of furniture.

'Don't be ridiculous. Raj's not a physical medium. His powers are strictly mental.' She got to her feet, impatiently wiping the blood away from her face.

'John, you tell her,' Carter said. He knew McKinley had been as vulnerable as he was to what was in the room.

'He's right,' McKinley said. 'He was controlling everything. It must have affected him when he opened up to the forces in the house.'

Jane glared at him. 'Well I'm not going to abandon him.' She reached for the door.

Carter pulled her back.

Jane spun on her heel and slapped him across the cheek.

'Get your bloody hands off of me!' she said and lurched for the door again.

As her hand gripped the handle the noise stopped. The silence was almost as deafening.

Jane took a breath and turned the handle. The door swung open.

Raj sat on the floor in the middle of the floor, head bowed, one fist rammed into his mouth as if to stop himself from screaming. The library was devastated. Bookshelves were bare, the books themselves turned into confetti that littered every flat surface. Furniture had been turned into kindling, and the drapes, unmoving now, were shredded.

Jane glanced back at the others. 'Wait here. I don't want to freak him out.' She stepped into the room. Raj didn't move, not even to raise his head to acknowledge Jane's presence.

'Raj,' Jane said softly, then spun around, sensing someone behind her. 'I said wait outside,' she said to Carter who had followed her into the room.

'Jane, I really think . . .'

'Just get out of the room, Robert, and leave this to me.' She said it quietly, but her tone left no room for argument.

Carter's shoulders sagged slightly in resignation and he returned to join the others.

'Shut the door,' Jane said.

He looked back over his shoulder. The expression on his face said, *I hope you know what you're doing*. Then he pulled the door shut behind him.

'Have we got a live video feed to the library?' he said to Kirby who was sitting on the floor, hands still clasped to her bleeding face.

Kirby nodded.

'Can you get it on your laptop?' Carter's voice was urgent; there wasn't much time.

Kirby nodded her head again.

'Bring it here. Now.' His voice raised, the manner not allowing any discussion or argument. There could be no delays.

'I'll get it,' Kirby said, casting a concerned glance at Carter.

Kirby returned moments later and flipped open the laptop, punching a few keys. 'There you go,' she said, handing the computer to Carter.

Carter studied the image on the screen. Raj was sitting in the middle of the floor, head bowed, Jane two paces away from him. Jane's mouth was working.

'Can you get sound as well?' Carter said.

Kirby reached across and hit another two keys. Jane's voice issued from the laptop's inadequate speakers. She sounded tinny and far away.

'. . . blame yourself for this, Raj. We're all under a lot of stress.'

Silence. Jane took a step towards him.

'We must talk about it,' Jane said. 'Or at least talk to Robert. He'll know the best way to proceed.'

Carter winced at this. He had no idea what had just happened, and was at a loss to know what to do next. He watched Jane move closer still to Raj. The man wasn't responding. He could be carved from stone. Carter squinted his eyes to get a closer look at him. He was starting to get a very bad feeling about this. 'Can we zoom in on Raj?'

Again Kirby reached over and pressed a couple of keys. The image of the man sitting on the floor filled the screen. Carter studied the image closely, and then froze. 'What's that in his hand?'

Kirby zoomed in closer.

Clenched in Raj's bloodied fingers was a shard of glass, six inches long and wickedly pointed.

'Pull back,' Carter shouted.

The camera retreated in time to show Jane crouching down in front of Raj.

'Jane, no!' he shouted and, tossing the laptop to Kirby, ran to the door, wrenching the handle. Locked. He started beating on it with his fist. 'Jane! Get out of there!' He remembered the broken window. There was still a chance. He pushed through the others and ran to the front door.

In the library Jane glanced back at the door with irritation. She turned back to Raj who had now raised his head and was staring at her. Raj's lips moved and Jane leaned in closer to catch what he was saying. And as she leaned in Raj lashed out, swinging his arm in a wild arc.

The shard of glass sliced through the soft tissue of Jane's arm, missing the artery but causing blood to pour from the wound.

Jane slapped Raj around the face. The blade of glass fell from his fingers. With an angry roar Jane picked up the glass and swiped it across Raj's neck, severing his windpipe and cutting his carotid artery. As blood pumped from his neck Raj tumbled backwards, hitting the floor, the impact sending a fresh spray of blood into the air. His fingers scrabbled at his throat, trying in vain to close the wound, but the more he struggled the more the air pumped from his lungs and he could feel the warm breeze from his windpipe on his blood-wet fingers.

As he lay there on the carpet, his life draining away in a crimson pool, Raj was changing. His face was shifting, stretching and ageing, until Jane was staring at her mother's disapproving features.

'Such a disappointment, Jane.'

'I know, Mum. I'm sorry.' She moved her lips but spoke the words in her head.

'Such a disappointment.'

Raj's eyelids fluttered shut.

'Raj!' Carter was at the window, frantically trying to haul himself over the sill, but there was still enough glass in the shattered window to impede him. 'Jane!' he shouted.

'You're too late,' Jane said. She was standing now, the bloody shard of glass still gripped tightly in her hand.

Carter stared at her, torn between revulsion and uncertainty. A slow smile spread across her lips. 'Much too late,' she said, and started to sink through the floor. A few feet away from her Raj Kumar gave a final red-speckled exhalation and quietly died.

CHAPTER THIRTY-FIVE

The telephone next to Jessica Anderson's bed rang, waking her from a deep and dreamless sleep. She rolled over and clamped a pillow over her ears but could still hear the shrill electric tone through the thick pad of duck feathers. Eventually she could bear it no longer. She threw the pillow across the room with a curse and grabbed the receiver, pressing it to her ear. 'Yes?' she snapped.

'Jessica, darling, it's Celeste. Did I wake you?' It might have been midday from the alertness in the woman's voice.

'It's three o'clock in the morning, Celeste. Of course you woke me.' She tried to inject a small amount of affection in her words but she felt murderous.

'Good. Be at the airport in an hour.' The alertness was mixed with cold instruction.

Jessica sat upright in bed, the pillow falling onto the floor. 'Are you out of your mind? Why the hell would I want to go to the airport at this time in the morning?'

'Because I have my Lear there, fuelled up and ready to

go. We're going on a trip.' She sounded like a mother presenting an errant daughter with a rare treat.

'A trip? A trip where?' Was this some romantic interlude?

'Scotland. Well, the Lear will take us to Aberdeen Airport; from there we're getting a helicopter to Kulsay.'

Jessica picked up the glass of water sitting on her nightstand and took a sip, washing away the fur on her tongue. 'Celeste, you *are* out of your mind.'

'I've just come from a meeting with the Sorority. It's been agreed that we need a presence on the island, to oversee what's happening there.'

'No, I'm sorry. I'm not flying to Scotland at three o'clock in the morning.'

'Sorry, sweetie,' Celeste said in her honey voice. 'It's a done deal. We're going. Unless, that is, you want to upset the Sorority,' she added silkily. The menace was floating on the surface.

Jessica took the phone away from her ear and glared at it venomously.

'Are you still there?' Celeste said after a long moment.

Jessica sighed and put the receiver back to her ear. 'Yes, I'm still here,' she said, resignation in her voice.

'Fine. See you in an hour then.'

'Yes,' Jessica said, and placed the receiver back on its antique-style cradle.

She threw back the sheets and padded through to the bathroom.

Fifteen minutes later she'd showered and washed her hair. She wouldn't have time to dry it so she pulled it back into a severe ponytail and secured it with a band, then she threw a few changes of clothes into a suitcase, and added half the contents of her dressing table.

When she was packed and dressed she picked up the phone again and hit the intercom button.

It was an age before Jennings, the chauffeur, answered. His voice sounded sleepy.

'Sorry to wake you,' she said. 'I have to go out. Bring the Mercedes round to the front of the house.'

'Where are we going, ma'am?'

'The airport.'

'The airport,' he repeated. 'Very well.'

The Lear was waiting on the runway. Celeste Toland had met her at the entrance to the airport and swept her through passport control with the ease of the heavily in-fluential. As she walked across the tarmac Jessica looked up into the Lear's cockpit. The pilot was young, fresh-faced and wore heavy dark glasses, despite it being the middle of the night. He was reaching up and adjusting something above his head. Then, as if aware he was being watched, he glanced down at Jessica, smiled slightly and threw a salute.

'He looks very young to be flying planes,' Jessica said to Celeste. 'No more than a child.'

Celeste took her arm and guided her towards the steps. 'Don't worry,' the older woman said with a smile. 'Jack-son's very experienced. And I don't just mean his piloting skills.' She gave a throaty chuckle. 'Jealous?'

'What, of Flyboy? Hardly.'

'Good. You needn't be. It's you I love.'

And Jessica didn't believe that either.

At the steps to the Lear, Jessica was surprised to see the rest of the group that called itself the Sorority. They all greeted her warmly but none made a move to get onto the plane.

Eventually Jessica lost her patience. 'You've got me up at the ungodly hour. Can't we at least get on board?'

Several of the women laughed. Celeste laughed with them, which angered Jessica.

Celeste stroked her face. 'Poor Jessica. We don't need to get on board.'

'Celeste, I'm tired. I just want to sleep. What's going on?'

Miranda Fry had opened her purse. 'Celeste, do you want to use mine?'

The older woman shook her head sadly. 'Thank you, no. It has to be mine.'

She opened her own purse and took out a small revolver.

Jessica backed away. 'What . . .'

Celeste sighed. 'I do genuinely regret this Jessica, though you won't believe me. The Sorority doesn't need you anymore. We have our passage to Kulsay. You'd only be, I am afraid to say, a hindrance.' She hesitated, almost as if there was genuine regret in her actions. 'I would always have to doubt your allegiance wouldn't I, Jessica?'

With that she shot Jessica three times in the chest and once in the head.

As Jessica slumped to the tarmac, quite dead, the group of women sank slowly into the ground until there wasn't a sign of them having been there save for the gentle waft of Chanel No. 5.

CHAPTER THIRTY-SIX

Robert Carter stood at the broken window and watched Jane Talbot disappear. There was nothing he could do; no way he could turn back the clock. He gave a howl of anguish and sank to his knees. The only woman he had ever truly loved was gone and the man she had just killed was lying dead just a few yards away from him. First Sian, now this. A hand rested on his shoulder.

'There was nothing you could have done.' John McKinley's words echoed his thoughts.

He looked up at McKinley's handsome black face. There was compassion in the other man's eyes; compassion and sadness.

'I watched it on the computer,' McKinley said. 'It all happened so fast.'

'Did you see what happened to Jane?' Carter said. Had it all been recorded?

'Gone. If it was Jane. I'm beginning to doubt that it was. Come on, let's get back inside.' He helped Carter to his feet and together they walked back to the front door.

Kirby and Bayliss were sitting on the floor. Bayliss's hands were covering his face; Kirby was weeping, fat tears rolling down her cheeks. She made no effort to wipe them away.

'Have you tried the door again?' McKinley said, as they stood outside the library.

Bayliss shook his head. The laptop was on the floor beside him, the picture on the screen a moment frozen in time. Raj lying dead on the floor of the devastated library. He looked peaceful in death, as if he was merely sleeping. Only the red gash at his throat tainting the image. Carter bent down and closed the screen, then went to the door and turned the handle. The door opened easily.

Crouching down beside Raj's body he reached out and brushed a strand of hair away from his face. As he stared down at the serene face his heart wrenched and a choking sob broke from his throat. Awful as he felt about not being able to save Raj, he couldn't help but feel more grief at losing Jane. He closed his eyes and let the memories of her come flooding back into his mind; memories he'd repressed since the end of their affair.

Jane, eyes wide with awe as she stood, staring out over the city from the top of the London Eye. Jane, laughing with abandon at the Marx Brothers when he'd taken her to a National Film Theatre screening of *Horse Feathers*. Jane, her face illuminated with soft candlelight, gazing at him lovingly across the table in their favorite restaurant in Soho. His fingers tracing the line of her cheek as she lay beneath him the first time they'd made love. The petulant tilt of her chin when he'd said something that displeased her.

So many memories jostling for space in his mind. How could he have let her go? Why did he let the work they shared come between them? He realized suddenly that he had wasted much of his life. It was a crushing thought, but a true one. Priorities. He'd always made them, shuffling the elements of his life into a certain running order. As their relationship continued, and he started to feel comfortable and secure in it, he'd let her slip down that list of priorities and allowed other elements to take her place. And as he let her slip through his fingers, she'd been easily seduced by the attention of someone else—her husband.

The others stood back in the doorway, allowing him this private moment.

It was McKinley who took charge. He instructed Kirby to copy whatever images and sounds were on the laptop so they had backup records. It gave him great pleasure to tell Bayliss to make coffee for them all, and after what had happened he wasn't surprised he got no resistance.

In the library McKinley helped Carter move Raj's body. For want of any better ideas they rolled it in a Persian rug and laid it as gently as they could on a couch.

'Let's go get that coffee,' McKinley said.

'I'm not sure . . .'

McKinley clasped a large hand on Carter's shoulder. 'It wasn't an idle suggestion. You need to be with the others.'

Carter half nodded, half shrugged and followed the big man out, through the hallway, and into the bar area.

Bayliss had four mugs of coffee lined up on the bar counter. Kirby was warming her hands on one of them.

Carter walked across to her. 'How's your face?' There were a few cuts and scratches on her cheeks and her forehead was coated in blood.

Kirby attempted a smile but it looked more like a grinning Halloween mask. 'How could Jane kill Raj?'

He walked behind the bar, wet a clean cloth with cold water, and then began to wipe the blood from her face. 'It wasn't Jane . . . not consciously.'

Kirby leaned her face to one side so he could finish cleaning her up. 'Is she dead?'

Carter laid the cloth down on the counter and picked up one of the coffees. 'There, that's as good as new.'

Bayliss was seated at one of the tables, spinning his finger in a warm wet circle made by his mug. 'He can't answer your question because he doesn't know.'

Carter led Kirby across to a chair near Bayliss and motioned for McKinley to join them.

When all four were seated Carter said, 'We've heard your story, Bayliss. Now it's my turn to tell you what I know.'

CHAPTER THIRTY-SEVEN

Carter wrapped his hands around the mug of hot coffee and looked at the faces staring at him. He had no idea what they were expecting from him. They were going to be told a mixture of speculative conjecture based on what he had read, facts extracted from his recent research, and intuition. Personally he trusted the last one the most but doubted they would share his faith.

Kirby looked younger than ever; almost like a child waiting for her father to tell a favorite story, only Carter wasn't sure this time there would be a happy ending. McKinley was impassive, his strong features seemingly relaxed, although Carter could tell by the pulses at his throat and temple that he was struggling to keep his emotions inside. Only Bayliss seemed relaxed, smiling as he breathed in the aroma of his coffee.

Carter took a sip of his drink, breathed out through his nose and summoned his thoughts. 'Judaism originated in Israel about four thousand years ago; Christianity, both Protestant and Catholic, takes a lot from Judaism. Incidentally so does Islam.

'Jews believe there is only one God, who created the Universe, and keeps it going for all time. God has always existed, and always will. God cannot be seen or touched but can be reached through worship. God chose the Jewish people as his special people and to be an example to the world.

'Judaism doesn't have any set doctrines, or creeds; it's a religion that follows *Torah* which is guidance from God found in the scriptures. Humans are made in the image of God, and should try to seek holiness in everything they do every day.'

Bayliss caught Carter's gaze and rolled his eyes to the ceiling. 'There's a point to this?'

Carter ignored him. 'All Jews have an affinity to Israel, the land God promised to Abraham and to the holy city of Jerusalem. Jews are divided according to their beliefs and practices and also to their racial origins; some, the *Ashkenazi* Jews, having roots in central Europe, and others from Spain and the Middle East, the *Sephardic* Jews.

'DeMarco was a *Sephardic* Jew.'

Bayliss snorted in derision. 'There's no evidence for that.'

'None that you found,' Carter said quietly.

Bayliss placed his mug untidily on a small side table and stood. 'I've researched him for years and there are no suggestions that he was anything other than Spanish. Spain has a rich history of explorers and in his way that's what deMarco was about. Only he took it to extremes.'

'I haven't said he wasn't Spanish. Sit down and let me continue. I admire the work you've done, you told me things I hadn't pieced together, but accept that I have an advantage.'

McKinley laughed, a gentle bass rumble. 'He means his psychic ability.'

'It allows him to get into corners ordinary research can't reach,' Kirby said.

When Bayliss was seated again Carter began speaking. 'During the time of the Spanish Inquisition Jews living in Spain were persecuted for their faith. To continue living there many of them lived a double life of pretending to be Catholics but secretly practicing their real religion in private. Because Catholicism was considered the one true faith many Jews became *conversos*, people who actually converted to Catholicism but still practiced Judaism underground. Those who refused conversion were tortured and killed.

'Those who converted but secretly maintained their true faith were called *Marranos*. In Spanish this means pig; it's taken from the Arabic *muharram,* which means ritually forbidden, based on the Jewish, and Muslim of course, habit of not eating pork.

'Many Jews did actually convert to Christianity but they were never fully accepted. The *conversos* on the surface were practicing Catholics; they went to Mass, but didn't embrace the faith. They still ate no pork, celebrated Passover, and gave oil to the synagogue. The *Marranos* employed a man to slaughter the animals, drain away the blood and deliver the meat, and another man to secretly perform their circumcisions.

'The large numbers of the *conversos*, and especially their wealth and influence naturally aroused the envy and even the hatred of the Spanish Catholic population. The New Christians, those who actually converted, were hated the most, but all the *Marranos* were persecuted. In the fifteenth and sixteenth century there were many attacks and riots because of religious bigotry.'

Carter paused while Kirby and McKinley made some fresh coffee and sandwiches.

'Smoke?' Carter offered Bayliss while they waited for the others.

Bayliss shook his head. 'One of the few vices I've managed to avoid.'

'You see where I'm headed with this?' Carter said, drawing the smoke deeply and dangerously.

'You can't have positive proof. Most of your conclusions will be supposition at best.'

Another cigarette was lit from the end of the first. 'Partly, but don't underestimate my powers. They've let me research this in ways you won't have been able to. You've done well; what you told us confirmed most of what I've found out.'

McKinley and Kirby came back in with two trays, one of coffee and one of ham and cheese sandwiches.

'Cigarette out please, Robert,' Kirby said as she brought over a mug of coffee and plate of food. She smiled at him as he took them from her.

When they were settled again, and Carter had devoured half his sandwich, he began talking.

'In Spain the Jews were gradually placed in ghettos and

ended up living apart from the *Marranos*. The two communities continued to communicate, with the unconverted Jews trying to keep the *conversos* faithful to Judaism.

'Constantly persecuted during the Inquisition, most *conversos* tried desperately to leave the country. This wasn't easy, although many fled to Italy, ironically the country that houses the Pope. Fanatical Popes imprisoned the *conversos*; those who didn't convert were burned in public executions.

'In Spain a certain group of *Marranos* began to embellish their Judaism. Living in houses of secrets they looked for outlets beyond their Jewish faith. Practicing in secret meetings they began to adopt the ancient and mysterious ways of Kabbalah.

'Kabbalah is considered to be the world's oldest set of spiritual wisdoms. Believers say it contains the long hidden keys to the secrets of the universe as well as the ways to unlock the mysteries of the human heart and soul. Kabbalah details how to navigate the whole world, physical and metaphysical, to stave off every form of chaos, pain and suffering. It teaches that every human being is born with the capacity of greatness and that Kabbalah is the way to activate that greatness.

'Kabbalah is meant to be used every day; remember how that links to the Jewish ideal. Kabbalah has as its purpose to bring clarity to the world, make people free to live to their full potential and ultimately to erase even death itself.'

Carter finished his coffee, lit another cigarette, and looked at each of them in turn. 'DeMarco was a *Marrano*. He took the path to Kabbalah but he twisted it out of all recognition. Bitter at the persecution he saw against his family he pursued the path towards erasure of death, and . . .'

'And succeeded,' Bayliss said, with a kind of awe.

CHAPTER THIRTY-EIGHT

'Kabbalah literally means *receiving* and what it does is interpret the Hebrew Bible or *Tanakh*, as well as classical Jewish texts such as *halakha* and *aggadah*, and various practices or *mitzvot*. By doing that it tries to be a doctrine by which people can live full and satisfying lives within God's omnipotence.

'The eighteenth century saw an explosion of Kabbalah, but by then deMarco was already well established and practicing his own brand of the faith. One of the aspects of Kabbalah is the belief that Jewish and non-Jewish souls are different. While all human souls emanate from God, non-Jewish or gentile souls originate from the left side of God and therefore all non-Jews have a dark or demonic side to them that is absent in Jews.

'That probably started as defense against the persecution suffered over the centuries by Jews who were called the servants of Satan, and characterized as nonhumans. But at the time Kabbalah taught that Jews had additional layers of the soul that others did not. Obviously this interprets itself as sounding superior and they were perceived as arrogant.'

Kirby leaned forward, holding her hand up uncertainly as if a pupil in class. 'Sorry to interrupt, Robert, but there are almost two hundred years between the Inquisition and the events on Kulsay between deMarco and *The German*.'

'He's saying deMarco went deep underground as a *Marrano* in the sixteenth century, twisted his Judaism into a version of Kabbalah, especially the escape from death bit, and then proved that Jews have a dark and demonic side as well,' Bayliss said. 'It's fascinating stuff, Carter, I'll give you that. You'll expect me to poke fun at your theory but I'm going to disappoint you. Rather than what I told you earlier confirming what you already thought it's the other way round. You've just given me a way that deMarco could achieve eternal life.'

'I'm not your enemy, Bayliss,' Carter said.

McKinley stood and walked across to the window. 'So I've got this straight,' he said. 'DeMarco became bitter at the treatment his people received from the Catholics. He had to be a Jew in secret but that wasn't enough for him; he found Kabbalah, only he used what he wanted from its teachings to escape death. He left Spain, eventually winding up in Scotland and Kulsay. Even there he was pursued by the forces of the Pope.'

'So his hatred of Catholics was doubled,' Kirby said.

Carter nodded. 'When he disappeared after the battle with *The German* my guess is he didn't die. I'd put money on him hiding underground, literally, using ley lines.'

Bayliss stood and crossed over to the bar. 'Drink, anyone?'

Kirby went across to help him. 'Okay, so if we believe deMarco is still alive somewhere, what's he been waiting for?'

McKinley banged the glass of the window and everyone looked at him.

'I went to see my wife after she died,' he said. 'They take you to the morgue and lead you through to a quiet room. It's very cold, and smells of swimming pools and toilets. A green sheet covers the body, and the lights are very bright and the walls are very white. I could see blood dripping from the walls but it wasn't really there. I just imagined it coming out of her and coating the walls. They ask you if you're ready and you say you are, but you'll never be ready, and then they pull back the top of the sheet and ask you if this is the person. And it was. Only when the man pulled the sheet back over her head I could see that there was someone else on the bed with her, a kind of shadow man. I shouted and tried to pull the sheet off again but of course they just thought I was hysterical and dragged me away. Then I saw him slip down from the trolley and smooth himself into a corner of the room. He was dressed in black and was very thin so no one else could see him, and he was pointing.

'I looked where he was pointing, and there were other shadows. I'm sure the shadow I saw scurrying beneath a bed was just that, a shadow, but it seemed real. The lighting in the ward was dubious, and no one likes the atmosphere of hospitals. It's always a bit disturbing even for the most levelheaded of people. But I was upset and everyone else was calm but very insistent. I was ushered away but not before I saw a black shape take up its position directly at the foot of my wife's bed. Not before I saw the man shadow pull himself as close to the bed as he could. As the room fell into a hospital slumber the shadow at the foot of the bed sloped forward and covered my wife like an eiderdown, but one that soaked into her body until it disappeared and my dead wife swelled slightly from within.'

McKinley suddenly sat on a chair away from the others. With head bowed as if in prayer, he seemed shrunken.

Carter turned to Kirby and Bayliss. 'John is telling me that he thinks I'm right.'

'Come on then,' Bayliss said. 'Right about what?'

'DeMarco has been recruiting people for one more battle. Dead people mainly, but if there weren't enough of those he takes them anyway. Like the management team from Waincraft. Like the crofters. Like Jane.'

Bayliss walked to the bar and poured himself another

large whisky. 'And deMarco is performing this recruitment drive here on Kulsay, is that it?'

Carter pointed to the floor. 'Not *on* Kulsay; under it.'

Kirby coughed. 'What I don't understand, well there's loads of it really, but if deMarco is Jewish, a convert or whatever, and his grievance is against the Catholic Church, why is he recruiting non-Jews, and even Catholics?'

Bayliss threw his glass to the floor where it smashed like childhood dreams. 'Come on, deMarco!' he shouted at the top of his voice. 'Come on, Alphonse. Are you up for recruiting a shit like me? I'm a true challenge, a real non-believer. Can you . . .'

There was a sound like jelly being poured from a jug and McKinley called out, 'Carter.'

Everyone turned to the window where McKinley was sitting; only he wasn't seated comfortably. His feet had sunken into the ground almost up to his knees so that he was slumped forwards, half on and half off his chair.

Carter stood but before he could move across to him McKinley motioned him to stay where he was.

'I tried to stop myself from sinking into the floor,' McKinley said. 'But it didn't work. I had to use my ability to keep whatever it is at bay. You won't be able to pull me out without using your psychic power.'

Kirby put her hand on Carter's shoulder. 'Which means opening yourself up, and making yourself vulnerable to attack.'

'Come on,' Bayliss said. 'We can pull him out if we work together.' He bustled over to McKinley, standing behind the chair, and grasped the large man's shoulders. 'Push back, John.'

'No,' Carter said. 'You'll break his concentration and we'll lose him.'

Kirby took Bayliss by the arm and guided him away. 'Leave Robert to deal with it.'

Carter closed his eyes. McKinley stared at him for a moment and then closed his. Kirby was certain she could feel an energy buzz in the room, like an electric generator humming a monotonous tune. McKinley began to move his head up and down like a mockery of nodding. Then his upper body joined in so that he was rocking forwards and backwards in the chair as if demented. Carter raised his arms in the air, spread them and then thrust them hard against his side.

McKinley rocked forwards so far that it looked as if he was going to fall on his face. Then he propelled back again, hit the chair hard, and his feet and legs reared up until they were over his head. The floor where he had been encased was rippling as if liquid. It looked like a crystal clear surface of water and Bayliss couldn't take his eyes away from the figures and shapes he could see. The motion of McKinley's body carried his legs over his shoulders and he fell backwards out of the chair.

His eyes opened at the same time as Carter's.

'Did you see them?' Bayliss said. 'Did you look into the . . .'

McKinley walked over to Carter and thrust out his hand. 'I owe you.'

Carter shook his hand and then sat down. The forces that had been pulling on McKinley were powerful; not just physically, but their mental strength was strong.

A roar of cracking masonry ripped through the room like the cry of a wounded animal. The walls of the Manse began to buckle as if being squeezed, and slowly but certainly a hole began to form in the floor at their feet.

CHAPTER THIRTY-NINE

The hole was perfectly symmetrical. Small at first; gradually it widened out, never deviating from its circular shape, never getting distorted. If the movement of it opening had been accompanied by music it would have been Mendelssohn's Scottish Symphony, the lavish Fingal's Cave.

McKinley placed an arm across Bayliss, indicating they should both move away from the lip of the hole. Carter took hold of Kirby's arm and all four of them moved towards the door. The floor was all but gone now, and the hole opened almost as wide as the room. From within the hole they could see flames, though there was little heat; and there were screams.

'It's Dante's Inferno,' Bayliss said.

'Only it's deMarco, not Dante,' Carter said, and as he spoke the outer wall of the room broke in two and pieces of the masonry fell into the opening. Great plumes of smoke and flame billowed up, eager tongues of fire.

'The ceiling,' McKinley shouted, and the whole of the ceiling began to collapse downwards.

They rushed out of the room and into the entrance hall. The staircase had fallen in on itself; the windows were shattered, great panes of glass hanging in cracked arrangements of irregular pattern. The marble floor tiles were popping up, one by one, as if pushed from beneath.

Carter turned to face the others. 'We need to get out of here, and fast.'

'What are we waiting for?' Bayliss said and moved to run.

Carter held a hand to the man's chest. 'They'll try to stop us.'

The front door crashed open, the force flinging the heavy oak hard against its hinges, pulling them from the wall.

Bayliss pointed. 'That doesn't look like we're being prevented from leaving. That looks like an invitation to me.' Then he heard a voice calling his name. 'Did you hear that?'

Then his name again, ahead of him now, through the door, a faint hissing voice, terrifying in its malevolence.

'Doesn't sound like an invitation now, does it?' Kirby said. The voice was angry and demanding.

Carter could see the trees and the garden to the front of the Manse, but it was in the distance, and the scene seemed blurred, out of focus, as if his eyes were covered in gauze.

Despite the dangers he knew they couldn't stay in the house. At first he had thought the collapse was intended to kill them all. Now he realized it was merely designed to get them out into the open. 'Come on,' he said. 'We'll have to risk it. We can't stay here.'

He clapped Bayliss on the back, and lightly took hold of Kirby's hand.

He ran on, as the sudden silence of the house overwhelmed him. There was no sound in the place at all, no screams from the opened floor in the bar, no loud rumblings as the walls crumbled. He was conscious of a slapping sound as his feet hit the floor, but even that sound was sucked away until all he could hear was the blood rushing in his ears.

Progress was painfully slow. Although he was conscious of running with all the speed his body could muster, the front door never seemed to get any nearer, and gradually he became aware that the floor under his feet was becoming soft. He seemed to be sinking into the tiles with each step he took. Almost as if he was running through sand, and at the edge of the sand was water, deep water waiting to claim him.

Voices began to clamor in his head. *Let yourself go, Robert. Let your body sink into the floor. We're waiting for you.*

He looked around at the others and it was as if they were running in slow motion, fierce effort burned into their faces, but they didn't seem to be moving.

The voices whispered in his ear again, joined this time by other voices, each calling his name, cursing him, vilifying him. Too exhausted to reply to them he ran on, wanting only to reach the outside.

The floor tiles confounded him. They were rippling and buckling, pitching and twisting, sucking at his feet, tripping him. His foot caught on the edge of a tile and he tumbled forwards, splinters of cracked marble embedding themselves in his palms as he stretched out his hands to break his fall. All around him the air was alive with whispers and cries, and gradually the visibility was diminishing.

He felt strong hands lifting him. 'Come on, man,' McKinley said. 'We're almost there.'

Carter looked back to the entrance of the bar, where the walls had gone and black flutters of what looked like burned paper floated in the air.

Kirby screamed. A pillar of mist was spinning towards them, thrusting forward along the walls as if for support. A gray swirling vortex coming at them with great speed, all the while hissing their names over and over again in a whispered chant. It was as if there were thousands of voices caught up in a swirling dance, shouting and calling out in every language on earth.

As the vortex drew nearer Carter could see that it was far more solid than he had imagined. The mist wasn't spreading across the entrance hall, as he'd expected, but was confined to its center, with a definite purpose about its course, which was directly towards him. The mist had a raw shape, which Carter realized was the shape of a man, though the edges were indistinct, with flailing arms and the appearance of a roughly defined mouth.

What the hell is that?

McKinley spoke the words directly into his thoughts, but his mind was so concentrated he couldn't reply.

Bayliss and Kirby were out of the house. They flopped down on the grass, panting like greyhounds after a race. McKinley was at the door, waiting for Carter, who was a few feet behind. He turned and knew that the mist had him trapped, pushing him along the wall, forcing him into it; he was terrified to touch it or to let it engulf him. He felt the wall at his back, and looked down in horror at the floor. It was beginning to dissolve. Behind him the wall was starting to give way, embracing him, welcoming him inside.

'Take my hand,' McKinley shouted at him, struggling to be heard above the noise.

Carter reached out, and stretched his fingers towards McKinley's.

Long flailing arms extended out from the mist, cracking forwards, clawing through the air at Carter.

McKinley had one hand on the frame of the door, the other pulling out towards Carter. The long black fingers were accentuated against the pale gray mist. Carter aimed his hand at them and felt the rough tips of McKinley's fingers.

It felt as if the wall was sucking him into it, while at his feet the floor was spinning out of control.

Carter's fingers locked onto McKinley's and with a

fierce pulling motion McKinley peeled Carter away from the wall; he carried on pulling and the swirls of mist began to melt away. Carter forced his other arm onto McKinley's and with a final effort both men were out of the house and lying on the grass with the others.

They all watched in silence as the house imploded. It fell in on itself with the roof wavering with indecision before collapsing inside the walls. Then the walls, already moving as if reeds blowing in the wind, fell forwards in a tired and slow fall from grace. Dust and debris heaved up into the air, mimicking the mist that had threatened Carter.

'That's that then,' Bayliss said.

Carter shook his head. 'Far from it. That's just the beginning.'

'But the Manse is the center of deMarco's world. Now it's gone,' Bayliss said.

'The house was the center but it's not the entrance. That's somewhere else.'

They sat on the grass as the dusk slowly surrounded them, shimmering with shadows.

Kirby plucked blades of grass and split them with her fingernails. She was thinking about Jane Talbot. What she had done, and where she might have gone. Would they see her again? Jane was the only person she had been able to talk to, really open up to about her feelings. The things she had shared with her about Malcolm and the baby had been locked inside her for so long that it had been a welcome release to let it all out.

Bayliss realized he had been terrified during most of the preceding hours. For all the research he had done, for all the knowledge he thought he possessed, nothing had prepared him for the reality once the horrors had begun. All the stories his grandfather had told him came flooding back, washing over him like exhaustion. The truth was that up until a few hours ago Kulsay had been something of a myth to him. A fairy story conjured in his imagination from old tales and whispered recollections. Now that reality had been tasted the sourness of what he'd seen was far worse than what he had learned.

Carter stood. 'I know where the entrance is,' he said. 'Where we have to go to finish this.'

McKinley turned round on the grass so that he was facing him. 'I'm ready. Where are we going?'

'The abandoned church,' Carter said. 'It's about fifteen minutes from here.'

CHAPTER FORTY

'Hang on,' Bayliss said. 'Finish it? Who says we want to do anything other than get the hell out of here?'

Kirby was brushing the grass from her jeans. 'We're here to do a job, Nick, we need to find those people.'

Carter lit a cigarette, the flame from the lighter emphasizing how dark the evening had become. 'Kirby's right, but it's more than that now, surely you must know that?'

There were some dull thumps as the final death throes of the Manse played out behind them. The grass beneath their feet felt cool and fresh after the heat from the house. A full moon gave some light but ahead of them the woods were black and filled with trees waving like masts of sailing boats at harbor.

Bayliss had a worried look on his face. 'You talk about "an entrance." An entrance to what?'

'To wherever deMarco is; to wherever he's keeping

Sian . . . and . . . God knows who else.' Carter couldn't bring himself to say her name, just in case Jane was lost to him forever.

'I've lived and breathed deMarco for as long as I can remember,' Bayliss said. 'When my grandfather wasn't filling my head with fanciful stories about Satanists and devil worship on Scottish islands, I was filling in the gaps from reading and surfing the Net. Remember those poor kids that got taken into care a few years ago because an overzealous social worker had found out a surefire way to check for sexual abuse? A whole community on the islands was forced to lose their children into care for years. Some of them still haven't been returned even when the woman was shown to be wrong, so wrong.

'I thought I was waiting for my chance to ride onto Kulsay on my white horse and save the day. Only it's night, not day, I haven't ridden a horse in over twenty years, and I'm scared to investigate anymore. I'm frightened of what I'm going to find.'

McKinley shifted his legs on the grass, where he was sprawled out as if at a leisurely picnic. 'I used to be like you,' he said.

'What? White?' Bayliss said.

A shadowy smile that touched his eyes showed McKinley took no offense. 'No, scared. I thought too much. Before any investigation, any possible haunting, I used to wonder, what if it gets me this time? What if it wants me and I'm not strong enough to stop it? Then I realized what the *it* was.'

Bayliss looked at the night-black face and was impressed by the calmness contained in the features. Whether the control went further than skin deep he couldn't tell but it was impressive to even appear relaxed under their circumstances. 'Go on then; what was your *it*?'

McKinley grunted, a kind of resigned acceptance. 'My

own limitations. I was scared I wouldn't be able to handle whatever was thrown at me. I was limiting my actions by imagining boundaries. Once you realize you can take on anything, if you react in the right way nothing should be able to restrict you.'

'I didn't take you for the "positive thought conquers all" type.'

McKinley shook his head. 'It's not that. It's being open to all possibilities once you're in a situation. Don't let fear or convention put shackles on your ability to improvise and take effective action.'

Bayliss let out a long drawn-out sigh. 'Sounds fine, except for one thing.'

Carter had been listening to what they were saying, and it was him who said, 'What thing?'

Bayliss stood and looked at the trees and their suffocating blackness. 'You three have abilities to help you handle what we might come across; I don't.'

'Just use your sarcasm,' Kirby smiled. 'That'll get them every time.'

CHAPTER FORTY-ONE

Carter only had a vague idea where the abandoned church was; so as they set out they took it slowly and carefully. After what they had experienced already they were wary of every step they took, fearful the ground might open up in front of them. Nervous the night might swallow them and they would join the legion of the lost.

There was something else that scared Carter. Since Jane had gone he couldn't concentrate. He had nearly paid the penalty for that inside the house. However hard he tried he couldn't shake thoughts of Jane out of his head. It was as if she had lodged there like a physical entity, stopping him from thinking clearly. He tried to picture the church in his mind to pinpoint its location, and all he could see was Jane in her wedding dress running back down the aisle, away from the altar and the priest, running from her husband; returning to Carter. It wouldn't happen now, and probably never would have.

He edged his way through the bracken beneath the trees and in his imagination he was walking hand in hand with Jane through a wood of dappled sunlight, the branches letting the rays of the sun filter through softly, like sifting flour through a sieve. Her loss was a dull ache inside him and he realized that the years he had spent without her had been a huge mistake; a loss he would never be able to recover.

'How much further do you think?' Kirby asked, and her voice brought him back to the present, to reality. Jane had gone and he would never see her again. The others, the remaining three people relied on him. Sure, McKinley and Kirby had powers they could use, although Bayliss didn't. But even with their combined skills Carter knew they were in for one hell of a battle.

'Robert?' Kirby prompted. She was behind him, with Bayliss behind her, and McKinley bringing up the rear.

'We've gone east since the house, and we've been walking about fifteen minutes. By rights it should be just ahead.' It was difficult to see clearly in the dark, although the moon was almost full and lent enough light to see the trees and the shadows around them.

'He's right,' Bayliss said. 'I passed it on my way to the Manse, and I recognize these rocks.' He pointed to a linear formation of granite rocks on the perimeter of a small clearing. 'I think these were some early form of staging post.

Marking the route from the crofters' village to their place of worship.'

Carter bent and examined the larger of the rocks. 'These predate the crofters. These are more the kind of markers that lined the early indicators for the Leys.'

McKinley looked behind, back through the trees. 'I guess we thought the ley lines you were talking about centered on the house, seeing as that's where deMarco spent his time. What if we were wrong? The ley lines converge on the church?'

Standing and stretching, Carter said, 'Many churches are built on ancient sites of worship. Most can be traced back beyond even their earliest apparent architecture. In England, don't forget, those are Protestant places of worship. The Catholic churches are much more modern affairs, and they get built wherever local council planning permission can be granted.'

'So the ley lines are nothing to do with it?' Kirby said.

Carter shook his head. 'On the contrary; the ley lines are how the Jesuits travel from Rome to wherever they're needed.'

Bayliss sat on one of the rocks. He looked tired. 'Physically travel along them you mean?'

'Absolutely,' Carter said. 'I've traced them over Britain, through Europe, even across the Atlantic.'

McKinley whistled softly. 'The U.S.?'

Carter nodded. 'Probably further afield than that; Asia, China . . . I didn't have the time to research it for long enough.'

'And the church here on Kulsay is a key point of the ley lines that converge from Rome . . . and where else? Much as I'd love to believe my precious island is the cornerstone of all that defines evil . . .' Bayliss said. He was fighting for more energy, a second wind so he could keep up with the others.

Kirby smiled at him. Despite her better judgment she liked the sarcastic Scot.

'Believe it, Bayliss,' Carter said. 'What we're going up against is going to make everything you've found out about your island seem like a stroll in the park.'

CHAPTER FORTY-TWO

A few minutes after they left the clearing, a few minutes more walking through the trees in the dark, the contours of the ground changed and rough scree replaced the spare grass and coarse thistle. The land dipped away before lifting in an embankment that rose up like the gentle swell of a wave at sea.

Here lay the ruined walls of the old church. Dull green ivy crawled over the damaged walls, righteousness reclaiming its devotion. Pale blue heather dotted the doorway as if it were confetti after a wedding, although it had been a long time since this place had witnessed happiness. An air of sadness hung over the whole area, a desolation that might be annotated on a Victorian mezzotint of the scene with the inscription: *Abandon Hope All Ye Who Enter Here.*

'Can you hear it?' McKinley said.

Kirby shook her head. 'I can't hear a thing.'

'Exactly. For the past half hour or so we've heard an owl, loads of shuffling about in the undergrowth that Carter here told us was foxes, and badgers, and God knows what British wildlife. We heard our own footsteps on the brush, snapping twigs, pushing back branches. Now we can't even hear our own breathing.'

Bayliss stamped his foot on a thistle. It slumped beneath his boot but there was no sound. They all listened and realized McKinley was right; the night sounds had stopped outside the perimeter of the church. It was as if the night was holding its breath, paying its fearful respects.

Carter walked across to the door of the church. It leaned drunkenly against the remains of the side wall, the heavy oak weathered but solid. He paced around the outside wall, peering in as best he could through the stained-glass window. Back at the door he moved a few paces inside.

'Careful, Robert,' McKinley warned.

The inside of the church was damp and dreary. The few remaining pews were upended, a couple of mildewed hymnbooks strewn across the flagstoned floor. Mould crept up one wall, while what seemed to be a colony of bats made a black smudge in one corner of the half-collapsed roof. The altar was smashed; pieces of stone laid about like broken teeth. A large bronze cross was upside-down in the center of the altar, embedded in the stone as if it was Arthur's sword.

At the far end of the nave was what seemed to be a faint light.

Carter pointed. 'That's where we go in.'

Bayliss stood shoulder to shoulder with him in the doorway. 'Surely it'll just lead to a vestry? A room where the minister would have put on his sacraments, and kept his records.'

'That was the original purpose, but since the church was abandoned it's become the entrance.'

Bayliss took a step backwards. 'Entrance to what?'

Carter called the others forwards. 'That's what we're going to find out.'

CHAPTER FORTY-THREE

An odor of dead things wafted through the gray air, seeping into their clothes, making their eyes water.

There was only faded light coming from the far end of the church, behind the ruined altar. The rest of the interior of the ancient building was cloaked in darkness, from the night and from the memories of past deeds. Spirits of evil danced around them, unseen, touching their faces like a soft summer breeze, but tainting and taunting them, mocking their readiness for what lay beneath the ground.

Carter led them. He had confined his thoughts of Jane to a locked compartment in his brain, sure it would be opened, and stay open, when this was over, but determined to focus all his powers on fighting the good fight.

He had risked probing with his mind, sending his psychic swords into the opening behind the light. There had been fierce energy, flashing and fizzing without restraint, but ill defined, just a mass of uncoordinated movement.

Together, as a group, they reached the back of the church and entered the small damp room that used to serve the various clergy as a changing and store room. Dusty shelves against the walls were empty now of everything apart from mouse droppings. The floor was strewn with leaves and mould, the combination making it slippery underfoot.

In here it was apparent where the source of the light was coming from. The end wall had a fissure in it several feet wide; it was only still standing because it leant drunkenly on the sturdy side walls. Through the break in the wall there shined a bright white light that seemed artificial in its intensity.

'Where the hell is the light coming from?' Bayliss asked.

'Hell might be right,' McKinley said.

Carter placed his hand on one edge of the cracked wall. It felt cold to the touch, like a long-buried corpse. The light was intense but it wasn't blinding, and he was able to see beyond it. He could see rough sides of what looked like a long stone tunnel that sloped downwards so that he could only see the first few yards before darkness took over.

'There's a tunnel,' he said.

'Do we have to go down it?' Kirby said, and the tone of her voice gave its own response.

There was a sound like knuckles crunching and the front door of the church fell off its hinges and crashed to the ground.

'There's your answer, if you needed one,' Carter said.

The remainder of the portion of the roof over the main body of the church dropped to the floor and gray dust billowed upwards like empty shrouds tossed in the air.

Carter looked at McKinley and the big American nodded. McKinley lightly took hold of Bayliss's shoulder and Carter gently folded his arm around Kirby's waist. As a group, shoulder to shoulder, they stepped through the gap in the wall and entered the light.

The white light swallowed them as if they had stepped into the belly of a whale. The tunnel sides dripped with moisture, but it was warm inside. Under their feet the floor was uneven but dry, the stone worn and smooth.

Behind them they could hear masonry crumbling as the remains of the church tumbled like so many old building bricks abandoned by a child, the purpose of them forgotten and insignificant.

The deeper they moved into the tunnel the less bright

seemed the light. The tunnel began to meander in all directions, snakelike, but constantly it took them downwards. In places it widened so they could stand in pairs, but for the most part they had to move along in single file. They were all wrapped up in their own thoughts, occasionally noticing the strange chiseled marks on the stone walls that probably meant something if they had had the ability to interpret them.

It was getting colder and their breath started to mist in front of them. The floor became more uneven, the ridges in the stone higher and more likely to catch a careless step. Water dripped from tiny faults in the walls, the stone beneath it green with algae. Once or twice they came to a fork where it was almost uncertain which direction to take, but each time Carter moved them forwards, certain he knew the way. No one doubted him.

'What will we do if the light fades completely?' Kirby said, but no one wanted to reply. They were all too busy trying to stay calm, trying to keep fear at bay.

And then the tunnel came to an abrupt end in the shape of a brass-hinged oaken door.

Then the light went out and it was totally dark.

CHAPTER FORTY-FOUR

Carter took control.

Darkness wrapped itself around them, an ardent lover, whispering and caressing, stroking and claiming.

'Everyone hold hands,' Carter said calmly.

Behind them, back in the entrance to the tunnel, clawed feet could be heard crackling over the stone floor.

Do it.

McKinley spoke the words directly into Carter's mind.

Strange high-pitched sounds were filling the tunnel, pursuing; Carter opened his mind.

Drawing on the others, especially Kirby and McKinley, he sent rhythmic pulses scattering down the tunnel, drawing on the strength of each of them, pulling out from them what he needed. The pulses met dozens of small masses of resistance.

'I'd guess it's the beetles that attacked when I was with Sian,' he said.

McKinley turned his attention to the door barring their way. 'Let's see if we can get through this.'

It was difficult in the dark but his hand located the handle, and he feathered the fingers outwards on the wood so he could feel across to the lock.

'There's no key.' He turned the handle. The door opened inwards.

Kirby screamed.

Beetles had leeched onto her neck, needling into the skin, trying to burrow inside.

Bayliss grabbed her arms, propelled her round so she was facing away from him, then slapped her hard on the back. He sensed rather than saw her body as it lurched forwards. She stopped herself from hitting the wall by bracing her arms against the rock.

Some of the beetles had fallen off as he slapped her. Now he ripped off as many as he could locate on her neck and shoulders.

Carter took Kirby by the hand. 'Come on,' he said.

With McKinley pulling at Bayliss they pushed at the open door, shutting it behind them as dozens of the rattling beetles scraped against the other side.

'Are there any still on you?' Bayliss said.

Kirby shook her head. She was quivering with terror.

You'll be fine. You did well.

Carter injected the words into her brain and she smiled. She hadn't done well at all, she knew that. If it hadn't been for Bayliss she'd have let the things . . . she pushed the thoughts out of her mind.

'Thanks, Nick,' she said.

'I never did like creepy crawlies.'

This side of the door the air was warmer, slightly stale, as if it was a long-closed cellar. The tunnel was still evident but it was wider, opening up like a river delta. The floor was still stone but smoother; more care had been taken when it was built.

That was the conclusion Carter couldn't expel from his mind. This had all been *built*. He hesitated to use the phrase 'man-made' because he suspected man had very little to do with the construction. He was in no doubt that the natural ley lines that flowed beneath the island had been amplified over the years by whatever had used them as a line of transport.

They moved slowly along, feeling the walls with their hands, noticing the rock was becoming less rough as the tunnel progressed. Gradually light began to filter around them, so visibility became easier.

A slight bend in the tunnel took them round an outcrop of rock, and when they could see straight ahead again they stopped and stared.

They couldn't believe what was in front of them.

CHAPTER FORTY-FIVE

It was as though the inside of Planet Earth had been scooped out, hollowed and emptied, leaving just this vast cavern that soared above them to a ceiling they could barely see.

A pale gray mist floated through the air, concealing the walls except for occasional glimpses of black stone. Set in the stone at regular intervals were high stained-glass windows, through which piercing sunlight flooded, even though they were deep beneath the earth.

The rays of light picked out features half hidden in the mist. Row after row of ornately carved wooden pews, on each of which sat an embroidered cushion, ready for kneeling at prayer. The pews were large and sturdy, but carved with delicacy, the figures and motifs unclear; they needed to be closer. There seemed to be flowers and trees depicted in the wood, amongst which creatures moved, some seeming to have horns on their heads, others apparently half human, half beast. The cushions were brightly colored, scenes of ritual and elaborate worship. Where there might be a crucifix there was an inverted cross, where there might be a Bible there was a skull.

'This isn't just a huge cave, is it?' Kirby said.

It wasn't possible that this far underground there could be light entering through the windows, but the sunlight was pure and bright. As they moved a little further into the cavern they began to see the images captured in the stained glass. They were all mockeries of the scenes familiar in any Christian church. The nativity scene of Mary holding baby Jesus in swaddling clothes was shown as a huge misshapen goat figure giving bloody birth to a monster, while all around creatures bayed and celebrated. These were not shepherds and wise men bearing gifts; these were twisted abnormalities leering and ranting. A scene that would normally be of Jesus on the cross was shown as a grinning devil clinging to the wooden cross by its lizard's tail.

High above them the ceiling could be glimpsed as the mist began to fade. Somehow they could breathe easily, far more comfortably than back in the winding tunnels. There was a source of fresh air despite the depth. The ceiling was carved out of wood, unseasoned oak by the look of it. Huge chandeliers hung from crossbeams, black candles of thick wax set in holders, flickering flames casting sullen shadows onto the floor below.

As they made their way further inside they realized that they were walking along what in a church would be the aisle. Ahead of them, yards in front of them, was a wide altar, where more candles burned, next to incense burners and decanters of filmy red liquid. To one side of the altar was a font, the large stone lid removed and propped against the side. Steam rose from the water in the font.

'This is a vast underground cathedral,' Bayliss whispered. 'I never read about this.'

Keep your mind closed.

McKinley heard Carter's words spoken inside his head. It was the right advice. They didn't know what they were walking into.

Along the stone walls, between the windows, were what seemed to be huge nets, hung from iron hooks set in the walls. The nets were coated in a wispy, grayish white material that resembled dried frog spawn. Inside the nets things were stirring.

As they reached the end of the aisle and stood in front of the altar lowly pitched, discordant organ music began to play. It was a twisted theme on Wagner's Wedding March. The mist had almost cleared now, and they looked around them, once more experiencing a kind of awe at the sheer magnitude of the place. It was huge, but the perspective was unreal, the walls seeming miles away yet close enough to touch; the ceiling barely visible yet crowding in over their heads.

Noises behind them made them all turn. Kirby gasped.

'How did we miss those?' Bayliss said.

On the pews were dozens, hundreds, of shapes. Coated in the off-white material, cobwebbed and cocooned, they became visible as people. Hundreds of people seemingly stored, seemingly in suspended animation, sitting on the pews in mock devotion, waiting . . . but waiting for what?

They wouldn't see them, there were too many there, but Michael Bennett, Farrant, Anderson, Casey Faraday, Sheila Thomas and Jo Madley were amongst those preserved.

Rustling above them made Carter and the others look around the walls. The nets were shaking, layers of the web-like material slewing off as the people inside struggled to get free. There was a low murmur as they moved, combined voices creating a hum of anticipation.

'We should get out of here,' Kirby said, her voice shaking with barely contained fear.

Carter wasn't listening. He walked back down the aisle to a pew about ten rows from the front. 'Sian?'

Staring sightless into space, tears cascading down her face, there was a ghost of a smile on her lips. It was Sian, wrapped in the restricting material, sitting calmly while all around her the others were shaking back to life. Suspended in the moment of their death and now being brought back to some kind of existence.

Carter put his hand on her shoulder and felt the viscous stickiness of the gauzelike webbing that coated her. Her mouth opened but no sound came out. She began shaking her head from side to side in a futile gesture of denial.

'Sian, let me help you,' Carter pleaded.

Someone coughed and a cultured voice with a pro-nounced Spanish accent said, 'I am afraid she is beyond even your help, Mr. Carter.'

Kirby gripped Bayliss's hand, and both of them moved instinctively closer to McKinley. Carter looked at Sian, who had sunk back within herself at the sound of the voice. The movement in the pews and on the walls also stopped, and it was as if the whole cathedral was holding its breath. Carter walked back to the others and stood next to McKinley.

The man in front of them was of medium height, aver-age build; nothing about his physique was in any way re-markable. His thick black hair was swept back from a noble forehead, and his strong nose merely heightened the effect of his piercing blue eyes. A smile danced on his full maroon lips, a small neat beard emphasizing the line of his jaw. He was handsome but looked ordinary. He wore ex-pensive clothing from centuries ago, the silk and velvet re-vealing he was a man of wealth. At his side was a sword sheathed in an ornate scabbard encrusted with jewels.

He affected a small bow. 'Allow me to introduce my-self,' he said, the accent originally from the Valencia re-gion of Spain. 'My name is Alphonse deMarco. Welcome to my home for the past few hundred years.'

Sounding like a thousand cicadas waking simultane-ously the figures on the pews and on the walls began their struggle to get free with renewed energy. The noise was almost deafening but deMarco had no difficulty in making his voice heard.

'You are curious, naturally, especially you, Mr. Carter, as to why I have gone to such lengths to attract you here. Such elaborate planning, such extreme effort to recruit people you might wish to . . . to save. People like Mrs. Tal-bot.' He flung his arm out to the right and Carter and the others automatically flicked their eyes in that direction.

Laid out on the altar, smothered in the hazy material,

was Jane Talbot. Her eyes were opened, and she was tearing at the coverings. Her eyes were staring at Carter.

Carter began to move forwards but deMarco held up a hand to indicate he should stay where he was. 'All in good time; a time to reap and a time to sow, as your good book says.'

'If it's me you wanted why did you have to . . .'

'Why take Miss Davies, Mrs. Talbot . . . why take the many hundreds I have recruited through the centuries? The dear ladies ensured you would grace me with your presence; the others . . . the others are my soldiers, my army. I have been collecting them, recruiting and storing them, here in my humble cathedral; waiting for the moment when I can unleash them on my enemies.'

Bayliss stepped forward tentatively. 'How can you have enemies? Those you fought are long dead, and no one else has ever heard . . .'

DeMarco laughed, and for an instant the writhing figures on the walls and the pews were still. 'Please don't accuse me of nonentity, Mr. Bayliss, it doesn't sit well with my ego. You have heard of me, with your ceaseless research, though I accept that the world at large is unfamiliar with my name . . . for now.' He walked a couple of steps from the altar and Bayliss shrank back. 'Ask in the corridors of the Vatican, ask His Holiness, even now, even after centuries have passed, and my name is known.'

DeMarco allowed a cold smile to twist his mouth. He raised a hand and snapped two fingers.

The huge room seemed suddenly to be active, yet Carter couldn't immediately see anyone or anything. At least nothing that stayed still long enough for him to identify it. The writhing figures were frantic with action now, some beginning to tear free of their bindings. In dark corners beyond the nave, hidden by stone pillars and arches, scuttling shadows darted about.

A sound like liquid flesh squeezing and pulling made him look upwards. From the ceiling indistinct shadows were erupting above his head and dropping like rain. Globules of darkness forced their way out through the wood and the plaster until they were in the open, and as they floated down they coalesced into shapes that were nearly human.

Then a large shadow fell upon him from behind and he was pulled to the floor. In the increasing blackness Carter thought he could see a black-robed form lying motionless on the floor beside Jane, holding her. Candles flickered around them, and quiet, frightened figures tried to hide in the shadows. The robed form had the shape of a man but was no longer a man. There was no face, just ruffles of hanging white skin, crinkled like paper, no eyes, and no mouth. The black robes hung deformed from the shriveled body, wasted, lifeless. The figure was like a cloud of smoke formed into a man-creature, a withered husk on the brink of death.

Carter felt pressure around his neck, as cold claws clamped into his skin. Talon fingers gripped the flesh, cutting deep, drawing out blood. He swung and turned to try to prize the fingers from him, and as he turned he saw what was attached leechlike to his neck. It was large, folded wings hanging to the ground, misshapen horns protruding from the head. The skeletal arms wrapped around Carter were covered in coarse black hair that had worn away in places, to reveal dark, paper-thin skin.

As Carter struggled against the creature he began to feel weaker, and the shadows reflected his weakness. And as the beast was draining the life from him, so the figure on the ground was stirring into new life, the black robes filling and swelling as Carter drifted into the darkness. All the time Jane lay quietly conscious, but her mind was switched off from the horror she was watching.

McKinley opened his mind and sent flashes of power

surging into the creature attacking Carter. At the same time he probed into Carter's brain, trying to send additional strength.

Carter felt the grip of the talons weaken as McKinley's psychic surges began to take effect. He stoked energy in his brain, letting it coil like a snake until with a fierce flash he poured it into the creature. At once the skeletal arms fell away and the wings drooped to the floor.

By the altar the stirring figure lay still, larger than before but seemingly still weak.

DeMarco looked concerned, and a look of almost fondness masked his face. He turned to Carter, barely glancing at the creature floundering in the aisle. 'My . . . my friend, Prime,' he said, indicating the altar. 'He has not survived the years as well as I.'

Carter kneaded the back of his neck. The claws had opened a wound but it didn't feel too deep. Kirby took off her sweatshirt and was dabbing at the blood. 'It's just superficial. So long as there isn't any infection.'

The creature that had attacked Carter still flopped on the floor. Kirby stood over it, raised one leg, and brought her foot down on the throat. Moments later, after she leaned all her weight into it, there was a snap of bone.

DeMarco turned and looked all about the cathedral. The shadowed figures that had seeped from the ceiling were pulling at the webbing on the walls, tearing it from the hooks that held it in place. As the material tore, the figures captured within were able to jump free, onto the stone floor, where they milled about like a crowd at a railway station. They made very little sound; Bayliss watched them for a few moments until he realized what was strange about them. Although they were clearly all human beings, men, women, some young, others older, and all were naked, there was blankness in their eyes. It was as if they were dead but hadn't been told to lie down.

McKinley probed into the minds of some on the pews nearest to him—numbness rather than emptiness. It was a kind of suspended life that hovered between existence and death itself.

'A technique I found in Haiti,' deMarco said. 'Not yet tested in battle but I have no fears about its efficiency. We have done several tests.'

When all the people on the walls had been released the gray-shrouded figures began to free those in the pews. Soon there would be thousands of them, silent but waiting.

'When I say Prime has not fared as well as I have, I omit to reveal I do have a slight advantage. Prime is of course only human.' DeMarco let a strange expression settle on his face, neither a smile nor a frown. It was the kind of expression that speaks of acceptance, of the end of resistance. He made a movement that looked as if he was scratching the back of his neck. Gradually the skin around his lips seemed to loosen. The folds of skin on his neck draped forward like a woman letting a silk nightdress slide to the floor. The shifting of his skin was accompanied by the most odd noise—the sound of wet tissue paper being folded, very quiet, very soft. The skin on his head flopped forwards onto his chest. With imperceptible movements behind his back deMarco continued to ripple his skin away from his body so that after a few moments it fell in rivulets from his waist. Still it continued to cascade away from him, the sound of faint tearing joined now by sighs of almost sensual pleasure. Carter realized the sounds were coming from the creatures around him, a kind of worship. As the skin finally peeled from the torso and dropped obscenely without a sound to the floor Carter was astounded when he bent casually, picked it up like a discarded towel, and hung it from a hook on the wall. What was left, without the cloak of human skin, was a nightmare.

There have been many depictions of the Devil over the

years, from horned goat-beast, to sophisticated man about town. What stood in front of them was nothing at all like the artwork, nothing seen in the movies.

The face was ghostly pale, life long since extinct. Tatters of raw skin hung from the forehead and cheeks as if torn billboard posters that advertised an event that was a vaguely restored memory. Thin tufts of hair coated the bloated skull, coarse and gray and congealed at the sides where there should have been ears. Instead of ears a pair of thick, dark brown horns pointed upwards and slightly forwards. The body was heavy at the chest, bulging with muscle; beneath the ribs and across the stomach the skin protruded outwards where things captured inside the body were pushing for escape. Simian arms folded across the knees of legs that were powerful and long. The hands were thick at the wrist, with elegantly tapered fingers that waved in the air with talon-sharp nails of deep yellow. The legs were bent at the knees, hiding their length and width. The feet were webbed between stubbed toes that were curved into claws at the ends. From the pronounced backbone two white, withered wings hung forlornly, as though distant relatives long forgotten.

By far the worst aspect was the eyes. Burning red like the hot fires of Hell, they flared with anger and hatred. Ceaselessly open, with no lids or lashes, they were pools of evil that beckoned like beauty to embrace them.

The voice, when deMarco spoke, was, like the body, devoid of the cultured façade he had adopted. 'How the devil are you, Carter? Welcome to my future.'

Without warning Carter felt his left arm rise from his side until it was pointing at right angles to his shoulder. Then the right arm did the same until he was standing in front of the altar, his arms outstretched as if crucified.

'An undignified pose I grant you; but it serves my purpose,' deMarco said.

Bayliss was terrified but brave enough to step between deMarco and Carter. When he was closer to Carter he could see the effort and energy he was extending to resist. 'You're not Satan,' he said. His tone was challenging, hiding the fear he felt. 'Nothing I've read about you suggested anything other than you as an acolyte, another wannabe Satanist with delusions of grandeur.'

DeMarco laughed, a brittle sound of torn metal. He flashed his red eyes and Bayliss slumped to his knees, the pain in his chest so fierce he could hardly breathe. 'Hurts, doesn't it? That's just the onset of the pain you'll feel in about ten years when the lung cancer spreads to your liver. If you live that long. You really should have given up the cigarettes and the whisky, you know; don't you read the packets? *Smoking kills . . .*'

Carter was being held and stretched. His arms were flung wide now, his chest straining against the force holding him.

Most of the people in the pews were released by now, and they stood with the others freed from the walls in a vast crowd, expectant, swaying slightly. The shrouded figures were placed at intervals on the periphery of the crowd, ready to herd them when deMarco instructed.

Kirby was helping Bayliss to his feet, pain and breathlessness etching lines into his face that hadn't been there before. McKinley was delicately trying to probe inside Carter's mind, feeling for the force that was controlling him.

'Nick Bayliss is regrettably correct. Although I do seem to fit most of the characteristics, I am but a humble servant. Loyal and determined but a mere employee; and with few corporate benefits either . . . ah, well, eternal life has its compensations I suppose. But down to business; I needed you, Carter, for your mind; linking it with mine, along the Ley we are standing on will allow me to generate sufficient power to summon . . . you called him Satan, Bayliss. I call him Father.'

With sudden speed deMarco stalked down the aisle and grasped Carter's left hand. The sparks that flew when their skin touched were like a power cable striking water. Carter flinched as if a dozen knives were penetrating his spine, and his organs felt as if they were swelling within him as the surge from deMarco began to build.

Before McKinley could attack him deMarco shouted to the gray-shrouded creatures at the back of the cathedral and seven or eight of them leapt upon McKinley, pinning his arms to the ground, covering his face with the drapes of their robes.

'And now we can begin the Ascent,' deMarco said, elation tingeing his voice.

As Carter braced himself, searching for an opening to exert resistance, there was a loud crash and one wall of the cathedral burst open, like the parting of the Red Sea. Through the wall poured hundreds of people, some holding incense burners, others flicking water from ornate containers, others reciting passages from the Bible.

With their attention diverted McKinley took his opportunity to free himself, his large frame and strength easily overpowering the bony creatures.

Carter felt deMarco yield and he managed to loosen the grip, but the force holding him in place was too strong and his arms remained outstretched, even when deMarco released his hand, watching as the wave of people flooded the cathedral.

The cathedral was now awash with people. Those nakedly released from storage milled zombielike, spilling out along the pews as the newcomers marched in, forcing the others back.

The shrouded followers of deMarco massed in front of them, two forces setting themselves for battle. Prowling like a caged tiger deMarco walked a few feet one way, turned, and stormed back. He was searching the intruders for someone he knew would be there; someone who *had* to be there.

Then he saw him. 'Meyer!' he shouted. 'Klaus Meyer.'

'*The German*,' Bayliss said.

'Muscular Christianity,' Kirby murmured.

McKinley shook his head. 'That isn't any German. I've seen that guy's picture in magazines back home. That's Carl Anderson. He's the father of Jessica Anderson, the woman Crozier introduced to us.'

An uncertain silence fell over the cathedral.

Meyer motioned his troops to be still and wait. He walked past the shrouded guards and advanced on deMarco. For his part deMarco moved past the font to meet him.

With a guttural growl of greeting, deMarco said, 'Klaus Meyer, after all these years.'

Meyer gave a small inclination of his head and shoulders in a bow of acknowledgement. 'I've gone by the name of Carl Anderson for the past sixty or so years, a successful businessman in America. Before that I was Clint Sybert, a respected surgeon working out of Canada. Before that I was in Europe, but these details are not of importance.'

With a wave of his hand deMarco offered disagreement. 'On the contrary old friend . . .'

Meyer took two steps forward, his temples throbbing with anger. 'Do not, ever, call me *friend*. You feign genuine surprise to see me, but we both know you've been stalking me all these years, as I have done you. My life has been long and under the protection of the papal authorities it has been prosperous.'

'How is your lovely daughter?'

'Jessica was a wonderful daughter in many ways but she was under your spell since the day she was born. I always knew it but she was my only daughter, and I loved her, even though I knew her every action was to serve you. It took much pleading with His Holiness to allow it, but eventually I was able to recruit women into my Jesuit order. So long as they remained a separate order the break with tradition was overlooked. My sister Celeste Toland formed the Sorority and Jessica joined eagerly, imagining I expect that she would be pleasing you by keeping close to the enemy. That is what you made my own daughter, de-Marco, my enemy. No one ever suspected, not even Jessica, that Celeste and I are siblings; we managed to exude a facade of personal loathing. To the outside world we disliked each other intensely. Celeste and I did business together but because of our supposed hatred for one another, Jessica conducted those transactions. It helped Celeste keep track of what Jessica was doing in recent months. Perhaps having a fling with her was taking things a bit far, but Celeste gets wrapped up in her work.'

'And the ladies are with you?'

'All except Jessica; she can't attend, she didn't have time to send her regrets. But as you can see from my many companions, you are not the only one who has been assembling an army of followers.'

Carter tried once more to free himself but deMarco still held him firm. His whole left side was frozen by whatever power deMarco was exerting on him. Then, without warning, Carter felt a fierce surge down the right side of his body. Another force was joining in the control of him. As the right side and the left side burned with the intrusion it felt as if his body was being pulled in different directions.

Meyer had joined deMarco and they were using Carter's powers as a conduit; battle had commenced. Meyer pulling in one direction, deMarco in the other.

DeMarco turned his back on Meyer; it was the signal.

Heavy black rain began to fall from the ceiling, pricking skin with needle-sharp points where it touched. The floor began to vibrate, and then started to ripple like waves upon the shore.

The gray shrouds of deMarco's followers were discarded and the winged demons that hid within were unleashed. They whipped and prodded the naked soldiers from the pews, urging them forward against the Jesuits.

Celeste issued her instructions and the well-drilled army deployed itself into position and began the fighting. Both sides had prepared for centuries, and neither would be satisfied with surrender.

The cathedral was filled with screams as blood spilled onto the stone floor, soaking into it as if into tissue paper. The light flooding through the stained-glass windows was like spotlights onto a stage, picking out thrusts of swords, slashes of claws. Everywhere were performances of hatred and anger. Limbs were severed, throats torn, as two beasts of armies clambered over each other.

On one side of Carter stood Meyer, on the other side stood deMarco. As deMarco thrust his power into Carter's mind, trying to unlock the psychic strength, so Meyer probed, seeking to gain control so that he could send this Satanist back to the depths from which he was trying to summon further demons.

As the twin forces pulsed through his body Carter seemed to glow, his skin translucent. His back arched from the pain pulsing through him.

Carter could feel the ley line beneath his feet swelling and moving like an electric cable. Both deMarco and Meyer were trying to harness it to bring ever more troops into play. He was summoning all his strength to keep his abilities locked away so that neither side could use them. If weakened, he wouldn't be able to predict what effect his powers allied to theirs would have.

He could feel the Ley expanding; something large was moving along it. He remembered what deMarco had called it, *Father* . . .

Suddenly Carter felt Meyer's influence lessen. He opened his eyes and saw a flour-white and spindle-thin demon latched onto Meyer's back, pulling his hands away from Carter's. Like a hungry animal deMarco pounced. He shot bolts of electric energy through Carter's arm, up along his spine and into his skull. The sparks flashed over his brain causing pain and confusion. With a roar of triumph deMarco pinned Carter's consciousness and directed their joint powers into the opening of the ley line.

The lights dimmed, the candles fluttered, and the warring armies momentarily halted battle. Tongues of flame flicked from the dark opening of the Ley. The stench of open graves wafted out, as a black cloud of flies hovered over the entrance. And something very large began to force itself into the cathedral.

Carter felt a bolt of lightning enter his head, the pain so intense his heart seemed to shrink inside his chest.

It's always been you, Robert.

On the altar Jane Talbot was sitting cross-legged, her eyes closed, her full attention on Carter.

I can't compare with that but I can help.

McKinley had made Bayliss and Kirby hide down beneath a front pew, and he was standing beside Meyer.

The ley line had ripped open and claws more than six feet in length were scrabbling to gain entrance.

Carter, using McKinley and Jane, directed a fierce pulse of energy at the demon attacking Meyer and within moments it was killed.

As the immense head and shoulders emerged as if from the womb of the Ley, and the army of deMarco renewed battle with revitalized vigor, so Carter pulled in the others and for the first time he opened his mind fully.

It was a risk, as deMarco was still there, but he moved quickly.

Jane was as powerful as Carter had predicted she would be. With McKinley using his power to the full they began slowly but systematically to repel deMarco. Piercing him with combined surges of psychic energy they gradually weakened him until he dropped away from Carter's mind, and within moments dropped Carter's hand. He was no longer in control.

DeMarco was on his knees, damaged, but he was crawling towards Jane.

Meyer was concentrating. There was a blinding light from above. It was as if the ceiling had evaporated and un-filtered sunlight was pouring down on them. It had a dramatic affect on deMarco's followers. The naked conscripts folded at the knees and fell forwards as the bindings of darkness that had held them in suspended death dissolved and left them to their natural passing. The gray demons shrieked as the skin bubbled and flaked off them in the intense heat and brightness of the light.

The Jesuits recognized the source of the light and revered it, but took strength from its purpose and seized their victory.

As the brightness intensified so the ley line began to shrink, and as if cowering away from the pure source of the light the huge entity that had sought freedom slunk back to the dark depths.

The battle lasted a few moments more before stillness insinuated into the cathedral. The intense light receded and Celeste began shepherding her army away.

Carter and McKinley helped Jane from the altar. Her face was drained of color but to Carter she had never looked more beautiful.

Meyer said, 'If you come with me there'll be transport back to London, although even for the Department I think your report is going to make waves.'

'You may want to file your own report first. Crozier thinks he's God but your boss takes precedence.'

Meyer held out his hand and Carter shook it.

'I'm afraid Sian Davies is amongst those who didn't survive. Like my daughter she's one of deMarco's victims.'

'So am I the only one concerned?' Bayliss demanded. 'There's no sign of Alphonse anywhere.' Kirby put her hand on his shoulder but he shrugged her off.

Meyer sighed. 'It shouldn't involve you anymore but I'll track him down. If he escaped I'll find him. He's alone now.'

Carter looked at the others, felt Jane's hand tighten in his.

'We're professionals. When we start a job we like to finish it.'

JOHN SKIPP
AND CODY
GOODFELLOW

Pastor Jake promised his followers everlasting life…he just didn't say what kind. So when the small-town televangelist and con man climbs out of his coffin at his own wake, it becomes Judgment Day for everyone gathered to mourn— or celebrate—his death. Jake is back, in the rotting flesh, filled with anger and vengeance. And accompanied by demons even more frightening than himself. What follows is a long night of endless terror, a blood-drenched rampage by the man not even death could stop.

JAKE'S WAKE

ISBN 13: 978-0-8439-6076-1

BRIAN
KEENE

They came to the lush, deserted island to compete on a popular reality TV show. Each one hoped to be the last to leave. Now they're just hoping to stay alive. It seems the island isn't deserted after all. Contestants and crew members are disappearing, but they aren't being eliminated by the game. They're being taken by the monstrous half-human creatures that live in the jungle. The men will be slaughtered. The women will be kept alive as captives. Night is falling, the creatures are coming, and rescue is so far away. . . .

CASTAWAYS

ISBN 13: 978-0-8439-6089-1

BRYAN SMITH

Beautiful. Sexy. Inhuman. Jake McAllister knows that his brother Trey's new girlfriend is a bad influence, but he doesn't know what Myra's really after—Trey's soul. Trey is just one of her new playthings, a pawn in her centuries-long game. One by one, Myra has seduced and enslaved the young men of the town. The women have joined her cult as eager priestesses, lured by promises of sex and power. But Myra's unholy plan is almost complete. Can one man hope to battle such seductive evil? Will he be able to resist the…

SOULTAKER

ISBN 13: 978-0-8439-6193-5

RICHARD LAYMON

For two families, it was supposed to be a relaxing camping trip in the California mountains. They thought it would be fun to get away from everything for a while. But they're not alone. The woods are also home to two terrifying residents who don't take kindly to strangers—an old hag with unholy powers, and her hulking son, a half-wild brute with uncontrollable, violent urges. The campers still need to get away—but now their lives depend on it!

DARK MOUNTAIN

ISBN 13: 978-0-8439-6138-6

GORD ROLLO

AUTHOR OF *THE JIGSAW MAN*

The small town of Dunnville is no stranger to fear. Evil has stalked its dark streets once before. These days, no one in the town likes to talk about it much. Some folks deny it ever happened....

But four boyhood friends are about to discover the truth, though no one will believe them. Their parents think they've been listening to too many scary stories. But what the boys have released from an icy well is no legend, and it will soon terrify Dunnville to its very core. Unspeakable horror is running free...and the nightmares of the past are about to begin again.

CRIMSON

ISBN 13: 978-0-8439-6195-9

To order a book or to request a catalog call:
1-800-481-9191
This book is also available at your local bookstore, or you can check out our Web site **www.dorchesterpub.com** where you can look up your favorite authors, read excerpts, or glance at our discussion forum to see what people have to say about your favorite books.

☐ **YES!**

Sign me up for the Leisure Horror Book Club and send my FREE BOOKS! If I choose to stay in the club, I will pay only $8.50* each month, a savings of $7.48!

NAME: _____

ADDRESS: _____

TELEPHONE: _____

EMAIL: _____

☐ I want to pay by credit card.

☐ **VISA**　　☐ **MasterCard**　　☐ **DISCOVER**

ACCOUNT #: _____

EXPIRATION DATE: _____

SIGNATURE: _____

Mail this page along with $2.00 shipping and handling to:
Leisure Horror Book Club
PO Box 6640
Wayne, PA 19087
Or fax (must include credit card information) to:
610-995-9274
You can also sign up online at **www.dorchesterpub.com**.

*Plus $2.00 for shipping. Offer open to residents of the U.S. and Canada only.
Canadian residents please call 1-800-481-9191 for pricing information.
If under 18, a parent or guardian must sign. Terms, prices and conditions subject to
change. Subscription subject to acceptance. Dorchester Publishing reserves the right
to reject any order or cancel any subscription.